Creature
Cozies

D1528524

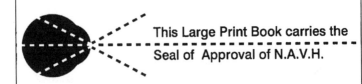

This Large Print Book carries the
Seal of Approval of N.A.V.H.

Creature Cozies

Edited by
Jill M. Morgan

WHEELER PUBLISHING

LPSC
Cr

This is a work of fiction. Names, characters, places, and incidents either are the product of the authors' imaginations or are used fictitiously, and any resemblance to actual persons, living or dead, business establishments, events, or locales is entirely coincidental.

Published in 2005 by arrangement with The Berkley Publishing Group, a division of Penguin Group (USA) Inc.

Wheeler Large Print Cozy Mystery.

The text of this Large Print edition is unabridged.
Other aspects of the book may vary from the original edition.

Set in 16 pt. Plantin by Christina S. Huff.

Printed in the United States on permanent paper.

Library of Congress Cataloging-in-Publication Data

Creature cozies / edited by Jill M. Morgan.
     p. cm. — (Wheeler Publishing large print cozy mystery)
    ISBN 1-59722-039-6 (lg. print : sc : alk. paper)
    1. Detective and mystery stories, American. 2. Animals — Fiction. 3. Pets — Fiction. 4. Large type books.
I. Wheeler large print cozy mystery.
PS648.D4C686 2005b
  813′.087208362—dc22   2005011114

Creature Cozies

As the Founder/CEO of NAVH, the only national health agency solely devoted to those who, although not totally blind, have an eye disease which could lead to serious visual impairment, I am pleased to recognize Thorndike Press★ as one of the leading publishers in the large print field.

Founded in 1954 in San Francisco to prepare large print textbooks for partially seeing children, NAVH became the pioneer and standard setting agency in the preparation of large type.

Today, those publishers who meet our standards carry the prestigious "Seal of Approval" indicating high quality large print. We are delighted that Thorndike Press is one of the publishers whose titles meet these standards. We are also pleased to recognize the significant contribution Thorndike Press is making in this important and growing field.

Lorraine H. Marchi, L.H.D.
Founder/CEO
NAVH

★ Thorndike Press encompasses the following imprints: Thorndike, Wheeler, Walker and Large Print Press.

Contents

Introduction: Writers and Their Pets

by Jill M. Morgan

I don't know if I'd call my cat, Griffin, a muse. He amuses me, but is he a source of writer's inspiration? More often, I am inspired to tell him, "Griffin, get off the printer!" He leaves bite marks on the corners of paper in the loading tray, chews on wires behind the computer, steps on the off button to the fax/printer when he walks over it, and stands across my keyboard purring when I'm trying to type. Some call this cat critique or feline editing.

My cat provides me with a continuous source of interruption, taking me away from writing to shoo him off the canary cage, or to rush into my living room yelling, "Don't even think about climbing those drapes," or to feed him. He is a connoisseur of taste, preferring to gnaw the leaves of my orchid plant to expensive cat kibble, but that, too, provides another break from my writing. Such frequent breaks might be just what was needed to prevent the story from being too slowly paced.

To the writer, distraction can be an open door to creativity. Who's to say that throwing a crinkle ball for Griffin over and over again, because he fetches and never gets tired of this game, isn't what inspires my mind enough to dig myself out of the deep hole in my plot? Would I have come up with this escape on my own? Maybe. Then again, I might owe my silent collaborator more than a tray of clean kitty litter and a cat tree with a view by the window.

In recent years, I have been fortunate enough to have the love and companionship of two pets. My sheltie, Sassy, has been my writing buddy for fourteen years. She kept her comments on my work to herself (smart pup) and settled down next to my chair each morning, causing me no more trouble than a rug that breathes. It was comforting to know I was not on my own, and if I was stuck on finding the perfect ending for a difficult chapter, petting the soft coat of a dog who loved me no matter what I wrote kept my angst in check. I was inspired by her loyalty, protectiveness, and beautiful brown eyes. Sassy died this week and my writing space seems cold and lonely without her. I still get up every so often to let her outside, throw her a ball, or give her a biscuit. It seems she's still here, and the memory of her inspires me.

Pets keep us company when we go into the uncharted territory of our imagination. They remain beside us, faithful companions, or maybe just hungry for their share of our next snack break . . . toast crusts, a dropped potato chip. The computer chair pushed back from the desk and my dog's brown, soulful eyes would go into action, begging for the last bite of that angel food cake.

We all have our rewards. For the pet, it is a pat on the head, a kind word, and okay, a variety of well-chosen snack foods from that type-and-nibble person. For the writer, the reward is the companionship of a true friend during moments when we doubt our ability to create a complete sentence, much less a mystery story. Cats and dogs take us as we are, frail writer beings, without a glance at our last royalty statements. They are above such things, bless them.

If pets are such benefit to writers, and they are, are writers of any particular benefit to pets? We writers are, for the most part, a sedentary group of humans, attached almost physically to our computer chairs and keyboards. Scooting back on our roller-legged chair and eying the monitor from a different angle, as if the words might somehow change from this new perspective — no, that boring paragraph is still boring, even five feet away — is the writer's version of a high impact workout. Scoot, two-three-four. Stare, two-three-four. Tossing those balled up pages into the waste basket (stuff even ten feet of scooting away can't gain a new perspective on) is our aerobics event. The real athletes are our fingers, dancing over the keyboard like an alphabet ballet. We are, in short, computer-chair potatoes.

And the benefit to our pets?

Got me.

If our dog wants to go for a walk to smell the neighbor's fungicided, sterilized, color-enhanced lawn covering that some call grass, it may be next week before she gets there. Ideas strike a writer like a fit of apoplexy, rendering him unaware of his surroundings, including the dog standing by the door with a leash in his mouth. Deadlines pop up out of nowhere. Who knew six months could speed by so fast? Writers now shackled to their computers for the duration have not a thought to spare for the doleful-eyed dog or the clamorous cat.

They love us, it seems, in spite of our addictive, one thousand-words-a-day habit. They forgive our blind, uncomprehending stares when ideas take us somewhere else. They share us with unembodied characters who command both our attention and our time, and they do this every day with constancy and love. They are there for us when we put away the written words that give us the means to fly, and when later we slip back into our bodies like wingless moths returning to our caterpillar selves.

Within the pages of this anthology are twelve mystery stories that speak to us of the love of authors for their pets. Outstanding authors such as Jane Haddam, Dick Lochte, Jan Burke, J. A. Jance, Ed Gorman, Carole Nelson Douglas, and others introduce readers to their pets in these creature cozies. Plots center on canines and kitties, and like a loveable mutt with more wags to his tail than pedigrees, each story in this book is unique and a paws'-down winner Best in Show.

Junior Partner
in Crime

by Carole Nelson Douglas,
with Midnight Louie, Jr.

Once upon a time in 1973, a stray cat called "Midnight Louey" lived at or about a motel in ritzy Palo Alto, California, one of the nation's wealthiest suburbs. Cats abandoned at motels, no matter how upscale, become feral. They go untreated if injured, often starve, and live short, brutish lives.

Midnight Louey, however, frequented the motel koi pond for lunch, and weighed a strapping eighteen pounds. This hairy lothario hung out by the Coke machine in the evenings to pick up lonely ladies who would take him into their rooms and out of the northern California chill for the night.

When the motel management decided to send this feline gigolo to the local pound to preserve their expensive decorative fish collection, a visiting Minnesota woman couldn't stand to see his superb survival instincts rewarded with certain death. So she shipped him two thousand miles back to her St. Paul home.

That's where Carole Nelson, a metropolitan daily newspaper reporter, saw the thirty-dollar ad in the classifieds offering Midnight Louey, who was "equally at home on your best couch as in your neighbor's garbage can," to the right home for a dollar bill. Intrigued by the fiscal contradiction, she wrote a feature article about Midnight Louey. By 1985, Carole had left Minnesota and journalism for full-time fiction writing in Texas, but she revived the black cat as the part-time narrator of a romantic suspense quartet of novels. And nineteen years after Carole met Louey, Midnight Louie, P.I. debuted as cover boy and star of his own mystery series in 1992's *Catnap*.

Obviously, the "real and original" Louey would be a very senior citizen of the cat world by now. We don't think about that. We know he's still out there somewhere, copping koi and seducing dames.

But Louey's inimitable beat goes on. During the first Midnight Louie Adopt-a-Cat book signing/cat adoption tour sponsored by Forge Books in 1996, Carole Nelson Douglas met Midnight Louie, Jr., in the Lubbock, Texas, shelter. Oh, he wasn't called that then, and he was an entirely different kettle of fish from the real and original, but he was as good at picking up dames as his name-sake, and he eventually came home with her to join the Douglas household.

How he got to the shelter is the real mystery.

— Carole Nelson Douglas

Act I:
Legend

It's hard living up to a legend.

Especially a legend that's mostly a fig-ment of some author's imagination, as most legends are, if you ask me.

The trouble is, nobody does. Ask me, that is.

I am just a cat.

I am not a hard-boiled, hairy-chested Las Vegas P.I. who's had serial tangles with murderers, like my old man, Midnight Louie, Sr. I do not write books, interrogate neighborhood dogs, visit casinos, or chase Persian showgirls.

There is only one way I take after my old man: I do like a little nip now and then.

I mean, what can the average dude do to ease the pressure? How would you like to be the son of Superman? All the kids would want to know if you'd hopscotched over any tall buildings lately.

I get asked if I've nailed any big-league baddies.

How is a house-bound soul supposed to do that?

I think about these matters often these days as I lounge about one of my many condos, polishing my handsome spats to the sheen of black patent leather.

Yeah, I am strictly a hot-house cat these days. I loll by the water fountain, nibble from fine crystal, unwind on the king-size bed, and enjoy naps on the custom-built screen porch over the kitchen sink.

Unlike my supposed sire, I am politically correct to the tips of the whiskers on my chinny-chin-chin: I do not wander the mean streets, I had the required surgery (nut cut) early in life, I almost had a claw draw, too, but my post-street blood numbers were a little iffy and prevented it, plus I am such a little gentleman at nail-trimming time that I retain the "four on the floor" that Senior boasts of.

Nevertheless, I am a peace-loving type, even though the platinum-blonde who was here first didn't warm up to me at first. But Summer, the silver Persian, has come around. The other cats, Smoke, the mother-daughter act of Victoria and Secret, and our token dog, Xanadu, have always been friendly. I don't much like that upstart roof rat, Amberleigh, that the humans plucked off a neighbor's eaves last fall, but I suppose in time I'll soften my stance.

I basically like being the good guy.

So my main role in life now is acting as a body double for my old man, being he's so camera shy: Miss Carole poses with me in photographs, and my mug has been on posters and dust jackets. Everybody says what a handsome fellow I am. And I am. Miss Carole boasts of my short-cropped black-velvet head and limbs and the flowing long fur on my body and tail.

I do get a perverse little kick out of thinking that Midnight Louie, Sr., the Sam Spade of pet detectives, is being repped by a dude who was once seriously mistaken for a girl.

Of course that wee misapprehension saved my life, so I try not to take it too personally.

My life has had its ups and downs.

The downs explain why I was to be found in the Lubbock city shelter at the tender age of one year, give or take a couple months, with my tail broken in two places, my tummy shaved, my midnight coat as dull as ditch water, and the name "Jasmine" written on a tag attached to my cage. Jeez, might as well have had my nose tattooed with the name "Rosie," although my nose, like the rest of me, is a solid, no-nonsense black.

Every guy and gal in a joint like a shelter, whether accurately labeled or not as to gender, has a story. Like the fancy Himalayan huddled on the highest perch with a deep gash on his aristocratic nose. Lubbock isn't a big town, and the shelter director managed to find his owner. "Oh," she says, "as long as you've got him, you might as well keep him." So here he sits with the usual lowlifes, scared to death.

Our holding cell is pretty nice for a shelter. We have a big open room, with perches and condos scattered between our nighttime cages. You could call it a colony. We are free to move around, stretch our legs and our territorial instincts. That's why Mr. Himalayan is so nervous. He's not used to establishing territory in a common holding cell.

Frankly, it was no piece of catnip for me, either, being I'm small for my age, and downright skinny. Not to mention that "girl" part.

I had a home once. They meant well, or at least they liked kittens in a kind of careless way. But they didn't keep us inside because they never thought about all the dangers waiting outside, even if they got me "fixed."

So I ended up footloose and fancy free, and I even had One Big Case before I was shoveled into stir and then worked my way out of the Big House.

Here is how it all went down:

Act II:
The Sting

It was a day like any day. My owners went to work and let me out for the duration.

Frankly, I never did like these day-long outings. I am just a little guy and there are a lot of big, tough cats and dogs in the neighborhood that my owners never see.

After cavorting for an hour or so, I was ready to find a safe place to hunker down.

It is April in Lubbock. The sidewalks are already hot, and I had to amble through a few neighboring yards in search of water. Nobody was watering their lawns because my neighborhood didn't exactly have lawns so much as dirt patches with weeds.

While I might stumble over a birdbath in the shade, which had a little gruel in the bottom mixed with water and, er, bird droppings, my best bet was breaking into the plastic bags at the curbs and finding those big plastic water bottles with a few drops left in the bottom. Sometimes I had to work their caps off, but if I put a lot of effort into it, I could almost wet my whistler enough to make it worth the effort.

So there I am, curled up like a dead roach around this empty plastic bottle that is bigger than I am, kicking and chewing and working that screwtop loose, when I feel a hot breath of wind singeing the nape of my neck.

This is no ordinary high plains breeze. As I turn around to look, I see the huge face and fangs of a drooling English bulldog.

Only mad English bulldogs go out in the noonday sun in Lubbock, so I scoot upright, kick the bottle into the bulldog's stupid toothy kisser, and take off across the hot pavement.

With a yowl and a bay and scrabble of nails long enough for Nosferatu (I have watched a lot of late-night cable television and have a vivid imagination), the dog is on my tail.

I dash through yards, forced to bypass familiar hiding places, knowing nothing will fool this infuriated hound. Before I know it I am in foreign territory where there is not a safe house to be seen.

I finally claw my way up a mesquite tree behind a dilapidated shack. Now mesquite trees are not very high, or wide, or handsome. It is a good thing I am a lightweight, I think, as I sway to and fro on a top branch in the hot sun. My coat is black and thick, and I soak up every sizzling ray.

Luckily, even a white-coated bulldog can't take the Texas heat. After an hour of howling and bow-legged leaping, it goes swaggering off like it has actually accomplished something.

I skitter down the tree trunk and head for the nearest shade by a wooden house, which is deserted.

Well, the bulldog has accomplished something nasty, after all, I realize as I survey my situation. I am far from home and I am lost. And there are not even plastic bags at the curb in this neighborhood. There are not even curbs! In fact, there are not even other houses, be they ever so humble.

You have no doubt heard of remarkable journeys made by lost pets across half the country to return to their homes. Forget it. That is all Disney propaganda.

It's not easy to sniff your way back to your old neighborhood when you've run willy-nilly away from it without having time to mark any territory along the way.

Besides, I don't see any pressing reason to find my way back. The food was pretty mediocre, the kids teased me without any parental objections, and I was fending for myself outside all day, anyway.

So I wait until evening shadows fall, then start hoofing my way back to town. That darn bulldog has chased me halfway to the Great Salt Desert.

My pads are pretty tender, but I know I need to find civilization to find garbage. The more civilization, the more garbage. I believe this is the motto of some political protest groups, but I am too hungry, foot-sore, and thirsty to be a political animal at the moment. *Vive le garbage!* It is all Chef Surprise to me.

To make a long story short, I pad it back to more occupied territory and get seriously into a career of garbage inspector. Frankly, I have not been brought up to hunt wild game, although there is some wild game out here that has been brought up to hunt me. Besides coyotes, there are domesticated dogs and feral cats.

For the next few days, I manage to scout up enough rank food and liquid to survive, but not well. I hole up and sleep by day, hunt the polyvinyl chloride herds at the curbs by night.

I am not doing well. My sides are concave and I have fleas. I am doing so poorly that when I run into some homeless people, they set aside their bottles of Mission Bell muscatel to give me pinches off their soggy Quarter Pounders. This is like getting a sawdust sandwich drenched in radiator fluid, but I gobble it down. Any port wine in a storm.

Then one day I am looking for a place to go to ground and I sniff a little something gourmet on the breeze. A window is open in the Land of Air Conditioners!

I run around to the back of a neatly painted bungalow to discover that there is a window with a screen and inside the screen is a raised sash and inside the room is a hot meal. With meat.

I bound up to the sill and hook my front shivs in the screen. I am so weak I can barely balance there.

I hear a creaking sound, and then this old lady comes wheeling toward me in a moving chair. Her hair is white and fluffy like popcorn.

"Kitty," she says, like she knows me.

Well, "Kitty," is my middle name. Me and a million like me.

"Poor Kitty," she purrs at me, and I know she can be trusted.

In a minute, *she* is clawing at the screen, too, except that she is making a much better job of it. Maybe it is those cuticle scissors she wields like a single wicked claw. Clever, these humans.

Before I know it, a few fresh pieces of roast beef are sitting on the sill, waiting for my delectation.

I delectate rapidly, and get more. And more. More is not enough.

Then there is another creak, of a door to the room.

The old lady quickly shuts the inner glass window and her chair spins around.

I blink, watching a shadow advancing to the window.

Down. Fast. Trust no one.

I huddle at the cool, damp stone foundation beneath the window, burping. A voice, muted, wrangles above. I cringe at its grinding tone. I have heard that sound many times in my journey. The raging of an angry human.

It is not shouting at me, I realize, but the old lady who fed me.

Who would shout at a kind old lady?

I stick by the window, not willing to give up the drive-through at Chez Grandma.

When darkness comes, I have to go out scouting for water, and finally score a dead sprinkler still sitting in a small pond of liquid.

I return to the window. I want to know the old lady is all right. Hopping up to the sill, I see the room is quiet and dark.

I meow softly.

Something stirs. Something creaks. The old lady is at the glass, struggling to lift it. "Kitty," she whispers. I see her eyes in the moonlight as if they were behind maroon-tinted lenses. They are sad and confused. I know the feeling.

"I saved you something, Kitty. Now, shush. Oh, I'm so tired. Here, I have to push open this bit of screen I've worked loose. Maynard and Lucille would be so mad. Here. Pork patty."

Bits of meat are pushed through, and I gobble the first bit. It tastes stale. Or something. I take the rest up in my teeth and jump down.

I must have overeaten earlier. My stomach rebels. I'll save it until later, bury it somewhere. Under the house where there's a crack in the stone.

Easily sated, even queasy, I slink off to a nearby outbuilding, and shelter behind some piled stones. There may be snakes, spiders, and scorpions, but I have to hide somewhere.

I sleep, and in that sleep my stomach undergoes earthquakes. I wake and spit up, not a hairball, but liquid I can't afford to lose. I know I am in trouble if getting food makes me sick. I am not just hungry, but starving.

Yet I must eat something, so I stumble back to my cache. *Eureka*. A dead mouse has fallen into my fangs. It lies there in the moonlight. *Fresh. Dead. Mine!*

Then I look. The meat I hid is gone. The mouse's belly is high and round . . . an acrid pile of vomit lies near it.

I draw back, all hunger turned to dread.

The meat is bad. The meat is fatal. The old lady!

I lope back to the window.

The room is dark with night. There is no sound, no motion. I sit vigil until the skies blush blue with dawn.

I see the old lady in her bed, tossing and moaning in her sleep. A furrow grows in the short fur on my forehead. I don't like what I'm thinking.

Later, I hear the other people enter the room. A rangy, raw-boned woman is crooning at my benefactor, pushing a tray of food onto the bed.

The minute she leaves I yowl plaintively at the window.

The old lady's eyes light up as they focus on me through the round spectacles that sit crookedly on her nose.

She pushes out of the bed into the wheeled chair, takes a dish from the tray and comes wheeling toward me.

In a minute the inside window is pushed open a few inches, and sausage meat decorates the windowsill.

I yowl and pace back and forth until her fingers push through the screen and manage to pat my sides.

"So skinny," she cries. "Here, Kitty. Eat all this. I have more."

The sausage has the same musty taste as the pork. I nibble delicately, then take as much as I can into my mouth and jump down to the ground.

In a moment I am on the sill again, begging, pacing, yowling. I get more, taste a touch, then grab the rest and disappear beneath the window view.

I am not eating this bounty, of course, much as I could use some easy protein. It is tainted, and not accidentally. Luckily, the old lady is so kindhearted that she eventually gives me the whole mess.

The only bad part is that I have to take a

few morsels into my mouth to make her think I'm gobbling it all up, and my stomach is already burning.

Once it's all gone, she shuts the window, eyes the door to her room uneasily, and rolls back to the bed. A few minutes later, the big-boned woman is back for the tray, and clucks with pleasure at the short work I have made of the breakfast sausage. The old lady has only eaten toast, but I'm betting that it is not spiced and suitable for poisoning.

I bury the sausage deeper than diarrhea.

Then I walk around to the front of the house. We are in a row of houses at least, though they are modest. I hear a TV blaring in the front room.

"She eat?" a man's voice asks.

"Some toast and all the sausage," the woman answers triumphantly and softly, but I have big ears I can manipulate to pull in whispers as well as mice scrabblings.

"Meat seems to work with her."

"And it's easy to fix, too. Just like handling a stray dog in the neighborhood."

"I'm sure glad we heard about your widowed aunt needing some live-in care," he says. "I'm ready for retirement."

"It won't be long now," Lucille comments, popping the top on a soda can dewed with water.

I salivate from my watching post in the parlor window.

"Sure is hot and dry in this damn place," Lucille adds. "Maybe I can hurry it up."

"Don't want to overdo it," Maynard says. "We can wait a little while."

But I can't. What's a homeless, inconsequential, mute dude to do? I have not yet even heard of He Who Is Soon To Be My Old Man. I do not know a private eye from a privy. I am just a youngster and in trouble myself. But I can't let someone who wants to help me go undefended.

I've got some time. It's clear I can cadge the old lady out of her meat indefinitely, although I doubt I can safely tooth that lethal stuff much longer without succumbing myself.

I settle under an oleander bush to rest up and think.

A couple hours later I hear the stomp of big, soft-soled shoes. Someone is coming up the cracked sidewalk to the house!

That's what I need! A human helper.

I peer out and like what I see: a big girl, tall and solid, with a long red braid down the back of her shirt and a broad, friendly, freckled face. She looks cheerful, strong, and confident. She is carrying a big leather satchel like it is cotton candy.

Best of all, she is wearing a U.S. government uniform.

I could use a little official help.

I waylay her before she gets too close to the door, throw myself down on my side in her path and cry piteously. Believe me, the piteous cries are not faked at this point.

She stops on a dime, which is good because the next thing she would have stopped on would have been my concave guts.

"Why, Kitty! What a sweetie!" My empty tummy is being tickled. It is all I can do to avoid the dry heaves, but I must appear to be a happy, healthy cat.

She unbends and clomps up to the door, pauses at the big metal bin nailed up next to it, then knocks.

"Yeah?" Lucille doesn't look or sound happy.

"Sorry to bother you," my savior says. "I was just wondering if Mrs. Sargent had gotten a new cat."

"That?" Lucille eyes me like I am a case of the clap. "Some darned stray. Mrs. Sargent don't need no cat. She needs a miracle."

"I'm sorry to hear that," the mail carrier says, sounding it. "I used to enjoy chatting with her on my rounds. She'd always wheel up to the screen door just before I got here, and we'd talk."

"What about?" Lucille sounds suspiciously suspicious.

The mail carrier blinks. "The weather, her health, my aching feet. I'd think a cat would be just the kind of company Mrs. S would need in her situation."

"She's lucky to have me and Maynard, and between us, she won't be in her situation for long, so you'll have to mark that mail RETURN TO SENDER. Last thing she needs is a damn stray cat. If I have anything to say about it, that animal will be gone before my aunt will."

"I'm so sorry to intrude." The mail carrier has stuffed a fistful of catalogs and flyers in the box and backed away. "You must be very sad right now."

Lucille looks about as sad as a striking rattlesnake.

"Tell Mrs. S that Erin the mail girl called, and I wish her the very best of everything."

Lucille mumbles something ungracious under her breath, and my strapping cohort walks away.

★ ★ ★

For lunch we have hamburger, and I con the whole patty out of Mrs. S in four minutes flat. I bury it next to the breakfast sausage near the foundation, musing that the property will be vermin-free for a very long time.

Dinner is meatballs. All mine. But I've had to tongue too much and can barely jump up onto the parlor sill after dinner.

Maynard and Lucille are watching *Touched by an Angel*, of all things.

"Meat go down?" Maynard wants to know. He is a beer belly with a five o'clock shadow and that's about it.

"Every last crumb. But it's not working fast enough. She seems to be doing better, oddly enough. I don't get it."

"Maybe we need a concentrated form. Something liquid."

I quail. There is no way I can keep Mrs. Sargent from drinking something.

Lucille gets up, goes into the kitchen and returns with a bottle of Ozarka spring water.

"Maybe a hypodermic. We could always say one of those nutso product tamperers had done it."

"Gad," says Maynard. "That crap tastes like fairy juice. Tropical fruit flavor. That

35

ought to cover up anything. We'll bring her to the parlor tomorrow morning, and make a damn toast out of it."

I more fall than jump to the ground. I am very hungry, very thirsty, very weak. And very desperate.

There is more sausage for breakfast, and more sausage buried by the foundation, and more sausage in my system than there should be.

I save my strength by snoozing in the oleander shade. Oleander leaves are poisonous to animals, you know, but I could not open my mouth to eat even a filet mignon at this point.

Mrs. Sargent is in the parlor. She had wheeled herself to the front door and asked that it be opened. She doesn't know that this is a last request.

Maynard and Lucille shrug.

"I'm glad you're feeling better, Aunt Betty," Lucille coos in that meat-offering voice. I've heard people trying to trap me and they sound just like that, all honey and hypocrisy.

"How about a nice tall cool glass of spring water?"

I am on the front stoop peering through the screen. They have left the latch off. I paw it open, slip through. Better.

"I'm feeling poorly lately," Mrs. Sargent says, eyeing the Ozarka askance. "That stuff is all bubbly. It might upset my stomach."

"It might soothe your stomach," Lucille urges, lifting the bottle.

Well, I am nearly dying of thirst.

I launch myself into the air, right at the Ozarka bottle.

We land like paired ice-skaters, the bottle in my arms as we go spinning across the hardwood floor together. I am kicking, I am unscrewing the cap faster than I have ever before. It is a world record. In a minute a sizzling flood of adulterated spring water is washing over the floor and over me.

"Get that cat!" Lucille screeches. "Kill that cat!"

"No!" the old lady yells. "Don't touch it. It's my friend."

My ears prick up as I leap to avoid the arc of Maynard's kicking work boot.

Other boots, coming up the walk.

"Shut the door," Lucille screeches, rushing for the heavy oaken slab that stands ajar.

I rush to beat her to it.

It's swinging shut like a steel safe door, momentum behind it.

Before me I see Erin's open, puzzled face nearing the mesh of the screen.

Mrs. S is screaming, "Don't hurt it! Don't hurt it!"

If that door closes, everything will remain hidden behind it. Everything bad that can happen, one way or the other, will happen.

That door must not close.

I dash through with no inches to spare. It is a good thing I am so skinny. My forelegs push open the screen door, inviting, drawing Erin in. Her face is alarmed, confused, and grim. She is not going to go away.

I grit my teeth. I stop on the threshold, close my eyes, and leave my tail trailing behind me like a doorstop.

Then all goes black and bright white. I hear howls of pain. I rocket into the front yard, pursued by agony.

Erin has pushed the ajar door open and is filling the front room. "Mrs. S? They said you were too weak to see company."

"Weak! A little, but that's from the food they give me. Mush like you've never seen before. Oh, the poor kitty, where is the poor kitty?"

"They said you couldn't see anybody," Erin goes on, talking as if Maynard and

Lucille weren't there. "I missed our talks."

"They said you had a different route, and never came anymore —"

So there it was: they said, she said.

I am out of there, but I knew that Maynard and Lucille soon would be too.

Act III:
The Great Escape

So what do I get after saving the day and the old lady and ingesting enough acid rain to be the Great Lakes? The Big Boys on the street are waiting for me when I finally stop panting in a vacant lot.

Death, taxes, and tomcats are unavoidable. Unfortunately, two of those negative outcomes were right in front of me, snarling and hissing and mincing sideways with their backs up and their tails and ears down. (And I don't mean the IRS.)

Luckily, the excruciating pain in my tail means that I was having a Very Bad Hair Day. It is standing up all over my body as if I'd stuck my tongue in an electrical outlet, which I know better than to do.

So I let myself really feel that pain-pulsating tail of mine, broken in two places the exact thickness of a hardwood front door. I yowl out my agony and run right through their ranks like a bolt of cold lightning . . . you know, that weird gray flash people sometimes see running along the baseboards?

I am an electrical phenomenon, all right. Wish someone had captured this Kodak Moment for posterity, not that I will ever have any.

I don't have the Big Boys' advantage of numbers (about nine), or the edge of body weight, 'cause every last and least one of 'em is twice my heft. But I do have speed and a tail that feels like the long, burning line of a firecracker fuse. I blast past them like the lead car in the Indy 500 and head right for sanctuary.

Some would call it prison, but at this point I need something between me and the cruel, cold world, not to mention about a gross of cold, cruel claws.

I dart right into the open cage and throw all my weight on the food holder.

Clang.

I don't bother eating the glop, although I feel hungry when I'm not hurting. I turn in a flash of pain and triumph and have the satisfaction of seeing the pursuing phalanx mashing their kissers into the metal mesh, ears and whiskers crumpled against steel wire. They all look like a bunch of Scottish Folds, that breed of cat with crimped ears. The tartan plaids impressed on their faces by the wire patterns go right along with the Caledonian theme. Scotland's burning, boys, and if my tail had to go for broke in the course of a humanitarian act, your pusses are gonna look like chopped haggis on a birthday cake with a rash of candles for a couple of days.

They scream and caterwaul and claw at me through the grid, but I am safe until the feral catch-and-cut crew come to retrieve me, and then I will be out like Flynn because I've already had my politically correct procedure.

So I squat on the unpleasant metal grid floor, which turns my tender pads into waffle-patterns, and watch the Big Boys raise their blood pressure to no avail. I would wrap my tail around my throbbing toes but it doesn't move so good. It finally dawns on me that I have sacrificed my pride and joy, my panache, my posterior plume, for all eternity. The cause was good, true, but the effect will be a lifetime maiming.

I would offer my tail a parting snuffle or

two, but I dare not show weakness in front of these bully boys, even if they are out of reach at the moment.

I have gravely underestimated the risks of turning myself in voluntarily. When the collection van pulls up as expected a couple hours later, the gang scatters like rats facing a Bengal tiger. I am left to stand alone, like the cheese in the old song. I am "It" in a game of tag, and all the players have vanished except the parents, who come to break up the game for the night.

A woman approaches my prison on soft cat feet to bend down and peer at me. These catch-and-cut types are usually women. My old man would call them "dames," but I am more enlightened.

"Got one! Oh, what a pretty cat," she says.

This sounds promising. The other woman bends down. I wait for them to un-latch the cage to move me so I can dash out and find another shelter before the Big Boys are smart enough to come back.

My world shakes, then spins. I am not to be removed, with an opportunity for fleeing, but will be transported in the trap.

Somebody has figured out that we street types are tricky.

But I am trickier than any "somebody" out there. Outwitted murderers, didn't I?

I stand and totter over to the cage side, rubbing against the grid, as close as I can get to Woman Number One.

"Merrrowwww," I say.

"This is a friendly one," she purrs right back. "We may be able to foster her and find her a home."

Her.

Thus it begins, the greatest masquerade of my crime-fighting career.

"Look," says Woman Number Two. "She can hardly hold her tail up. Something must have happened to it."

Duh.

"Oh, not the cage door closing, I hope," whimpers Woman Number One.

I mew piteously, small and wee. Nothing like a big lump of guilt to get humans on the right track.

"We'd better have the vet look at the tail before surgery."

Yeah, you'd better! The vet had better look *under* the tail, because I sure as heck do not want an unnecessary hysterectomy!

"Linda, I think we can place this one. She must be in awful pain, but she's still so sweet and friendly. I don't think she's feral at all."

Sweet and friendly does not cut it on the street, but among the Cage Set, it's the best pedigree there is. Even if you have to undergo a temporary sex change.

I purr so loud I sound like a snoring frog.

"Poor little thing!"

By now *my* eyes are watering. Well, my tail is a poor little thing, all right.

Soon I am ensconced, cage and all, in a van that smells like collies and cat-marking behavior.

Every jolt on the journey makes my tail quake, and I make the silent scream many times, which is the downside of the silent meow, but I grit my teeth. I do not want to scare anyone on the other end.

Frankly, the pain and the hunger and poison and the stress catch up with me, and I am pretty much out of it by the time I arrive wherever I arrive.

I recall much sympathetic cooing, and ginger inspections of my maimed posterior appendage. I am lifted and my weight is found wanting. I am turned upside down and my stomach is shaved.

This is when the cluckings become shock, and I am quickly turned right side up.

Voices say that I am "friendly" and a

"candidate." I am moved into another cage, and then another van, and then another cage.

I wake up in a room with a window wall on the bleak high plains emptiness of beyond-suburban Lubbock. A bare-naked tree, all trunk and limbs, awaits in a fenced area like a denuded traffic cop.

The room is crawling with my kind. All kinds of my kind, with but one thing in common: We belong to no one, and that could get us killed.

But we have one other thing in common, I know it in my bones. We have been chosen to live, at least long enough to get a chance at conning some human into a home.

Let us not kid ourselves. This is not a resort hotel. In a way it is as rough as the empty lot where the Big Boys rule.

A male attendant comes into the room, dispensing dry food. Finally, my cage is approached.

"So this is the new kitty."

The door opens. I am carefully lifted out.

"Bad tail," the young man says, squinting at the card affixed to my cage. "Name of . . . Jasmine. One- or two-year-old female. Yellow eyes. Long tail. Trapped. How'd you get yourself caught in a big ole trap, Jasmine? Must have been awfully hungry. You weigh as much as a six-month-old kitten in my hand. Here. You sit on this cat condo and make friends with the others."

I am left, high, dry, and handsome (if my tail were in any normal condition) for all the other cat eyes in the room to stare at. They are not mean, those eyes, but they are wary and hungry and hurt, probably like my eyes. Which are *green!* Or so my mama done told me, and I tend to believe her.

And my tail is not particularly *long,* but it is broken and hurts like hell.

And my name is not Jasmine, because I am not a girl, but I can see why with all the animals they have coming and going they made the mistake.

I am light on my feet, and jump down to try some food nuggets in a bowl.

Hisses, humped backs, and the delicate prod of nail-tips. I sigh. This may not be the Big Boys' lot, but I still will have to fight for every crumb.

Despite the initiation rituals, which leave me with minute scabs on my neck and shoulders, this place offers a certain routine. There are sunny times out scrabbling up the bare tree limbs.

There are the rare times a browser meanders through our quarters, eyeing each of us, murmuring at some, passing through, all too seldom picking . . . one.

We watch with round envious eyes as the lucky pickee is groomed, then handed over, never to be seen again. We hope the escapee heads toward the heaven of laps and Fancy Feast and a secure old age.

We know, of course, only that one is gone, and it is not us.

How long can they keep us? Others crowd to join us, many times more than the few who leave. A grain of sand sifts through the narrow neck of the hourglass, and a thousand new grains pour into the wide gaping maw at the top.

So many are called homeless. So few are chosen.

My tail mends, though it is still tender, and I am still underweight. I bask in the sun on the bare-limbed tree. I take my nicks of the colony's claws. I wait. I am looked at. And left.

Then one day there is a buzz of activity. Several shelter people enter our colony cage at once. They need, they say, a black cat.

Eight of us perk up ears, widen eyes, purr.

Someone laid-back.

Three flip over on their sides and purr. I am not normally a side-flipper, and I will not start now.

Good for media.

Four lift paws, blink.

I am too weary still to perform. I can only recline elegantly, my twisted tail hidden between my legs.

"Here," someone says. "Jasmine is so calm. She should do well under the hot lights."

I am picked, picked up, put into a small carrier that is dark and close and taken to a van. This time my tail doesn't hurt as much as we jolt to a strange place.

I sit for a long time in the carrier, ignoring the water, food, and cardboard box of litter.

I am finally extracted into the glare of fourteen suns and settled on someone's lap.

Someone's lap.

This is my Big Chance.

My moment in the sun.

A few precious seconds to impress, please, survive.

I knead my nails into the lap. I purr. I blink in the bright lights. I remain very, very calm.

I hear voices discussing an adoption event. For the first time I hear the name "Midnight Louie." I hear my "name" Jasmine and statistics given. I hear that I have a "good personality" and am available.

Then the lights vanish. The cage returns. The humans gather around me and talk above my head as usual. They think it went very well. The noon news show resumes. The attractive anchor lady says, "And now the latest on a shocking case of elder abuse. Mrs. Sargent is safe in a foster home after her niece and the niece's live-in boyfriend were arrested on charges of abuse and attempted murder. An alert mail carrier noticed that —"

An alert mail carrier indeed! What about an "alert male carrier" of a once-proud tail?

But I am happy to hear the outcome, and the journey in the van soon returns me to the shelter common room. It is all over. And after two days, no one calls my name. I have been on TV and I have not been adopted. I know that Mrs. Sargent and Erin have been too busy to watch TV, but still, I had hopes. . . .

Needless to say, I am a little depressed.

Then another flutter of activity. An eminent visitor. Again I hear the name Midnight Louie. I begin to curse it, for it is not mine.

A woman enters the common room. She is being shown around, a VIP. Many thoughts flash through my mind. Midnight Louie is one big wheel to be mentioned on television. This woman is associated with Midnight Louie. It would be a smart move to associate with this woman.

But so many cats occupy the space, high and low and in-between. All are sweet and deserving and variously attractive. What can I do?

I sit on the concrete floor by the woman and meow. My dry, dusty life on the Lubbock streets has left my voice scratchy and faint. I doubt she will hear me.

But she looks down. "Oh, this is a little one."

She bends down and picks me up.

Hosanna to Bastet! I purr. I rub my face on her shoulder. I am light (thanks to long-time hunger) and laid-back (thanks to weakness).

She cradles me like a baby, tummy up.

"The tummy is growing out from a shaving. She must be spayed."

The attendant agrees that it looks like that.

I agree, too. I am politically correct,

whatever gender I am taken for. I am quiet and friendly. I deserve a home.

I am put back down on the concrete floor and the woman leaves. The sun no longer shines on the naked tree outside and the high plains are empty, and evening comes.

The attendants arrive in a flutter. Many are chosen, lifted into carriers, carted away. I am one.

I end up in the bottom, floor-level cage in a Tic-Tac-Toe board of piled cages in a fluorescent-lit store somewhere in Lubbock. Kittens cavort above me, easily accessible. I am old, a year or two, and inhabit the lowest level where people have to squat on their knees to see me.

But suddenly I am released. The woman who knows Midnight Louie has asked me out on a date! I sprawl on her lap and purr. I knead my sharp claws into the fiber of pure silk. I sit on the table that is piled with books and rolling pens and a white foam cup that recently held water. I always tend toward water, like a cactus. I stick my nose in the cup, lift it up and everybody laughs.

"Robocat," the woman names me as I pose with the cup on my nose and head.

Later, she is on the phone discussing me.

I am a year-old female, she says, small and portable. I've been on TV and am ideal for media appearances. I have a wonderful purr-sonality, but my tail is a mess. I will never be able to loft it higher than a croquet hoop. But it won't show much; she didn't even notice it at first.

I am being discussed! The shelter director has brought a collapsible travel cage so I can fly away with the Midnight Louie woman tomorrow.

I am out of the cages and free to be me. (Even if it is Jasmine, the female impersonator.)

And then I am returned to the cage, the cages are loaded into the van, and we return to the shelter.

Nothing whatsoever else happens. I bask briefly in the tree. I accept and give my sharp-pointed badges of courage to my peers. A lot of cats come, a few cats go. And I wonder how long Jasmine of the Crooked Tail can be kept without disappearing into That Room From Which No Cats Return.

Days go by. Then a flurry. Maxie, a big black short-hair, is suddenly brushed and spiffed up. The lucky devil. Someone has adopted him.

My tail droops even lower than usual. Time must be running out.

Flutter. Visitors in the colony. Attendants, a man and woman.

Maxie is presented.

"This is the wrong cat," the Midnight Louie woman declares. "This is not Jasmine."

I am dredged up from the concrete floor. I am suddenly being combed.

"Oh," she says, "I was afraid for a moment —" She looks regretfully at Maxie, freshly brushed. "We really can't take two —"

While she worries, I purr. I rub my face on her shoulder.

Money is exchanged. I am worth something! I am put into the soft portable carrier I never left in before. We drive away, and I am released into a room with a bed and a window and a bathroom. I have my own little bathroom in a cardboard box, and my carrier is left open, and there is food and water in bowls, but I am too excited to use any of it.

The man and woman vanish, speaking of dinner.

When they return, I have examined the room from stem to stern and they are surprised that I am so calm. They go to bed.

Bed. A room. Night. I am home.

I jump up on the bed. I jump up on the

man and woman, only I cannot jump up on both at once, so I alternate every fourteen purrs. I meow. I alternate. I purr. I meow. All night.

I have a home! I've got a home!

I am hoarse by morning and the people have not slept much, but they are pleased with me for some reason. They have never seen such a happy cat, they say. I am so smart. I am so pretty. I am such a sweet, pretty girl.

Oh, well. I have a home. I would pretend to be Lassie to have a home.

To make a long story short, I am the new unofficial Midnight Louie body double. I drive home five hours to Fort Worth, and when I get there I eat, drink, and make merry. I gain weight. I go to the vet, who says that my liver numbers are bad and I must have eaten something toxic, but after a month they are on the money.

My coat goes from dull to glossy. My tail recovers full range of motion, even to the tip. Although I will never be able to hold it straight up like a pennant, my filling-out coat covers all signs of my heroic breaks.

But one thing bugs me. They keep calling me "Midnight Louise" and "she."

Otherwise, everything is perfect.

So I have to figure out what to do about

it and finally decide that the shortest route is the best.

When they are playing with me one day I roll over and leave nothing to the imagination.

"Louise!" they exclaim, as if I had done something wrong. Get with it! Different strokes for different folks.

"I can't believe it," he says.

"He . . . she was such a small little cat, and it's hard to tell a neutered male from a female in crowded shelters," the woman says. "Remember Goldie, the stray we took to a no-kill shelter and left spaying money for so she'd get a home faster? Then they called and said she was a neutered he?"

"But there is no other Midnight Louie than Midnight Louie," he says. "What can we call . . . him?"

There is a silence. "Midnight Louie. *Junior.*"

And that is that.

So I am out of the detecting business and female impersonator racket, and into the luxuriating indoor house-cat class. Permanently.

Highest, Best Use

by J. A. Jance

For years ours was a three-dog family with two elderly golden retrievers, Nikki and Tess, and an ugly but honest mutt named Boney, who was half German shepherd and half Irish wolfhound. When Nikki and Tess were finally called home to heaven at ages eleven and twelve, respectively, a grieving Mr. Bone (who makes cameo appearances in my two thrillers *Hour of the Hunter* and *Kiss of the Bees*) went into a great decline. Deciding he was lonely, we went in search of a companion for him. We intended to come home with one puppy, but of course, being softhearted ninnies, we arrived instead with two equally adorable — in our minds, anyway — red-dog golden retrievers.

It's six years ago now since those two tiny balls of fluff tumbled into our lives. In our view, they were virtually identical. For a while, the only way we could tell them apart was by the color of their collars — Aggie's was green and Daphne's, pink. Boney, however, had no difficulty at all in telling them apart. He looked at Daph and said to himself, "Hey, you're a little cutie." From then on, Daphne could do no wrong. She could pull Bone's ears and tail and all she would elicit from him was a long-suffering sigh. Aggie was a different story altogether. Boney took one look at her and said to himself, "You are the Devil's spawn!" From that moment on, it never changed. If Aggie came too close to Mr. Bone, she was greeted with a low-throated growl and a puppy-eye-level view of his two-inch long and very sharp fangs.

Four years ago, we lost Boney, too — after eleven short years. Like Maddy Watkins in the story, I'm greedy and think dogs should all live much longer. While Bone was around, he was definitely top dog, and he enforced an artificial pack hierarchy with Daphne in the middle and Aggie on the bottom. Once

Boney was gone, the two girls had to settle the top-dog question to their own satisfaction. They did it by way of a bloody battle that sent them both to the vet. My daughter, who was dogsitting at the time of the fight, broke it up by throwing a full Brita water pitcher into the fray. She, under-standably, refers to the Girls as "hooli-gans." My husband calls them "Angel Dogs."

I won't say which of those two names they answer to, but I will say that these wonderful little sixty-pound dogs have added immeasurably to our quality of life. I can only hope we do the same for them.

— J. A. Jance

The first day of school. Maddy Watkins sighed at the very thought of it. After all those years of teaching kindergarten and loving it, school was starting without her. Again. It was six years now since she had stopped teaching for good. It surprised her to realize that the first day of school still had the power to leave her feeling blue. *Oh well,* she thought. *No use sitting around feeling sorry for myself.*

Finishing the last of her breakfast coffee,

she set the dainty china cup down on its saucer. Instantly her red-dog golden retrievers, Daphne and Agatha, went on full alert, watching her intently, to see if Maddy's next move would have something to do with them — an after-breakfast treat, perhaps, or maybe, if they were lucky, a walk on the beach. Both dogs sat without moving while Maddy cleared and rinsed the breakfast dishes and put the milk carton back into the refrigerator.

"So what is it then, girls?" she asked. "A walk?"

After sprinting to the door, their toenails snapping and skidding on the hardwood floor, the two nearly identical dogs stood side by side with their tails wagging in unison while Maddy slipped a light sweater over her shoulders and gathered her walking stick and whistle.

"Now wait," she told them. Obligingly, the two dogs stepped aside while Maddy went first. Only when she said, "Okay," did they come gamboling and frolicking through the door, across the porch, and down through the yard where they stopped again, waiting expectantly, for Maddy to open the gate that allowed access onto the long stretch of private beach that Maddy Watkins shared with other homeowners whose property bordered Race Lagoon.

By the time Maddy made her way to the gate, the dogs were literally dancing back and forth with excitement. "All right, girls, all right," Maddy grumbled good-naturedly. "Hold your horses."

Once she opened the gate, the dogs raced headlong toward the beach and the water where there might be dead crabs or rotting starfish for rolling on and dead twigs suitable for chasing. Just watching the dogs run side by side, leaping over logs and sprinting through the knee-high grass, made Maddy feel better. Their happiness was so utterly uncomplicated and honest, and it was almost always catching. As they reached the water's edge, she gave a short blast on her whistle. Immediately Aggie and Daph whirled around and raced back, tongues lolling, faces smiling. "Okay," Maddy said as soon as they reached her, then she sent them galloping away once again, back toward the water.

Watching the joyful dogs running at breakneck speed, Maddy couldn't help but remember that snotty young woman at the animal shelter. It had been a year after Bud, Maddy's husband, had died of kidney failure, and six months after Maddy's eleven-year-old dog, Sarah, had died unexpectedly in her sleep. Maddy had gone to her local animal shelter thinking she'd come home with some nice puppy — one of those sad, abandoned creatures that the ads always describe as "free to good home."

"But you're seventy years old," the young woman had objected archly while scanning the information on Maddy's application. She made it sound as though Maddy were actually older than God. From the young woman's point of view, maybe that was true.

"So?" Maddy had demanded.

"But it says here you want a puppy."

"That's exactly what I want — a puppy that hasn't already been wrecked by someone else. A puppy I can train to do things the way I want them done."

"But wouldn't you rather have a nice sedate older dog? We have several of them here right now, ready for adoption."

Maddy didn't feel like explaining that she had done that once — taken in an older dog. Sarah had been at least six when someone had left her — sick, dirty, underfed, and barely able to walk — in a ditch alongside the road. That had meant that there were only five short years between Sarah's arrival in Maddy's home and the terrible hurt of losing her. Maddy Watkins was tired of loving and losing. She was greedy and wanted more time. "I said I want a puppy," she insisted.

"But puppies are so much hard work," the young woman said, speaking clearly and slowly as though Maddy were both deaf and developmentally disabled. "With house training and exercising. Puppies can be *very* demanding."

Maddy gave another short blast on the whistle. Again, Aggie and Daph tore back to her, running at breakneck speed. While Maddy took her own sweet time getting down to the pebbly stretch of beach, the girls would have run the entire distance six full times. So much for them not getting enough exercise!

"Young lady," an exasperated Maddy had responded. "I taught kindergarten for forty years, so I have some dim idea of what's involved in potty training. Kids or puppies — it's all pretty much the same."

"Still," the young woman had replied. "Our guidelines won't allow us to send animals to unsuitable homes — ones where we don't think they'll receive the proper kind of care."

"Care!" Maddy had exploded. "You're looking at my *age* and my cane and you think that gives you the right to judge whether or not I'm qualified to have a dog? I'll tell you what you can do then. You can take your animal shelter and go straight to hell, and don't expect any more donations of dog food from me, either!"

With that, Maddy had flounced out of the shelter, although flouncing was difficult to achieve with her cane as well as her newly remodeled hip. Within days she had gone from the shelter to a dog breeder where she had blown the better part of one month's worth of retirement income on two lovable full sisters from a litter of eleven fuzzy golden puppies. And then, because she had always loved murder mysteries, Maddy had named the two puppies after her two favorite authors, Agatha Christie and Daphne DuMaurier.

Maybe all those years of dealing with kindergarteners had shielded Maddy from what was going on outside the walls of her classroom and her home, but that confrontation at the shelter had been her first eyeball-to-eyeball encounter with age discrimination as it applied to Maddy Watkins. The unfortunate experience hadn't turned her into a raging Gray Panther on the spot, but it had certainly raised her consciousness. From then on, wherever she encountered it, she fought back as best she could.

Of course, her friends and her son had been as universally disapproving as the little twit at the pound. "Why on earth did you get two of them?" Tess McKnight had asked over their weekly bridge game. "Why not just one? Wouldn't it be easier for someone your age to take care of one dog instead of two?"

"Because two puppies will keep each other company," Maddy had returned. "And both of them will be good company for someone *my* age."

Rex, her middle-aged son the real estate developer, and his fashion plate wife, Gina, hadn't been any happier about the situation than Tess was. "You're getting up there, Mom," Rex had hinted darkly. "You shouldn't be out here all by yourself. It's dangerous. You never know who or what might come wandering by. There are all kinds of nuts running around loose these days, even out here in the country."

"I have your father's gun for protection," Maddy had told him. "I'll bet when it comes to target practice, I can still shoot circles around you."

Knowing she was right, Rex nodded in grudging agreement. Bud Watkins had been a lifelong member of the National Rifle Association. To Bud's dismay, his son had always been far more interested in shooting hoops than in shooting guns. Now Rex didn't bother arguing the point with his mother.

"Still," he continued, "one of these days, you're going to have to get out of this big old place and move into town. What will you do with two dogs then?"

Of course, the house wasn't big at all, not by modern standards. And Maddy knew what Rex really wanted — a huge waterfront lot where he could build some big rambling monstrosity on spec, one he'd be able to sell for a fortune to some willing Microsoft millionaire from Seattle.

"I'll cross that bridge when I get to it," Maddy had told her son crossly. "Besides," she added, "Ag and Daph are both a lot better behaved than you were at their age." *Or even now,* she thought, but she didn't say it aloud. Rex hadn't liked her parting comment very much, but it had served him right. He had some nerve, trying to force his mother out of her own home long before she was ready.

Maddy reached the beach and took up her favorite position — a seat on a worn old driftwood log. Later in the fall, once the rains and high tides came, that narrow strip of beach would virtually disappear under water, but for now, she sat high and dry. Early morning mist and fog had burned off, giving way to bright September sunlight. Maddy sat with warmth washing over her body while the dogs played a madcap game of tag up and down the beach and in and out of the water. Tiring of that, Aggie pounced eagerly on a piece of driftwood and brought it over to Maddy where she deposited it just within reach in a none-too-subtle hint.

This, too, was part of the morning ritual. It was Maddy's job to hurl the chosen piece of wood into the water as far as possible so the dogs could swim out, grab it in their mouths, and bring it back. After all, that's what they were — retrievers — and Maddy loved to watch them do their chosen work. Of the two, Aggie was by far the better swimmer. She was usually the one who swam out far enough to grasp the stick, but as soon as she brought it within range, Daphne would latch on to one end. Then, together, the two dogs would bring the stick out of the water, looking for all the world like a team of very wet, miniature plow horses.

The last time Maddy threw the stick,

however, she noticed that Aggie was the only one bringing it back for a change. Instead of lunging in to steal a piece of the prize, Daphne seemed to have lost interest in the game and was intent on something else. After a moment's hesitation, Aggie, too, abandoned the stick. When they came out of the water, what they dropped at Maddy Watkins's feet wasn't the stick at all. Instead, it was a purse — a woman's large leather purse, complete with a long shoulder strap trailing a skirt of seaweed.

"What in the world is this?" Maddy demanded, picking it up.

The dogs raced off, expecting Maddy to make another throw. When she didn't, they paused long enough to shake off excess water.

Maddy unclasped the purse and emptied it. Along with water and more seaweed, a clutch of items fell out onto the gravel. Included were several tubes of lipstick, three different pens, a compact, and a soggy passport. Maddy had to be quick in order to scoop up the booty before the dogs beat her to it. Once upright again, Maddy couldn't help but marvel. Dr. Mason had told her that after surgery, her hip would be as good as new. Two years later, it still wasn't quite perfect, but it was far better than it had been. Before the surgery, bending down to pick up anything would have caused her impossible agony. Now it was more of a serious twinge, unpleasant but not unbearable.

"Okay, girls," she said. "Enough. We'd better go back to the house and see if we can find the nice lady who lost her purse. It looks valuable. I'm sure she's going to want it back."

Aggie and Daphne may have been disappointed at having their outing cut short, but they raced up the path with the same uncompromising enthusiasm they had shown coming down to the beach. Back at the house, Maddy toweled off the wet dogs and ordered them onto their rugs to dry. By then Maddy had completely forgotten about this being the first day of school. She poured herself another cup of coffee, then she covered the Formica kitchen table with towels and laid out the wet purse and its contents so she could examine them more closely.

Maddy was no expert in purses; she usually bought hers from the bargain table at Ross Dress For Less, but this one looked expensive. It was made of fine-grained leather with what looked like a brass medallion hanging over the clasp. With the help of her best reading glasses, Maddy was just able to make out the words written there in raised letters. "Brahmin, Fairehaven, Massachusetts."

She used dish towels to dry what she could. The powder in the compact had dissolved and disappeared entirely, but the tubes of lipstick were still pretty much intact. Years of being an Avon Lady on the side had made Maddy a whiz when it came to women's cosmetics. The labels may have all been illegible, but she recognized the distinctive cases. These were expensive items — ones that came from upscale counters at Nordstrom and The Bon or from exclusive spa-type places, not from your neighborhood Bartell Drugs.

Putting a towel inside the purse to blot up more of the water, she noticed a zippered compartment at the back. Opening that, she pulled out a sodden mass of paper and gasped in surprise when she realized it was a thick wad of money. Bud had never been one for cleaning out his pockets, and Maddy hadn't been much better. Over the years, she had washed his wallet countless times. She had learned through trial and error the best remedy for repairing water damaged currency had been her trusty clothes dryer — turned to the DELICATE setting, of course. So that's what she did now. She put the fistful of money as well as the soggy passport into the dryer and turned it on. Then, feeling like a modern-day Miss Marple, she turned her attention to the contents of the small zippered wallet.

She hit paydirt almost immediately. The plastic cards inside the wallet were all impervious to water. Laurel Riggins was the woman's name. Age 43. Blond hair; blue eyes. Her address was listed as Double Bluff Road on the far end of Whidbey Island. The official Department of Licensing photo showed an attractive woman with what looked like a shy smile. "Now we're getting someplace, girls," Maddy said as she got up to go in search of the phone book.

Lying on their rugs, the damp dogs thumped their tails in grateful acknowledgment of that morsel of attention. Moments later, again with the help of her reading glasses — why did they insist on using such fine print in phone books these days? — Maddy had located the number for Hadley M. Riggins on Double Bluff Road. Her call to the Riggins residence was answered by the voice of a middle-aged male.

"Is Laurel there, please?" she asked.

"Not right now," the man said. "This is her husband. Is there something I can do for you?"

"My name is Maddy Watkins. My dogs and I were down playing on the beach this morning," Maddy explained. "I live on Race Inlet. And Ag and Daph — those are my dogs — seem to have found your wife's purse. I have it here now. It's water damaged, of course. I doubt she'll be able to use it again, but I thought she'd want the contents back at least."

"How very kind of you!" Hadley Riggins exclaimed. "Laurel lost it a number of weeks ago. We thought maybe it had fallen out of the car when she was taking the ferry. As I said, she's not here right now. She's in town at the moment, but she'll be thrilled to have it back. She's replaced her driver's license and so forth, but still, it'll be a relief to have it back. I could come over right now and pick it up — if that wouldn't be too inconvenient."

"Not at all," Maddy said. "That will be fine." She gave him directions to the house. It wasn't until after she got off the phone that she realized he had made no mention of the money.

The better part of an hour passed before Hadley Riggins drove into the yard in a white Lincoln. Leaving the dogs inside the house, Maddy went out to meet him, carrying the purse and its contents stowed in a plastic grocery bag.

"I hope you don't mind," she said. "I put the money in the dryer. But it's all there."

"Money?" he asked with a frown.

"Yes," Maddy said. "The eight thousand dollars that was in your wife's purse. It was in a zippered compartment. I dried it in the dryer just like I used to do when my husband's wallet went though the wash."

Hadley Riggins nodded. "Oh, that's right," he said. "I forgot about that."

But Maddy Watkins had been a kindergarten teacher for too many years not to recognize a lie when she heard it. Hadley Riggins had known nothing at all about the small fortune in cash that had been concealed in his wife's purse. And that seemed odd. If Maddy had ever had occasion to carry that much money around in her own purse, you can bet Bud Watkins would have known all about it. Losing eight thousand dollars didn't seem like the kind of thing that would simply slip a person's mind.

"I'm sure Laurel would want me to give

you something for your trouble . . ." Hadley Riggins began as he reached belatedly for his wallet.

"You'll do nothing of the kind," Maddy declared, waving aside his tentative offer of compensation. "Honesty is its own reward," she added, hoping that he got her disapproving message all the same. It seemed to her that the least he could have done was act moderately grateful, even if he wasn't.

That was on Tuesday morning. For the next several days, Maddy busied herself with looking after the dogs, caring for her jungle of houseplants, reading her Bible, and letting the warm September days slip over her like a soft, warm blanket. She had said she wanted no reward, and she had meant it. Hadley Riggins's unconvincing offer of monetary compensation hadn't set well with her. Maddy certainly didn't want money, but she did expect to receive a gracious thank-you note for her trouble. Her parents had brought up Maddy with a strict sense of right and wrong. Her mother had insisted that one of the hallmarks of good breeding was the prompt sending of thank-you notes. A full week passed during which no thank-you note was forthcoming. By then, Maddy was growing suspicious.

First there was the presence of all that money — a sum Maddy Watkins was convinced Hadley Riggins had known nothing about. And then there was the passport. Maddy had a passport of her own. She and Bud had gotten passports when they had taken a Caribbean cruise years ago. Maddy's passport was still valid, but she certainly didn't carry it around with her or put it in her purse whenever she planned to take a ferry off the island. The only time the document had been in her purse was when she and Bud were actually on their cruise. The rest of the time she kept it in the strong box upstairs along with the rest of her important papers. Had Laurel Riggins been running away from something with all that money and her passport? Her husband, perhaps? That might explain why Hadley Riggins had known nothing about his wife's eight thousand dollars.

Finally, on Wednesday of the following week, Maddy stopped off at the sheriff's substation in Oak Harbor when she went into town to buy groceries. The young officer at the desk, Deputy Pete Harris, couldn't have been more polite. "How can I be of service?" he asked.

Maddy had been considering what to say and how best to say it all the way into town. "I think I'd like to report someone missing," she said.

Deputy Harris sat forward in his chair. "You *think* you want to report someone missing?" he asked. "Does that mean you don't know if they're really missing or you don't know whether or not you should report it?"

"I *believe* a woman named Laurel Riggins is missing," Maddy said. "But I don't know for sure." She went on to tell the whole story. In the beginning, Deputy Harris took copious notes on what appeared to be an official piece of paper, but by the time Maddy finished, he had put down his pen and was actually grinning at her.

"You're filing this report based entirely on the fact that a woman you've never met hasn't bothered to send a thank-you note?" He made no effort to hide his mirth. Maddy, on the other hand, was not amused.

"So you don't think thank-you notes are important?" she demanded.

Deputy Harris sobered. "Of course they're important ma'am," he said. "But not a matter of life and death. It just doesn't sound to me as though there's enough here to warrant an official investigation. We haven't had any other complaints about this. I think it's possible Laurel Riggins just didn't have the benefit of the kind of upbringing you did. I'm sure she's fine."

It was the snotty young woman at the animal shelter all over again, only Deputy Harris was more polite.

"I'm sure she is, too," Maddy said. She got up and headed for the door.

Deputy Harris beat her to it and held the door open for her. "If there's anything else we can do . . ."

"Don't bother," she replied curtly, jabbing the sidewalk with her cane as she walked past him. "You've done quite enough."

Aggie and Daphne were waiting in the back seat of Maddy's Buick. They wanted to kiss her hello when she came back to the car, but Maddy wasn't interested. She was too provoked. "Not a matter of life and death," she grumbled to the dogs. "Well, we'll just see about that."

She went home and put on her Avon Lady vest, the one with all her sales awards pinned to it. Then after walking and watering the dogs, she loaded them and her cosmetics sample case back in the car and headed for Double Bluff Road. She avoided the Riggins's place, but she called on houses up and down the road. At several places there was no one at home. But when someone did come to the door, there was little reluctance when they saw a white haired little old lady standing on the doorstep leaning heavily on a cane. Usually she was asked in and invited to sit down and even offered something to drink. At each house she explained that she was in the neighborhood because she had come to deliver an order to Laurel Riggins. Finding no one home, she hadn't wanted to waste the trip. In the process, she did her sales pitch and managed to pick up an order or two along the way, probably because people felt sorry for her.

It was at the fourth house that she hit the jackpot. "Why, Laurel's in New Zealand," Tammy Wyndham told her. "She left about a month ago — to visit her daughter. Chrissy's a missionary, you know, working for some outfit that's headquartered in Auckland."

Laurel didn't go to New Zealand without her passport, Maddy thought, but she kept her face perfectly composed. "Oh, that's right," she said. "Now I remember her saying something about a trip. It's just that what she wanted has been back-ordered so many times that I completely forgot about her being out of town."

Maddy smoothed things over as best she could, sold Tammy Wyndham some lipstick, some foundation, and a bottle of perfume, and then headed back to Oak Harbor. When she returned to the sheriff's substation, Deputy Harris was still on duty. "Still no thank-you note?" he asked with a small smirk.

Maddy did not smile. "Her neighbors say she went to New Zealand."

"No wonder then," he said. "The mail from there probably takes a little longer."

"If Laurel Riggins left the country, she didn't have her passport," Maddy responded sternly. "It was still in her purse when I dragged it out of the water. The passport was there along with eight thousand dollars. I know because I counted the money myself. Not only that, when I called, her husband told me she wasn't home. He said it in a way that sounded as though she'd just that minute walked out the door to go to the store and would be back in an hour or so."

Deputy Harris grimaced. "All right," he said. "I'll send an officer out, but I still think it's a wild goose chase."

Relieved, Maddy went home. A fierce squall was blowing in off the water. The huge evergreen trees at the back of the house were shedding pieces of limbs around them as she and the dogs ran into the house. With the wind blowing the rain sideways against the windows, Maddy couldn't help being grateful for the hours of careful craftsmanship she and Bud had put into the building of their snug little house. Safe and warm, she made her evening meal — a small bowl of chicken-noodle soup, a slice of buttered bread, half an apple, and a single glass of Chardonnay. Then, with the two dogs at her side, she settled in for a quiet evening, sitting in front of the fire in Bud's old easy chair, re-reading Agatha Christie's fascinating auto-biography, and listening to classical music on KING-FM.

The hours slipped by. The living room with its handsome river-rock fireplace was the part of the house that reminded her the most of Bud and made her feel close to him. He had laid the fireplace himself. He had crafted the sturdy andirons in his machine shop/foundry. He had also made the little pair of bronze baby shoes that sat on a plaque on the mantel. Rex, of course, had never been the least bit interested in working with his hands, and he had been ashamed of his father for doing so. That was one of the reasons Maddy kept his baby shoes right there in plain sight — to serve as a reminder to both of them.

All her life, Maddy Watkins had been a night owl. Her propensity to stay up late had been the bane of her existence all those years when she'd had to get up the next morning or even later that *same* morning and go to school to face a classroom of exuberant five-year-olds. Now though, staying up as late as she liked and rising only when she was ready were some of the most worthwhile benefits of being retired. Unaware of time passing, she glanced at the clock and was surprised to see that it was already after twelve. There were only two pages left in the chapter she was reading, so she decided to finish those before letting the dogs out and making her way into the bedroom.

It was halfway through the first of those two pages when Aggie raised her head. Ears pricked and hackles up, she let out a long, low growl. The ferocity in the growl was enough to make the hair on the back of Maddy's neck stand on end. At once Daphne, too, was on full alert. Before the dogs could bark, Maddy stifled them. "Enough!" she ordered. "Quiet." It was something she had taught Sarah when Bud had been so sick and needed his sleep. When the girls had come along, she had taught them the same thing. Now they didn't bark, but Aggie was still growling.

Maddy reached over and switched off her reading lamp. Then she turned off the music as well. The fire had burned down to mere coals that left a dim, ruddy glow in the room. Maddy was sitting and holding her breath when she heard the tinkle of breaking glass coming from the direction of her bedroom. The tinkle of glass was followed by a huge *whump*. At once she smelled smoke.

She reached for the phone, thinking to dial 9-1-1, but the line was dead. Another breaking window and another *whump* told her a second firebomb had been thrown, this one into the guest bedrooms upstairs. If whoever was doing this was systematically working his way around the house, the living room would be next, followed by the kitchen. There was no chance of getting to Bud's gun. That was in the bedroom in the nightstand drawer. Maddy's only hope lay in making it out the back door without being seen.

Grabbing her cane, she hustled to the back door. "Come," she said to the dogs. "Right here."

They came at once, astonished at their good fortune that she would consider going for a walk with them so late at night. Her slicker hung on a peg beside the door — another piece of Bud's thoughtful handiwork. She grabbed the slicker and shrugged her way into it as she crossed the porch. Outside, the night was black. Rain still fell in pelting sheets, but that was good. It would make her more difficult to see — and hear. More breaking glass. This time from the living room. Her attacker was still around the corner of the house, but he wouldn't be for long.

With her heart pounding in her throat, Maddy did what she hoped her attacker wouldn't expect. Instead of heading for her nearest neighbors and help, she and the dogs made for the gate and for the wind-swept strip of beach beyond it. Afraid her attacker might catch sight of movement as he came around to the kitchen side of the house, Maddy hurried through the gate at the end of the yard and then ducked behind the massive gate post. Sure enough, she had barely hidden herself away when a shadowy figure emerged from behind the corner of the house. While he knelt with his back to her, Maddy turned and fled down the path toward the beach.

In the dark and rain, the narrow path was slick and steep. Once Maddy slipped and almost fell, imagining what would happen if she dislodged that incredibly expensive artificial hip. But somehow, scrambling desperately with her cane, she managed to right herself and go on. She knew that as soon as she finished descending the bluff, she would be out of sight of someone standing next to the house, but if he came to the edge of the yard or as far as the gate, he'd still be able to spot her.

The dogs, pulled by the lure of the water, threatened to dash on ahead. "Right here," Maddy commanded in an urgent whisper. And then, when they did as they were told and stayed at her heels, she added a grateful, "Good dogs. Good right here."

It seemed to take forever to reach the narrow strip of gravelly beach. Ducking down behind the driftwood log, Maddy grabbed the dogs and held them close. Panting, they lapped happily at her face with their long smooth tongues. Shaken as she was, it was all Maddy could do to hang on to them, but she didn't dare set them loose for fear her attacker would see them moving and come after them.

Huddling in the cold and wet, Maddy struggled to come to terms with what had happened. Someone had actually tried to kill her. But just when she had almost managed to convince herself that perhaps she was mistaken and had dreamed the whole thing — that it was nothing but a waking nightmare — a tongue of vivid orange flame shot high into the air. From her home. From the house Bud and she had built with their own hands and back-breaking labor and hard-earned cash.

No, it wasn't a dream at all. Someone *had* tried to kill her — someone who had thought a little old lady in her seventies would be safely in bed and sound asleep by midnight. And she knew without question who that someone was — Hadley Riggins. Maddy knew it in the same intuitive way Miss Marple must have known things. Hadley Riggins had murdered his wife, and he was willing to kill again in order to cover up that first crime.

Chilled, wet, and miserable, Maddy clutched the dogs to her and refused to move while her home on the bluff turned to ashes. Because of the metal roof, most of the flames were invisible from the place where Maddy huddled on the beach, but the dark clouds overhead turned orange in the reflected glow of the fierce flames. She didn't cry. There was no point. She and the dogs were alive and safe. That's what counted. Nothing else mattered.

After what seemed like an eternity and only when Maddy heard the sound of approaching sirens did she struggle to her feet and start back toward the house, toward the place where her house had once been but would be no more. She pushed open the gate at the top of the path and saw a small group of people huddled in the far corner of her backyard, far enough to be out of the way of the firemen swarming like so many ants around what was left of her house. Fanny Baxter, Maddy's next-door neighbor, was the first to spot Maddy and her dogs.

"Oh my God!" she exclaimed as though she'd seen a ghost. "Where were you? We all thought you were dead!"

"I was supposed to be," Maddy told her, and then let herself and the dogs be enveloped in the welcome comfort of her neighbors' outstretched arms.

By four o'clock the next morning, Maddy and the dogs were back at the substation. This time, however, instead of being left outside in the car, the dogs had been ushered into the office itself. A young officer who wasn't Deputy Harris had led Aggie and Daphne into a coffee room area where he promised them water and a few oatmeal cookies. Meanwhile, Lieutenant Caldwell, the supervisor who was taking Maddy's statement, listened carefully to everything Maddy said. And again, unlike Deputy Harris, Lieutenant Caldwell wrote it all down.

"So you didn't *see* anyone there in the yard?"

"No," Maddy replied. "Not at first. I heard glass breaking and the first fire start. It made a terrible noise — a huge *whoosh* kind of thing. I took the dogs and my cane and made for the beach. Later, I caught a glimpse of someone, a man I think, from the gate, but I was too far away to make out any details." She paused. "Have you sent anyone to check on Hadley Riggins?" she asked.

Lieutenant Caldwell nodded. "I did. No one seems to be home at the moment."

"He killed his wife," Maddy declared. "I'm sure of it. And now he's tried to kill me as well."

"You say his daughter is a missionary in New Zealand?"

Maddy nodded. "In Auckland. At least, that's what I was told."

"Do you have an address for her?"

"No," Maddy replied, "but you might check with the Riggins's neighbor, Tammy Wyndham. She lives on Double Bluff Road. She may be able to tell you."

"We've already done some checking," Lieutenant Caldwell said. "With the State Department. No one has been able to find any record that Laurel Riggins ever left the country."

"See there?" Maddy said. "I didn't think she had."

"We've put up roadblocks," Lieutenant Caldwell added. "Wherever Hadley Riggins is right now, I can assure you he won't be able to get off the island."

Behind Maddy, the outside door opened and closed. "Mother?"

Maddy turned to see Rex standing just inside the doorway. She hadn't called him, but someone must have — one of the neighbors, no doubt. It had taken him this long to drive from Seattle. The last ferry had already left Edmonds. He'd had to drive all the way around, through Mt. Vernon and down the length of the island.

"Hello, Rex," she said.

"Are you all right?"

"I'm fine."

"And the dogs?" he asked.

It gladdened her heart to think that he had actually asked about Aggie and Daph, that he'd gone so far as to inquire after their welfare.

"They're both fine, too," Maddy said. "They're out in the kitchen caging cookies from somebody's lunch."

Rex stumbled over to Maddy's chair. He pulled her upright and drew her into a heartfelt hug. Maddy could tell he was relieved and frightened, too.

"What happened?" he demanded.

"Somebody tried to kill me," she said calmly. "But I got away."

"Who?" he said.

Maddy shrugged. "It doesn't matter. This nice man, Lieutenant Caldwell, is going to catch him."

Rex looked at the man seated behind the desk. "Is that true?" he asked. "Somebody really did try to kill her?"

Lieutenant Caldwell nodded. "But don't worry," he said. "We *will* catch him."

Rex turned back to Maddy. "But what about you?" he asked. "Dennis Baxter called and told me about the house. He says it looks like it's a complete loss. What will you do? Where will you go?"

"Don't be silly," Maddy said. "The girls and I will be fine. I'll take whatever I get from the insurance company and buy myself a little place in town, maybe right here in Oak Harbor, someplace that's close enough to the beach that the girls will still be able to play in the water. And then you'll have your wish, too, Rex. You can build some humongous house on my old lot, sell it, and make yourself a fortune."

"But what are you going to do tonight?" Rex asked. "Do you want to come into the city with me? I'll be glad to take you. That's why I'm here."

"Certainly not," Maddy replied primly. "I wouldn't think of it. What would Gina say? There must be a motel around here someplace. When you call for a reservation, though, make sure they take dogs."

For a change Rex did come through. That night he found a room at the Seafarers Inn. It was there, in a shabby motel room with dingy wallpaper and bedding that reeked of cigarette smoke, that Maddy Watkins finally let herself think of all she had lost. She pulled the dogs up onto the grimy plaid bedspread and held them tight while she wept for her lost home, for her

90

fireplace, for that plaque with its tiny bronze shoes.

The next day, Rex and Gina managed to locate a quaint little B and B called The Oakdale, which was within easy walking distance of the beach. The B and B owner, upon hearing what had happened, allowed as how Aggie and Daphne would be welcome to stay despite the fact that hers was usually a no-dogs-allowed establishment.

A week later, on an autumn afternoon dripping with hazy, golden sunshine, Maddy and the girls returned to the B and B to find a patrol car parked near the front gate. When she saw the waiting officer was none other than Deputy Harris, Maddy was less than thrilled.

"What is it?" she asked.

"I thought you'd want to know," Deputy Harris said warily. "We found Hadley Riggins this afternoon."

"Where?" Maddy asked.

"In his car out in the woods. It was parked on a deserted road out by Coupeville."

"He's dead?"

Harris nodded.

"Suicide?"

"Yes."

"Was there a note?"

Deputy Harris nodded again. "It seems Hadley Riggins let his twenty-year-old daughter run off to New Zealand to marry an old duffer who's at least fifty years older than she is. The old man's a missionary of some sort. Hadley Riggins was all for it. He said he thought it was his daughter's highest, best use. Laurel Riggins evidently disagreed with her husband. She made plans to go to New Zealand on her own in hopes of bringing the daughter back. We know that's where she planned on going because she'd gotten herself a visa."

"Hadley found out and kept her from leaving," Maddy breathed.

Deputy Harris sighed. "According to the note, he pushed her off a ferry the night she was supposed to leave, and no one saw her go overboard. He must have figured the body would never be found. Then, he pretended that she'd gone off to New Zealand just the way she'd planned. Everybody pretty much believed him, except for you, Mrs. Watkins." Harris shook his head then. "If it weren't for you and that missing thank-you note, ma'am, it probably would have taken us a whole lot longer to figure out something was wrong."

"Well," Maddy said, relenting enough to give him a faint smile. "My mother always told me thank-you notes were frightfully important."

"Yes," Deputy Harris replied sheepishly. "You might say they really can be a matter of life and death."

Diamond Dog

by Dick Lochte

The animal shelter described in the opening section of "Diamond Dog" actually exists, which is more than I can say about the mythical town in which I have placed it. A number of years ago, when I became a first-time house owner, I took one look at my new large backyard and decided it was time I had a dog. Marriage and fatherhood were still in the offing. I wanted a loyal companion, a bodyguard, and, I suppose, the slightly stabilizing responsibility of having another mouth to feed.

That brought me to a rather remarkable animal shelter where, as in the story, an array of well-bred homeless dogs vied for attention. Beau, the giant black Bouvier who plays a key part in the following fiction, was there. But I didn't pick him. I signed up for a smaller dog, an eerie-looking toy collie that seemed more manageable.

Animals were held at the facility for fourteen days, allowing their owners time to find and reclaim them. During that period, those wishing to adopt a pet would place their names on a wait list, timed and dated. On the morning of their fifteenth day, unclaimed animals became available for adoption. Interested parties had to be there at eight-thirty a.m. when the shelter opened. If you were on time and your name was first on the list, the dog was yours. I was there that morning, bright and early. My name was first on the list for the toy collie. Second on the list was a six-year-old girl. When her father explained to her that I would be getting the little collie, she started to cry.

"What else have you got?" I asked the attendant. She took me back to a cage that was almost filled by a huge black dog I'd seen during my first tour.

"He's house-trained. He's obedient. And he's beautiful," she said, opening the cage door. The creature lumbered out.

"That's not a dog," I said. "I don't know what it is. A bear, maybe, or a Wookie, but it's not a dog."

"Bouviers are wonderful watch-dogs," she said, ignoring my outburst. "Police departments use them in Europe. They're intelligent and loyal. And, unless someone adopts him today, we're going to have to put him to sleep."

"You're not serious," I said.

But she was. Large dogs took up too much space and ate too much food, she explained. That's why they were hard to place and why the shelter was unable to provide unlimited care for them. Beau's time was up.

So, due to a couple of circumstances, or possibly con jobs, I wound up with a magnificent, handsome, utterly lovable animal with the body of a bear, the heart of a lion, and the appetite of a Great White shark. He has been such a large part of my life, it's high time he was introduced to Serendipity and Leo.

— Dick Lochte

1. Serendipity's Tale

The Bay City Animal Shelter is a one-story, U-shaped, pale orange brick building at the end of a drab little cul-de-sac named, appropriately, Wistful Street. With the Pacific Ocean only two blocks to the west, its four-pawed inmates, discarded, forgotten, or lost, can at least breathe some of the cleanest air in the Greater Los Angeles area. And, Lord knows, the city employees who staff the shelter are caring and knowledgeable and die-hard animal lovers to a woman or man. Still, what else but wistful could the dear little orphaned canines and felines be, knowing that they have only two weeks to attract new owners before facing the big sleep?

This particular shelter houses some of the very finest canines one could hope to own and love. Samoyeds. Weimaraners.

Beautiful collies, though I understand they tend to be snippy. I imagine the reason for this abundance of well-bred animals is that Bay City has become a stopping off place for the upwardly mobiles of Southern California. The downwardly mobiles, too, I suppose. Its highways and byways are filled with families leaving the area for loftier haunts like Brentwood or Pacific Palisades or Bay Heights, where my grandmother, the actress Edith Van Dine, and I live. Or they're moving on to less pricey locations like the Hollywood flats or the Valley or the tawdrier sections of Venice.

According to Officer Rina Rose, who handles the records at the shelter, these near-transients often forget their animals or simply leave them behind. How callous! Today's urban jungles are no places for helpless domestic animals. Those that manage to survive turn up at the shelter.

I discovered the house of the lost canines more than three years ago, when I still harbored the adolescent twelve-year-old notion that I would be spending my future in the field of animal husbandry (wifery?). This was before I discovered criminology to be my true vocation. Since then, I have sung the praises of the shelter and been responsible for several happy pairings.

That day in the middle of Spring Break, however, I was on my own errand, skating four miles down Bay Drive from the Heights to Wistful Street. The early morning traffic was surprisingly dense, and I arrived a few minutes late. Lieutenant Rudy Cugat of the Bay City Police Department, trim and dapper as always in a pastel lime suit, was in front of the shelter. He tapped his slightly vulgar gold wristwatch.

"In the wealthy land of the prompt, the tardy cannot raise a dime," he said, as I skated up to him. "Someone was here, demanding possession of the animal. I know the man — a miserable, mean-spirited cur. Claimed to be the dog's owner. But he had no proof. Still, I suspect Officer Rose would have awarded him the canine, if I had not been here to plead your case."

"Is the man still here?"

"He left. With blood in his eye." The lieutenant seemed to be savoring the memory.

"I wouldn't want to take anyone's dog," I said.

"Believe me, chica, the man is a lying *bas* — a teller of untruths. And he is a lousy writer."

Ah. A writer. That explained the lieutenant's hostility. I well understood writers' temperaments. The great private detective, Mr. Leo Bloodworth, and I had collaborated on two moderately successful books based on our adventures among the criminal element, *Sleeping Dog* and *Laughing Dog*. Not to be outdone, Lieutenant Cugat had written a novel, *Bay City Heat*, a rather fanciful tale about a superhuman police detective obviously modeled on himself. The softcover original had not earned back its obscenely large advance, and the foolhardy publisher had canceled his contract. But an orphaned writer was a writer still.

"Who is this teller of untruths?" I asked.

"Diamond Jack Barker," Lieutenant Cugat said with distaste.

"Oh." I knew the name, of course. How could one not? In a world seemingly filled with obnoxiously aggressive and obsessive self-promoting authors, Diamond Jack Barker was a nonpareil. So excessive were his stunts that the fact that his dark, well-researched true crime stories were rather elegantly written seemed almost beside the point. His last, *The Rapist*, had been based on events that had occurred in Los Angeles in the late 1980s — the search for, capture, and conviction of a serial rapist. Because the guilty party, who took his own life shortly after the sentencing, had been the son of a former governor of California, the story had been safely buried. Until Diamond Jack Barker unearthed it. That was his forte: digging up things that people hoped would remain hidden. "Still, if the dog is his . . ." I said.

"I have had dealings with Diamond Jack," the lieutenant said. "If it was his dog, he'd have brought the ownership papers, several copies of his latest tome, and a camera crew from *Entertainment Tonight*."

"Then what's he want with the animal?" I asked.

"I don't know and I don't care. The man is scum. Let's get this done, please, chica. The city is festering with criminals in need of my attention."

The lovely Bouvier des Flanders, a large black sheepdog, was waiting for us. He'd just been given a nice bath. He smelled of strawberry soap, and the dark curly hair on his huge frame had the shine of health. "He's a big boy, that's for sure," the lieutenant said as the animal was led from his temporary cage by the cheery Officer Rose. Though short and slight, she seemed to be having no trouble maneuvering the dog.

"Here he is, all seventy-eight pounds of him," she said. "I'm real happy you picked him, Serendipity. We don't always find homes for dogs as large as Bozzetto. They're a little more high-maintenance than the little Benjis."

The lieutenant raised an eyebrow and said to me. "You certain Leo is fine with this?"

I smiled and changed the subject. "Officer Rose, where did the name 'Bozzetto' come from?"

"On his collar," she said. "No address. No phone number. Just 'Bozzetto.' We checked the area directories to see if maybe it was a family name. Not around here, it isn't."

"Are we stuck with it?"

"He responds to it. If you decide to change it, you might want to pick something close. Bozo. Boz."

"Beau?" I asked. The big dog turned my way.

"Looks like that'll do," Officer Rose said.

The paperwork took only a few minutes. Officer Rose was explaining the importance of neutering when Diamond Jack Barker burst into the shelter. I had seen him on various TV talk shows, but he was much scarier in person. His thick black hair was poking out in all directions. His eyes, usually covered by aviator sunglasses, were naked and slightly bulging as they took in the dog, then the lieutenant.

"Okay, Cugat," he said. "A thousand bucks? That buy my dog back?"

"Is he really yours?" I asked.

The true crime writer stared at me as if I'd suddenly beamed down from the USS *Enterprise*. "Yes, he's really mine," he said, mocking me.

"What's his name?"

"Bozzetto, if it's any of your goddamn business." He turned to the lieutenant. "A grand do it, amigo?"

"It's not my dog, Diamond Jack." The lieutenant seemed genuinely amused.

"Damn right, it's not," Mr. Barker said, misunderstanding. "Now you're talking sense." He snapped his fingers, evidently expecting me to hand over the leash.

Instead, I asked, "What do you feed him?"

"Huh? Dog food. What else?"

"What kind of dog food?"

"I don't know. Chow."

"Wet or dry?"

He scowled at me. "I don't have time for this crap, kid. Gimme my dog."

"I don't think it is your dog," I said. "Every owner knows exactly what brand

and type of food their animal eats. Who's your vet?"

Mr. Barker's face was crimson. Suddenly, he grabbed the leash, tearing it from my hand.

Just as suddenly, he was on the ground, with the lieutenant's elegantly shod left foot pressed against his chest. "Naughty move, Jack," he said. "Where are all the photographers when you need them?"

"Let me up," the writer yelled.

"I'm going to remove my foot, now, Jack. And you're going to bid us adios."

Mr. Barker got up. He dusted himself off, glaring daggers at the lieutenant. "You blindsided me, Cugat," he said. "Nobody beats Diamond Jack when he's on guard."

"Bye-bye, Jack," the lieutenant said.

"Have your fun. You're going to pay heavily for it."

He slammed the door behind him.

"Wow," Officer Rose said. "Something is definitely eating on that dude. If he was a dog, I'd treat him for worms."

"His bark is worse than his bite," the lieutenant said. "I think."

There was no sign of Mr. Barker outside the shelter. Lieutenant Cugat's thoughts turned to Beau. "Chica, when I agreed to help you convey the animal to Leo's home in my brand-new Lexus, I did not envision quite so large a passenger. I assume he's car trained?"

"He must be, don't you think?" I said.

Beau, née Bozzetto, behaved himself admirably during the half-hour drive to Mr. Bloodworth's coach house on the far edge of Hollywood. He alternated from sticking his huge handsome head out of the window to feel the breeze, to slumping on the rear seat with his chin on my thigh.

When we arrived, the lieutenant surveyed the street and said, "I don't like leaving you here, chica. This is a high-crime neighborhood."

"I'll be fine," I said. "I've got this big boy for protection. I'm going to take advantage of Mr. Bloodworth's absence to do some tidying up and let Beau get used to his new home. I've ordered a little cake."

"Long as I've known Leo," the lieutenant said, "he's been like the Lone Ranger. Even when he was married. You sure he's gonna like this surprise birthday present?"

I nodded. "He told me he wanted a dog. He said, and I quote: 'You know, Sarah,' and I love it when he uses that diminution of my name, 'you know, Sarah, when a guy gets to be my age, he starts thinking of a pipe and slippers and a dog to bring the morning paper.' "

"You asked him if he wanted a dog and that's what he said?"

"Actually, his comment was in response to my observation that he was a bit overweight and needed an exercise program."

For some reason this seemed to amuse the lieutenant. "What's so funny?" I asked.

"Life," he said.

He watched me retrieve the front door key from under the plaster statue of Curly Stooge that Mr. Bloodworth used to decorate his overgrown garden. "Alas, chica, I must go. You can get home okay?"

"Gran isn't expecting me until dinner. If Mr. B. comes here right after work, he'll drive me home. If not, I'll take a cab. But I do hope I'm still here where he arrives. I want to see his face when he gets his first look at Beau."

"I wish I could see that myself," the lieutenant said.

2. Leo's Tale

Birthdays! Who the hell needs 'em?

I celebrated my latest at The Horse's Neck, a sports bar I save for those special occasions — income tax day, Christmas Eve, the anniversary of my getting booted out of the LAPD, and my birthday. Morning found me on the couch in my living room, dressed in my suit and tie. And shoes. If I'd been living on the East Coast and it'd been winter, I'd still be wearing a hat and topcoat and muffler.

It was not quite dawn. Chilly. I was in that awful in-between state — still a little drunk but hurting from the hangover. And there was a big black dog pissing on my living room throw rug.

At the sound of my groan, the dog finished up his business and trotted over to give me an eyeball-to-eyeball inspection. He was a goddamn giant, with hunks of pink and white stuck to his black beard. He opened his mouth, showing me a set of choppers that looked like a bear trap with gums and giving me a whiff of something vaguely liverish. I probably didn't smell so sweet myself at the moment, but I wasn't thinking about that. I was too busy trying to figure out how I could be having a nightmare with my eyes open.

The animal wasn't really threatening. I think he was trying to be friendly. He unfurled a tongue the size of a triple kielbasa, and before he could slap it against my cheek stubble, I rolled upright and shoved off the sofa.

My stomach flipped over and I realized that, with all the fun I'd been having listening to the depressed Russian bartender at the Neck describe the suicide rate in the Ukraine, I'd forgotten to take my Achiphex. Which meant I was not only drunk and hungover, I was having an attack of acid reflux. Staggering around the bemused dog on my way to the bathroom, I noticed there was a red ribbon hooked to its collar. Later for that. Later, too, for the remains of something that was probably a birthday cake on the freshly gouged and icing-smeared dining room table.

When I finally was able to begin gargling away some of the residue of another misspent night, I spied, reflected in the mirror above the washbasin, the big dog standing in the bathroom doorway looking at me with what I took to be disdain.

"Yeah, well, at least I don't have birthday cake all over my chin," I told him.

I wasn't the least bit curious about what he was doing in my house. The ribbon gave it away. I'm a detective.

I was hanging the urine-soaked throw rug on the back fence, preparing to spray it down with the hose, when the phone rang. Sighing, I walked past the dog into the house. The dog followed. I picked up the kitchen extension and said, "Hi, kid."

"How'd you know it was me?"

"Lucky guess. Look, about the dog . . ."

"His name is Beau. But that's not why I'm calling."

"Maybe not, but —"

"It's on the news. Lieutenant Cugat is in custody," she said. "They think he murdered Diamond Jack Barker."

"Well," I said, "it's high time somebody did."

★ ★ ★

They were holding Cugie without bail at the Beverly Hills lockup before shipping him downtown to Bauchet Street. He wasn't looking so hot. The guy prided himself on his appearance, but he didn't seem to care that he needed a shave, and his suit looked worse than mine.

"You up on this?" he asked me.

"Sarah told me about the scene at the animal house and Jamie just gave me the rundown on why they picked you up." The homicide detective in charge of the investigation, Jamie Hernandez, was an old pal of Cugie's and mine. He'd explained that Barker had called a press conference yesterday afternoon in which he charged Cugie with unprovoked assault and battery. It was a nuisance claim, but a nasty one that would tie up my buddy in legal and official police red tape for a while. Then, last night at approximately nine o'clock, Cugie showed up at Barker's condo on Charleville Street in Bev Hills. According to the doorman on duty, he looked drunk, an observation he made to Barker. Regardless, the writer told him to send Cugie back. The doorman did not see my buddy leave. Barker's corpse was discovered at nine in the morning with a letter opener stuck in its neck.

"Jack and I had our talk and I left through his garden out back," Cugie told me.

"Why not go out the front?"

"That was his idea. He said he'd sleep better if I snuck out the back."

"Sleep better why?"

Cugat shrugged. "Who the hell knows? Probably didn't want his neighbors to see a drunk greaser leaving his place. Hound, you know I didn't kill the *cabron*, right?"

"I know you sure wouldn't have used a letter opener with your Police Special on your hip. What the hell were you doing there, anyway?"

"I had a couple Cuba Libras and decided to explain to the man the serious mistake he made with those charges. See, two can play that game. We cut this deal a few years ago."

"What kind of deal?"

"I helped him write his 'masterwork,' *The Rapist*."

"Yeah?"

"I dug out all those hidden records of the case. He thanked me in his introduction. Didn't you read the book?"

"I get enough true crime every time I leave the house," I told him. "I don't go paying for it in bookstores. Especially not to make a weasel like Diamond Jack Barker a millionaire. How much did he pay you?"

"Twenty-five large," Cugie said.

"Not bad."

"For all I did?" he said with indignation. "He promised I would be the coauthor. My name was supposed to be on the cover, not on the acknowledgment page. It's in the deal memo, all signed and sealed."

"You shoulda sued him."

"I threatened. That's how I got the twenty-five grand. I let it go at that, but then the *pendejo* accused me of assaulting him. I went to his place to wave that deal memo under his litigious nose. He messes with my rep, I'll mess with his."

"And?"

"He agreed to withdraw his complaint. He sure wasn't happy about it, though."

"You guys do a little shouting?" I asked. "Something the neighbors might mention in court?"

Cugie gave me a sheepish look. "Maybe. I, ah, even made a move to slug the son of a bitch. But he pulled a gun on me. A little K3."

"He was carrying?"

"Had it on his desk." Cugie frowned. "I

guess that doorman's warning about me made him nervous."

"Going there wasn't such a great idea, amigo."

"Really? I was wondering about that."

"He didn't happen to mention what he wanted with the big dog?" I asked.

"No. He offered me another thousand bucks to get it for him, though."

"We could have split the loot," I said. "The dog's more trouble than my last wife."

"Forget about the dog, huh, Leo. Find out who killed the lowlife son of a bitch and get me out of this mess."

"Your brothers in blue should be helping. . . ."

"They've got their man, and that's that. I been a cop long enough to know how it works. All the effort from here on will be to build the case against me. Jamie's a pal, but he has to walk the line. You don't."

I stood up and signaled for the guard that I was through. "Jamie's feeling guilty enough he's promised to open a few doors," I said. "I'll see what I can do."

Serendipity was at my place, cleaning up the dog's assorted messes. When I'd finished filling her in on Cugie, we went into the backyard, where the King Kong of dogs was chasing butterflies. "Beau's definitely special," she said.

"I guess he is," I said. "He's not housebroken. He'll eat your shoes if you don't keep 'em on your feet. And, in an indirect way, he's responsible for Cugie being in the slams. Definitely special."

"You don't like him," she said, her face falling.

"I didn't say that. He just takes some getting used to." I looked at the big monster obeying nature on the crab grass. "You think I can just leave him out here during the day?" I asked.

"He's fenced in," she said. "He should be fine. Just make sure he has water and food."

"I wouldn't want him to get out and bite anybody." I was thinking primarily of the Vietnamese gangstas squatting in an empty house two lots over.

"He's a beautiful animal, Mr. B. But if you don't like him . . ."

"Stop saying that. I like him. I like him. I just don't . . . no, I like him."

She smiled. I couldn't remember exactly when her smiles had started meaning so much to me.

"How do you plan on helping poor Lieutenant Cugat?"

"Detective Hernandez has agreed to let me take a look at the crime scene."

"When?"

"Around five. He's tied up till then."

"Five. That works for me," she said.

The Prince Charles on Charleville Street was a three-story building with a fishbowl front and a revolving team of uniformed doormen who kept tabs on anyone who entered or exited. The elderly evening doorman paused in his contemplation of the ugly metal sculpture in the center of the lobby to tell us he'd just come on duty and wasn't sure if Hernandez was in the house. He was tall, a little bit more than my six-two, with white sideburns showing under his officer's cap and a matching white moustache and beard combo. In his dark blue uniform with gold piping and epaulets, there was something naggingly familiar about him. That was par for the course in Southern California, where the guy selling you auto parts probably had his own cowboy series in the Sixties.

The doorman, who I suppose could have been an ex-cowboy star, too, dialed Barker's number. After listening for a while, he said, "I'll give it a few more rings, in case Detective Hernandez is on the patio."

"It's okay," I told him. "He said he might be running late. We'll take a stroll while we wait."

Serendipity and I went on a tour of the outside of The Prince Charles. "It's always a good idea to get the lay of the land," I told her. "Unless Cugie turned psycho in the last twenty-four hours, somebody paid a call on Barker after he left without the doorman or anybody else seeing him. The question is, how."

The building occupied a corner of the block. To its left was a small enclosed garage for the condo dwellers. It required an electronic key to enter. As far as I could tell from the sidewalk, the garage was a separate structure from the main building. The only connection was a leaf-green canvas awning that began at an exit door near the garage entrance and fed into the matching awning in front of The Prince Charles.

Halfway along the right side of the building, the one exposed to the sidewalk and the street, there was a bolted fire door that someone could have used to exit. But there was no knob or handle, so no one could have entered through it without the help of a party inside the building. At the rear, a ten-foot wall topped with spikes separated the building from an alley wide enough for automobile access. The wall was broken by four metal doors behind which, I assumed, were the patios of the garden apartments. Barker had died in the one on the northwest corner.

"It's not likely anyone hopped over that wall," Sarah said as we stood near Barker's back door. She kicked the door with her flat-toed shoe. It responded with a deep solid gong and didn't budge. "Pretty formidable."

There was a wad of paper flattened on the asphalt by the day's traffic. I cracked my knees to give it a closer gander and then rose with a grunt. "Okay. Let's go see if Hernandez made it."

The elderly doorman was under fire when we got there. A woman his own age was on him like a rabid dog. "Your apology means nothing to me, Anthony," she said, her wrinkled face crimson, her deep blue eyes flashing. "I don't trust the streets at night, which is why I'm living in a building that has a doorman. I don't want my daughter and granddaughter to have to leave here when it's dark without someone watching their progress to their car."

"I really am sorry, Miz Palmer." The doorman looked like he was about to bend in two. Hearing the name "Palmer," I realized the old lady was Hildy Palmer, who'd won an Academy Award for a movie she made with Brando back in the Fifties. God, she'd been beautiful then. Now she was just another over-pampered ill-tempered old lady.

"Sorry doesn't cut it, you son of a bitch," she said. "I'm paying for security and I expect to get it."

She pivoted on her Joan and Davids and strode toward the thick glass inner door, seething. She stayed there, a foot from the door, facing forward, waiting for the doorman to unlock it. When he did, with the key attached to his belt, she marched angrily into the building.

"There goes the Christmas present, huh, Anthony?" I said.

"I was just away from my post for a minute," he said. He looked sheepish. "A fella my age, nature calls. Miz Palmer can be rather demanding. And the name is Tony, sir. Tony Prima. I never much cared for Anthony."

"Okay, Tony. Detective Hernandez show up yet?"

"Yes, sir," he held the inner door open.

"He said to just send you back. Suite One-D."

"Your 'nature call'?" Serendipity asked, "Was that last night?"

"Every night, ma'am," he said with a faint smile. "Even when I don't drink coffee."

"Did you mention it to Detective Hernandez?" she asked.

"Not to him, but to the officer who questioned me."

Detective Jamie Hernandez, small, wiry, and dark, met us at the door to suite 1-D. He seemed a little nervous and wasn't at all pleased that I'd brought Sarah. Watching her move past us to enter the study where Diamond Jack met his fate, Jamie said, "It's a crime scene, Hound. Not the Universal City Tour."

"She's a natural at this detective business, Jamie. Comes up with good stuff. She just found out that the doorman was away from his post last night."

"That's in the report," Jamie said, a little defensively. "Ten minutes to take a leak, at approximately ten-fifteen. The thing is, you still need a key to get through the inner door."

I followed him into the murder room. It was the sort of den you'd expect a bestselling writer to have. Books lined one wall. TV set and other electronic garbage along the other. There was a soft oxblood-colored leather couch, several stuffed chairs, and an antique desk of dark wood with gold accents. It and one of those chairs for people with back problems were facing away from French doors leading to the patio.

A dark-brown carpet covered the floor. It looked like it might have been nice and plush yesterday. Now it was splotched with powders and chemicals from the lab. White marking tape had been laid down, outlining the position of the absent corpse, head about two feet from the bookshelf. For some reason, there was a second out-line, a rectangle approximately eight inches by ten inches beside the body.

"Here's the deal," Hernandez said, keep-ing an eye on Sarah as she poked around the room. "Accordin' to the door guys, there was on'y four people to visit Barker yesterday. Cugat was the last in. At," he consulted a sheet of paper, "nine-oh-five in the pee-em. Barker was alive when Cugie went in; the door guy talked to him. Med-ical examiner says death occurred some-time between then and eleven."

Sarah had been looking at a paperback

edition of *The Rapist* that had been resting on Barker's desk beside a laptop computer. She replaced it and asked, "Anything missing, that you know of, detective?"

Hernandez hesitated as if he were wondering if he should bother to answer her question. Finally, he said, "Doesn't seem to be. But we haven't given the people who worked for him the chance to make sure."

She pointed to several reddish-brown drops marring the glass desktop. "Was there a lot of blood?"

"You see it," Jamie said. "The real damage was internal. He died fast, the medical examiner says. Weapon was a silver letter opener usually on the desk, next to the wooden in-out baskets."

"Did you find a gun, a little K3?"

"Yeah. In his desk drawer. The guy had handguns all over the place. Purchased and registered a couple weeks ago. They sure did him a lot of good."

"What's with the second outline on the carpet?" I asked.

"That's where the book was," Hernandez said. "The one that made him famous. *The Rapist.*"

"Is the size of the outline accurate?" Sarah asked.

"They know what they're doing," Jamie

said, a defensive edge to his voice.

"So how do you figure it went down?" I asked.

"Following the blood trail, it looks like he got stuck over there," Jamie said, pointing at the desk. He indicated the splotchy rug. "More blood drops form a line over to the bookcase. We figure he grabbed the book just before he passed."

"Then the book is pretty important," Sarah said.

"A dying man stumbles across the room for it. Yeah, 'important' fits," Jamie said.

"It was a hardcover?"

"Uh-huh. If you notice the shelf, all the books are hard-covers. On that top shelf are the ones he wrote, several copies of each. The others look like research. L.A. history. Organized crime. Books on poisoners, stranglers. Like that."

Sarah went to the shelf and took down one of the other copies of *The Rapist*.

"First printing," she said. "Doesn't look like it's been opened before."

"Any idea what Barker had in mind when he grabbed the book?" I asked.

Jamie looked glum. "Cugat's name is in it. It's part of the evidence against him."

"They're through dusting and everything, aren't they?" Sarah asked.

"Yeah, but don't go . . ."

Too late. She'd flipped open the black leather appointment book on Barker's desk. "This says that two people were supposed to meet with Mr. Barker yesterday," she said. "At three-thirty, someone named Tina. At six, Doctor L. *The Rapist* is dedicated to Tina."

"Who she?" I asked Jamie.

"The stiff's sister," Hernandez answered. "Tina Barker. Late twenties. Unmarried. Not much family resemblance, lucky for her. Kinda hot, if you like neurotics. She was his editorial assistant. Bottom of the suspect list. They seemed to get along. No apparent motive. Doctor L. is Doctor Louisa Lemay, a shrink Barker wanted to help him with his next book. Claims she barely knew the guy. Says she left him at six-thirty and that jibes with the doorman's memory."

"Anybody else here yesterday?" I asked, walking to the French doors that led to the patio.

"Young guy named Stephen Page. He's not on the calendar because he worked for Barker. A gofer. Did the computer stuff, answered the phone, ran errands. Like that. It was he who found the body this morning."

"He have a key?" Sarah asked.

"No. The sister says nobody did except Barker."

"The gofer mentioned in *The Rapist*, too?" I asked.

"Not in the front, which is about as far as I got."

"But his name *is* Page," Sarah said.

"Yeah." Jamie almost smiled. "That's good. But he's not our guy. He's a wimpy college punk. All shook up, like Elvis. Worked here mornings only. Part of an intern program at his school. Three other people saw Barker alive after Page went home yesterday. And as the old guy at the door is gonna testify, Cugat was the last he opened up for."

"Maybe another occupant let in the killer while the doorman was relieving himself," Sarah said. "Or maybe a neighbor did the actual killing."

Jamie looked at me and rolled his eyes. "First thing we did was talk to the other people in the building, the ones who were home last night. This is a high-end condo, Hound. One-bedrooms start at half a mil. Before the murder, this suite might have been worth as much as one point five mil. Notoriety plays hell with this kinda real estate. These folks would think twice before murdering their next-door neighbor."

"Even people who care about property values wind up committing crimes of passion," Sarah said. I wondered if she was trying to needle him.

"Where's the passion here, kid?"

"The killer used a weapon at hand, the dead man's own letter opener. That doesn't seem to suggest premeditation."

"Unless the killer had been here before and knew about the letter opener," Jamie said.

I was siding with him on that one. I pointed to the French doors. "Barker keep those locked or open?"

"Closed and locked," Jamie said, "except for the half-hour he spent sunning himself everyday."

"Any prints on 'em?"

He sighed. "Our pal's. Otherwise clean."

"If Cugie had just killed Barker, you'd have thought he'd have been more careful," I said. I opened the doors to the evening smog and a well-cared-for patio and garden. There was a chaise longue covered by a beach towel decorated with a drawing of the cover of *The Rapist*. Beside the chaise was a wrought iron table with a spotless ashtray, sunglasses, and a day-glo bottle of tanning lotion.

Beyond the brick patio, near the rear

wall, camellia bushes were in full bloom, their white and pink blossoms looking moist and healthy. On the brick walkway, just past the French doors, I spotted a wad of paper and bent over to look at it.

"That's like the one in the alley," Sarah said.

Before I could stop him, Jamie picked up the wad and unfolded it. "Just a hunk of white paper," he said.

"Could loosen up the case against Cugie," I said.

"How do you figure?"

"Fold it up like it was and see if it fits in the door slot opposite the latch bolt."

Hernandez obeyed. The wad fit neatly into the recess in the striker plate along the frame. When he swung the door shut, the paper stopped the latch bolt from connecting.

"There's another wad in the alley near the patio door," I said. "Any of Barker's previous visitors could have fixed it for a homicidal return without the doorman being any the wiser. So much for Cugie being the last person to see the dead man."

Hernandez nodded. "Not bad," he said. "Except that opens things up too much. Who's to say the doors weren't fixed two days ago? Or four?"

"That doesn't seem likely," Sarah said. "If Mr. Barker or anybody used the doors, they'd know right away that they didn't click shut. He sunned himself every day and the bushes look moist enough to have been watered very recently."

"The go-for, Page, says that Barker liked 'em wet down first thing every morning," Jamie said, nodding. "So I guess we're back to the people who were here yesterday. Cugat included, of course, only now he's got company."

As we reentered the apartment, Jamie looked at his watch. "Hell, I'm on golden time," he said. "I'm gonna invite the possibles down to Parker Center tomorrow to chew the fat a little more."

"Any way you can fix it for us to listen in?" I asked.

"You, maybe." He shifted his glance to Sarah and shrugged. "What the hell. You, too, I guess. Gimme a call in the ay-em, Hound, and I'll tell you when exactly."

Leaving The Prince Charles, Serendipity seemed distracted, but snapped out of her funk long enough to return the doorman's wave as we drove away. "Isn't one of your favorite singers named Tony Prima?" she asked.

"Louie," I told her. "Louie Prima."

"Oh," she said.

While she slipped back into her thoughts, I dug out a cassette and popped it into the player. Backed by the incomparable Sam Butera and the Witnesses, Prima and Keely Smith swung their way through "Just A Gigolo," "That Old Black Magic," and "Embraceable You" and were well into a stirring rendition of "Jump Jive An' Wail," when we arrived at the apartment Sarah shared with her grandma.

She didn't seem at all moved by the music. She thanked me for the lift, reminded me to pick up some flea powder for the dog, and said she would be ready and waiting the next morning by nine o'clock.

"I know you, kid," I said as she was getting out of the car. "Something's on your mind?"

"I just want to do a little cruising along the Information Highway, Mr. B. To check out an idea."

I waited until she'd entered her building, then burned rubber away from there. There was an idea I wanted to check out, too.

3. Serendipity's Tale

It was the Beau-Barker connection that was so puzzling.

As soon as Gran wandered off to bed — she retires early on the nights before the taping of her soap — I gathered the dinner dishes and placed them in the washer. Then I settled down in front of the PC for a workout with my favorite Internet search engine, Copernic.

That kept me up later than usual, which, I suppose, is why I had trouble waking up the next morning. Then Mr. Bloodworth called, doing the job better than any alarm clock. Detective Hernandez had scheduled a ten o'clock meeting with the suspects at Parker Center. Could I be ready in twenty minutes? Could I not?

The big sleuth was strangely quiet on the

drive downtown. Quiet but grinning like the Cheshire Cat. Odd.

We shared the elevator to the fourth floor with a pixieish, shaggy-haired blonde in black leather who turned out to be Tina Barker, the dead man's sister. Detective Hernandez and his partner, Detective Marcella Schott, a black woman, walked us to an interrogation room down a hall past the robbery-homicide bullpen.

I had seen the room once before. Then it had had just three chairs and a table. There were eight chairs that morning. No sooner had we occupied five of them, than another detective walked Lieutenant Cugat in and handed him over to Detective Schott, who purposely placed her chair between him and the door. The poor man didn't look like he could make a break for it, even if he were so inclined. He was depressed and pasty and unkempt. He moved as if his body had sprung a leak and all energy and confidence had drained away.

"Any hopeful news, Hound?" he asked Mr. Bloodworth.

"Hang in there, partner," Mr. B. replied. He was still grinning. Definitely up to something.

Detective Hernandez ducked out of the room and came back a few minutes later with the corpse's former part-time assistant, Stephen Page. The boy was as nervous as we'd been told. He was also making little gulping noises and, from time to time, clutching his stomach.

The final suspect, Dr. Louisa Lemay, was last to arrive, but even she made it before ten. She was a tall, full-bodied woman with a generous mouth and shoulder-length, slightly curled brown hair. I've often wondered what it would be like to be a brunette. They invariably seem more intelligent and serious than blondes, and Dr. Lemay was no exception. She wore a sedate skirt and jacket combination and no-nonsense glasses with tortoise-shell frames that drew attention to her lovely green eyes.

She stared intently at Detective Hernandez while he informed them that, since his initial chats with each of them had been one-on-ones, he thought he'd make it a group discussion today. "But before I begin," he said, extending his hand in Mr. B.'s direction, "I've agreed to let Mister Leo Bloodworth ask a few questions."

This was a surprise. I wondered what Mr. B. could possibly have told the detective to convince him to make such a break from police protocol. I hoped it didn't mean Mr. Bloodworth had leaped to the wrong conclusion about the book on Mr. Barker's floor and sold his assumption to Detective Hernandez. But as soon as he turned to Dr. Lemay, my heart sank.

"Doctor, you were working with Mr. Barker on his next book, right?"

"As I informed an officer yesterday, I met with him two days ago to discuss the possibility of my working with him," she said, speaking in a precise manner, with just a hint of a Southern accent. "Mr. Barker showed me a good-sized green box filled with clippings, notes, and audio tapes that he said pertained to an unresolved crime, a very famous — I suppose I should say infamous — one. Some of the material — he held up one of the tapes — contained information that he felt would provide evidence of a psychological nature. He needed an analyst's evaluation. It was an intriguing idea and I agreed to assist him."

"Which infamous unresolved crime are we talking about?"

"He . . . wouldn't tell me. He said that he feared it might prejudice my analysis. I assured him of my professionalism, but he remained adamant."

"Jack could be a real bug on secrecy," Tina Barker said.

"The police didn't find any green box," Mr. Bloodworth said. "Maybe that's because —"

"Did anyone else see the box?" I asked. I wasn't supposed to participate in any way, but I felt I had to do what I could to stop Mr. B. from making a serious mistake.

"S-s-sure. I've s-s-seen it," Stephen Page said. "It's b-b-been on his desk for the last couple of weeks."

"When my brother gets down to the nits and grits of a project, he puts the blinders on," Tina Barker added. "Lately, he's been in and out of that box constantly."

Mr. Bloodworth looked perplexed.

"Does anyone know which unsolved crime Mr. Barker was researching?" I asked, risking Detective Hernandez's ire.

"All my brother would say about it was that this incredible murder story had been laid on his doorstep. He was at the stage when he wouldn't dare even give a clue about the subject matter. There are so few really good stories that haven't been done to death and so many true crime writers out there sniffing around."

"We're getting off track here," Mr. Bloodworth said. "Let's take a look at what really went down the day of the murder."

Don't do this, I begged silently. Please don't.

"We know for a fact that it was one of you who decided Diamond Jack Barker needed killing," he said.

They gawked at him, registering an array of emotions — from incredulity (Dr. Lemay) to fear (Stephen Page). "Leaving motive aside for the moment, the main problem was accessibility," Mr. B. went on recklessly. "How do you dodge the door-man to get in to do the job? Well, you have to find another way."

Filled with confidence and, I'm sorry to report, displaying no small degree of smugness, he explained his theory about the killer sticking paper wads in the rear doors to keep them unlocked for re-entry.

"But, Hound," Lieutenant Cugat said, "Barker was still kicking when I left through the back. And I could swear I heard those door locks click behind me."

Then Stephen Page let even more wind out of Mr. B's sails. "Uh, those p-p-paper wads, they were mine," he said. "Mr. B-B-Barker liked me to water the p-p-plants in the morning and take out the trash. The study doors tend to swing open if they're not l-l-locked, and he wanted 'em shut, especially when the air conditioner was on. B-B-But he didn't want to keep getting up to unlock them for me. The alley door is self-locking and if I wasn't careful, I'd wind up having to walk around to the front of the b-b-building. So I just p-p-plugged the locks. I unp-p-p-plugged 'em, soon as I was finished with the p-p-plants."

The two police detectives exchanged glances and Detective Hernandez said, "Ah, Leo, maybe we should —"

But Mr. Bloodworth was not to be denied. "Okay, let's sideline the accessibility problem for the moment and move on to the clue to the killer that Barker left with his last strength. The medical examiner tells us that he must've died quickly. The killer had to have been there in the den to see him struggle to get to the shelf and grab his book. If the killer had thought the book to be in any way incriminating, it would have wound up back on the shelf, right?"

Tina Barker and Stephen Page nodded.

"So we can assume the killer was not someone connected to the book. That immediately eliminates Lieutenant Cugat and Tina Barker, both of whom were mentioned in the dedication and acknowledgment." It was good to see the light of hope return to the lieutenant's eyes, even temporarily. "It also eliminates Stephen Page," Mr. Bloodworth continued, "since his name has an obvious connection to any book."

"But, Hound," Lieutenant Cugat said, "if the book doesn't point to the murderer, why did Barker bother to grab it?"

"It points to the murderer, all right," Mr. Bloodworth said. "It points to Dr. Lemay, who was probably going to be the subject of Barker's next expose. Well, doctor, what nasty secret of yours did Barker uncover?"

The doctor's jaw dropped and she stared at Mr. B. in abject amazement.

"I still don't get what the book says about Dr. Lemay," Lieutenant Cugat said.

"Neither did Dr. Lemay," Mr. Bloodworth said with insufferable pride. "When she saw *The Rapist* lying on the floor beside the man she'd just murdered, she didn't realize what its title would spell if the two words ran together."

"Therapist," Lieutenant Cugat said, catching Mr. B.'s grin.

Dr. Lemay wasn't grinning. She'd risen to her feet, anger robbing her face of its natural beauty. "This is absurd," she said, heading for the door.

Detective Schott stood to intercept her, but she clearly wasn't certain she should.

Dr. Lemay said to her in a quiet fury, "If you are not out of my way in ten seconds, I shall notify my lawyer to sue you, your associate, the LAPD, the county of Los Angeles, and especially that fat buffoon who has just defamed me by accusing me of murder on the strength of a book title. By God, I'd love to hear what a jury would say about that evidence."

Detective Schott looked to her partner for guidance and got it in the form of a quick nod. She stepped aside, allowing the furious therapist to storm away.

Those remaining seemed thoroughly perplexed.

Mr. Bloodworth, to his credit, saw some humor in the situation. "Gee, that worked well," he said.

Detective Schott escorted Lieutenant Cugat back to the Bauchet Street lockup. Detective Hernandez told Tina Barker and Stephen Page that he was sorry he'd called them in for nothing and thanked them for their cooperation. He left to walk them to the elevator, then stuck his head back in to tell us to stay where we were. He did not look happy.

Alone with Mr. B. in the interrogation

room, I said, "You were right about the book being a clue."

"No kidding," he said. "The doc killed him."

"No. You were wrong about that."

"What are you talking about? 'The Rapist.' 'Therapist.' It's gotta be."

"Think back to Mr. Barker's den," I said. "What was on his desk?"

"The usual junk. A lamp. A laptop. Phone." Then he said, "Oh, yeah," evidently remembering the paperback edition of *The Rapist*.

"He was stabbed near the desk," I said. "If it was the book's title that was so important, he could have just picked up the paperback. He didn't have to go across the room. He wanted the hardcover edition."

"Okay. What does that tell us?"

"The murderer," I said. "I mean, there's some other stuff you have to know, too, but that and what Tina Barker said just a while ago should tell you who it is."

"Never mind the games," he said. "Let's hear it."

"Well, to begin, it's not just one murder, it's more."

"How many more?"

"Thirty maybe."

I wasn't trying to shock him, but I evidently did. He seemed to pale. "I know you catch stuff I overlook," he said. "But thirty murders."

"There's no way you could know about that part of it," I said. "Unless, like me, you were curious about why Mr. Barker was so interested in Beau. I did tell you that his given name was 'Bozzetto,' did I not?"

"Uh-huh."

"Well, I had two questions. Who was Beau's previous owner? And why was the beautiful dog set free? To find out the first answer, I fed 'Bozzetto' into my search engine and came up with an Italian cartoon animator and a French snowboard champion. I doubted Beau's owner had either of them in mind when naming the animal. 'Bozzetto' also turns out to be an art term, referring to a model that a sculptor might use in constructing a large work. This seemed a more likely possibility.

"As for question two, all the talk of murder made me think that Beau's owner might have experienced something bad around the time he wound up on his own. I checked the Web site www.socalcrimenews.com, which lists all major crimes in this area by date, and discovered that a sculptress had been brutally mur-

140

dered in her home on the Venice canal on the same day that the Bay City police spotted Beau dodging traffic and brought him to the shelter.

"Bouviers are notoriously protective of their owners. My guess is Beau chased the murderer's vehicle and wound up lost."

"This is all interesting stuff, kid. But what ties it to Barker?"

"The murdered sculptress was named Jenny Sargon. She was sixty-eight. I'd never heard of her before, but maybe you did?"

"I don't think so. But I'm not really into sculpture."

"Not even the Seaside Sculptor?" I asked.

"Yeeeaaahhhh," Mr. Bloodworth said, drawing the word out thoughtfully. "That was about thirty years ago, but it's not something you forget. Stanley . . . no, Sidney Furst. He was world famous. Became a multimillionaire forging realistic-looking bronze statues of people and animals. The Brentwood and Holmby Hills crowd coughed up the big bucks to have a Furst for their front lawn. A couple on a bench. A postman carrying a letter up the walk."

"Then came the San Fernando Earthquake in 1971," I said. "Seven point six. One of the Furst statues cracked. . . ."

"And there was a corpse inside. Furst was exposed as a nut case who'd been bronzing human beings in his foundry. They went after Furst, but he was in the wind. Thirty of 'em, huh? As I recall, they were homeless, most of 'em."

"Except for Harry Ambrose," I said, the Internet being my source.

"Right. 'Hurlin' Harry,' " he said. "Heisman Trophy–winner. Superstar. Pride of the Raiders. Got stoned one night with his pals and wound up a lawn jockey in Pasadena. People went nuts after they peeled the bronze off Harry. It was one thing to kill homeless people, even in those numbers, but it was a different deal with Harry. He was well-loved, and his killer was still out there somewhere. Pressure was applied. Heads rolled on the force. But they never found Sidney Furst."

"He left a fiancée behind," I said. "She claimed to know nothing of his crimes or his whereabouts. After a while, they left her alone. Like Mr. Furst, she was an artist and a sculptor. Her name was Jenny Sargon."

Mr. Bloodworth brightened. "I get it. She was helping Barker write a book about

Furst. And Furst killed 'em both."

"Looks like," I said. "That's probably what Mr. Barker was trying to tell us when he grabbed the hardcover edition of his book. The 'first' edition. Or maybe he was trying to get a true-crime book about Furst from the shelf below and made a mistake."

"In either case, Furst is the guy. And I bet you know where he is, right?" he asked.

"No, I don't," I told him. Then I smiled. "But I know where he will be at five o'clock."

4. Leo's Tale

We pulled up to The Prince Charles apartments a little after five. Jamie and Detective Schott were in their unmarked police car behind us. I could see old Tony Prima, at his post in full uniform. The big dog could see him, too, I guess. He started throwing himself against the door of my sedan. I wasn't sure the door would hold.

"Looks like you were right, kid. The monster recognizes Prima."

"Beau," she said. She was seated on the backseat beside the dog, holding his thick leather leash. "The dog's name is Beau and he's not the monster. Prima is."

"Point well taken," I said. I was proud of her, proud of the way she'd knocked Jamie off his high horse. When he'd returned from bowing and scraping to Barker's

144

sister and the go-for, he just wanted to vent. That's why he'd kept us, to have somebody to shout at. He wasn't interested in anything we had to say. I was ready to blow but Sarah stayed cool as a cumquat. Ignoring his insults, she told him her theory linking the Jenny Sargon murder to the Barker killing.

His eyes started to light up when she dropped Furst into the mix. The idea of catching the infamous Seaside Sculptor was so appealing, he started acting like a lap dog while she piled on the circumstantial evidence. The "first" edition. The name "Prima," Italian for "first." The doorman's absence from his post around the time of the murder. The murder of Jenny Sargon taking place in the early morning, an odd time unless the killer was just getting off a night shift. And there was the comment from Tina Barker that her brother had said his next book idea had been dropped on his doorstep.

Hernandez had been so impressed, he'd even gone along with the kid's plan to use the dog. "It's what Mr. Barker was going to do," she said. "If Beau recognizes Mr. Prima, that tells us something. If Mr. Prima recognizes Beau, and makes a run for it, that'll tell us even more."

The animal in question definitely recognized Prima. And he wasn't glad to see him, "You gonna be able to hold back Beau?" I asked Sarah. "We just want Prima scared, not eaten."

"I think so," she said.

Actually, the point was moot. As soon as Prima spied us heading for the front door with the growling animal, he made a beeline into the building. His keys would open all locks, but as the kid and I had learned, there were only five other exits. Sarah stayed at the car with the dog. Detective Schott took the side fire door, gun in hand. Jamie and I ran to the alley, scanning the four garden exits.

Prima pushed through the rear door next to Barker's. Age didn't do him any favors in the quick-getaway department. Jamie had him on the ground and in cuffs in jig time.

As they carted him off, I heard him ask Jamie if there was a good fine arts program at Pelican Bay Prison.

Sarah and I were waiting when they turned Cugie loose an hour or so later.

On the drive to his house, he took the passenger seat and Sarah shared the back with Beau. He listened quietly while we gave him a rundown on the events of the evening. Then he took a minute or so to digest it all. "Jack was an idiot," he said finally. "He should have gone to the police as soon as he began to suspect that his doorman was Sidney Furst."

"Mr. Furst had been working at The Prince Charles for nearly seven years without bothering a soul that we know of," Sarah said. "I guess Mr. Barker figured he wasn't a threat."

"But Jenny Sargon's murder must have wised him up. It meant Furst knew he was planning an exposé. He had to be next on the guy's People To Kill list. Hell, Furst even had a key to his apartment."

It was a point both Hernandez and I had raised earlier. Sarah gave Cugie the same answer she gave us. "I can't say for sure what was in Mr. Barker's mind. But we know he was adamant about keeping his story ideas a secret. He must have felt that going to the police would open up the possibility of his being scooped. Instead, he went out and bought a small arsenal. He must have thought that was all he needed. He was convinced he was the top dog. Furst may have been able to subdue Jenny Sargon, but no seventy-year-old man, not even one as seriously homicidal as Mr.

147

Furst, could get the better of Diamond Jack Barker."

Cugat nodded, "He was a conceited bastard, all right. He once told me that's why he was 'Diamond' Jack, because no one was any tougher or sharper or more valuable. What a fool. Diamond? He wasn't even a zircon."

He turned in his seat to face the rear. "But speaking of diamonds, Ms. Dahlquist," he said, "as far as this nearly railroaded hombre is concerned, your friendship is rarer than the brightest jewel. Thanks for saving me."

"That's very sweet, Lieutenant," she said, "but Beau is the one who flushed out Mr. Furst and sent him scurrying. He's a handsome, brave, intelligent animal. And he'll make a wonderful companion, don't you think so, Mr. B.?"

I flashed on my throw rug, drying on the line, my smelly backyard, the three-pound bag of kibble sitting in the middle of the kitchen, the upcoming trip to the vet for shots, the exterminators I had to call to get rid of the fleas, the prospect of accepting responsibility for another living creature. "A wonderful companion," I agreed.

Anything to see that smile.

Scratch
That One
by Jill M. Morgan

I intended to write this story about my dog, Sassy, who is gentle, sweet-natured, calm, and never bites. I would have done so, if my cat, Griffin, hadn't stood right in front of my keyboard while I was writing this story. He's pushy that way. Once he had forced his way into my thoughts, he managed to make his way into my story.

Lots of antique stores have cats sleeping on a counter, or curled up snugly on a chair. These cats are usually round as cushions, never awake, and barely above a stuffed-animal state of activity. I thought it would be fun to put Griffin — who is only a hair above feral in temperament, whose favorite snacks are moths he catches in midair, and who has been known to walk along fluorescent light fixtures inches below our ceiling for his own amusement — into the quiet setting of an antique shop.

Griffin never meows. Such pleading noises fall beneath his dignity. If he wants something, he manages to let you know in other ways. A paw tapping the chin of a person neglecting to continue petting him is effective. Nips on the arm work very nicely if he's had enough. He does make sounds. His voice is a trill when he's excited by the crinkly sound of his favorite ball, or a barklike huffing reserved for any male cat seen outside his window, and a low throated growl for the UPS carrier who delivers packages to our door.

He has attitude, which is admirable in a cat. I wouldn't want some pushover cat who meows for his can of salmon and shows no more personality than a sofa pillow with ears. If I have to chase Griffin away from the canary cage one time too many, or he bites holes in my printer paper, or he stalks my bare toes when I pass him, that's okay with me.

Griffin has entered the pages of this story with a pounce. Like the little wild cat that he is, may he leap right over these words, and into your heart.

— Jill Morgan

Sunlight warmed the box window of Two Sisters Antiques on Dolores Street. Morning shone through the window's crisscross lacing of narrow shelves, touching the blue silk scarf nested beneath the ornately patterned Royal Doulton vase. The same soft light brightened the mirrored silver surface of the Victorian tea set, with each piece's hand-hammered border of flowers and birds in flight.

Closest to the window, stretched out and hugging the warmth of the glass, was a large butterscotch-colored cat. He was long-haired, with untidy tufts of fur poking out between his toes, back legs furred like riding britches, and intelligent eyes that were a leonine golden yellow. His fluffy tail switched restlessly back and forth as he lazed in the sunlight watching cat TV, which was really only the tourists and citizens of Carmel passing by the shop.

"Griffin," called out Rose Hart, owner and caretaker of both shop and cat, "where are you?" A muted tinkle of kibble pouring into a small blue dish brought about satisfying results. "There's my good boy," Rose

151

said, stroking his back. She scratched him behind the ears and under his chin.

The big tomcat purred loudly. He tolerated the petting for a moment more, then signaled the end of such liberties with a small nip on Rose's bare arm.

"Hey, you monster," Rose complained, dumping him unceremoniously onto the floor. "Go find yourself a mouse."

Griffin eyed her with a glance that promised sweet revenge, but ambled off.

Rose stared at the blue-green bruise already discoloring the underside of her forearm, where twin imprints of cat incisors could be seen. The bite hadn't broken the skin, but hurt all the same. She rubbed at the soreness. She tried to understand the fact that Griffin behaved as if these were love bites. He always seemed to be purring happily whenever he bit her, brat that he was, but who really understood the mind of a cat?

The cat was a stray she had found as a kitten, abandoned by his mother in Rose's backyard. No more than five or six weeks old, he had yowled pitifully, loud and long, from beneath the hedge where he'd been left. Rose had listened to this for an hour or more, taking a peek at the kitten a time or two, but determined not to get involved in this meow-lo-drama. She would let his mother come back for him. The problem was, the feral mother never came back. By nightfall, Rose's resolve had weakened and she had taken the kitten a little bowl of tuna to hush him up. He ate it so hungrily, she fed him again. That was that. By eight o'clock that night, the kitten had bullied his way into Rose's house and her heart. She named him Griffin, because he was such a wild little beast. She'd thought about naming him Savage, but it didn't seem to suit his more affectionate side. Griffin he became, the lord and master of her home, antique shop, and Rose's heart.

It was two years since Griffin had come to live with her, two years since Rose had come to Carmel, following the inheritance of Great-Aunt Jewel's estate. At twenty-six, flat broke, and seriously in need of a not-so-ethical locksmith to open the padlocked door of her apartment, being three months overdue on her rent, Rose had taken the first bus out of L.A. and never looked back. The great-aunt had been a stranger to her, antiques had been unknown to her, and a bank account with more than twenty dollars in it had been unbelievable to her. All that had been changed by the arrival of one letter.

The memory of that time had barely registered in Rose's mind when she turned to see Griffin halfway up the staircase, poised on the sheer edge of one step, his bushy tail whipping back and forth and his body crouched in pre-pounce mode. She saw what he was stalking, a tiny moth fluttering below him. The muscles of Griffin's face twitched, and he gave one short, excited trill, more like a bird call than a cat's meow. Moths, his favorite.

"Griffin!" Rose called out sharply. Too late to prevent this cat-astrophe. His leap was fearless, right onto a small mahogany table. He caught the moth on the way down with one paw, and had it covered by both paws before Rose could call out, "Don't you dare!"

He was the mighty hunter. He was Griffin the Brave. He was, to Rose's consternation, "Bad, bad cat."

The moth escaped, flittering up to dance in the reflected light of a Chippendale scroll mirror hanging on the wall. Griffin leaped from the floor to the mahogany table. He clawed at the mirror, as if scratching it open might release the moth.

As if in slow motion, Rose watched as the mirror wobbled loose from its nail and began an irrevocable slide down the wall, smashing into a thousand pieces against the hardwood floor.

The cat vanished, no fool he.

Rose peeked out from between fingers protecting her eyes from flying glass. Shards of mirror were flung everywhere like glittering bits of diamonds. She allowed herself one small, pitiful whine. "It started out such a nice day," she said, fighting back a trembling urge to throw something at the retreating cat.

Sighing, Rose lowered her hands from her face, sighed deeper when she'd had an even better look at the mess, and said to herself, "Everyone warned me not to bring a cat into an antique shop. Did I listen?" The one-person conversation continued in this same vein as Rose dragged over a broom, dustpan, and trash can.

"Dumb, dumb, dumb," Rose fumed, glancing up from her labors every few seconds to see if she could spy out the cat. At last, she spotted him crouched beneath a desk, his yellow eyes wary. "You'd better hide," she muttered darkly. "That mirror was worth two hundred dollars." She had paid fifty for it, but that was beside the point.

Careful not to cut her knees on the shards of mirror, Rose knelt and lifted large pieces of the wooden frame into the trash. Jagged glass jutted from the broken wood. Although Rose handled the pieces gingerly, she still managed to jab her finger on one of the needle-sharp points. At this, she yelped in pain and looked daggers at Griffin, whose feral eyes stared back intently, and whose tail whipped back and forth in barely contained excitement.

"I am not bringing you here tomorrow," Rose told him. "Do you hear that? You are not coming, no matter how much you beg." Begging was not in Griffin's vocabulary. She knew this. The truth was, he had only to follow her to the front door of the house and wait patiently. Rose's worry about him pining away for hours — his little cat heart broken from loneliness and fear that she might never come back — always triggered her to scoop up Griffin, plop the cat carrier onto the passenger seat beside her, and bring him along on the short drive into town. She had to admit it, he had her well trained.

Badly needing something to staunch the blood from her finger, Rose left the room and came back with tissues clumped around the cut, only to find Griffin pawing at the backing of the mirror.

"You get away from there," she shooed,

waving her tissue-clumped finger in his general direction.

He scratched harder, getting in a few good swipes before she got there.

"Scoot," she insisted, and he took off.

When Rose glanced down at the broken mirror, she noticed something she hadn't seen earlier. The backing had come loose, and Griffin's furious scratching had pried it apart even further. Rose lifted it, and to her surprise, saw something wedged between the backing and the splintered frame.

"What's this?" Rose asked no one in particular, being alone in the shop.

It took some work to complete the separation a crash to the floor had started, but after a few minutes Rose had the frame fragments on one side of her, and the unbroken wooden backing on the other. Most interesting of all was what had been wedged between them. In Rose's hands was an old black and white photograph of a child.

The little girl had a dark drape of bangs dropping over her forehead, and blunt-cut bobbed hair that fell just below her ears. She had enormous eyes that seemed to be searching for something, almost speaking to Rose right out of the picture. The child wasn't smiling, but had what Rose's mother used to call a "serious look." It had been the fashion back then for children to be posed this way.

Why would anyone put a picture of a child inside a mirror? she wondered.

The answer was easy. *To hide it.*

Rose left the mirror fragments on the floor and carried the old photograph to the front window, where the lighting was better. Here, details only dimly visible at first now emerged from the photograph's shades of black and white. The picture was a formal portrait, not a snapshot. The child's hands were neatly folded on her lap. She wore a dark, solid color dress, relieved from complete somberness by a starched, white, Peter Pan collar at her neck, and a locket with a pretty Celtic design Rose had never seen before. The girl was seated at the edge of an expensive looking chair. *Queen Anne,* Rose noted, automatically appraising the value of the piece (*side chair, walnut, vase splat, cabriole legs: thirty-three hundred and change.*)

"Who are you?" she addressed the photo. "Not a butcher's daughter. Your family had enough money to pay for that chair."

She studied the photo more closely, the child looked so pensive and proper, every hair in place, every inch of her dress smoothed and pressed into starched stiffness. And yet, poking out from beneath the hem of the dress were the scuffed toes of the child's black boots, each pointed in a different direction.

It was the only touch of childlike playfulness in the picture, but to Rose, it was the thing that made the girl real, a child from long ago, stepping out of a broken mirror and the closed border of a photograph. She turned the photograph over, and on the back was an inscription handwritten in ink, *Virginia Louise, age five.* Rose read the date aloud, "November 7, 1941." Also on the back of the photograph, printed at the bottom, was the name of the photography studio — Breckenridge Portrait Studios, Carmel, California. She now had a name to put with the picture, Virginia Louise, but the date seemed equally interesting — November 7, 1941 — only a month before the bombing of Pearl Harbor and the United States entering WWII.

As Rose studied the picture, Griffin crept out of hiding on quiet cat's feet and jumped into the wide display window beside her. The muscles of his sides quivered as he landed and stood for a moment, judging her mood, ready to make a dash for it if she still seemed angry. Intent on the old photograph, Rose barely glanced at him.

"Watch out for glass," she warned.

He settled in, choosing the warmest spot for stretching himself out and basking in the morning light. One back paw, spiked with soft fur between the toes, nestled cozily onto the sterling tray of the Victorian tea set. His tail fell softly over the blue silk scarf. He rolled onto his back, turned his stomach to the sun, propped his head against the Royal Daulton vase, and lazily, slowly, closed his eyes for a mid-morning nap. The throaty sound of purring filled the space, as comforting as the rhythm of a mother's heartbeat.

In the days that followed, Rose tried to push away the haunting image of the little girl, but the child's eyes, lost and searching, remained with her. Like a ghost who would not disappear into the daylight, the hidden child lingered in her thoughts.

"You know what they say about breaking a mirror," remarked Blue, Rose's assistant at Two Sisters Antiques. Blue, the long-legged, boot-wearing, ruggedly handsome Texan who drew more women customers into the shop than any set of fancy dishes ever could, was always glad to offer his opinion on anything.

"A two-hundred-dollar write-off on my taxes?"

"Seven years of bad luck," said Blue, giving her a nod of his head to punctuate this dire pronouncement.

"And there's no way to avoid that?" she asked. "No salt I could throw over my shoulder, or something?"

"Heck, you think tossing a little salt over your shoulder could fix the serious damage done over a broken mirror? You don't know your superstitions. Nope, your future's ruined, I'd say."

"I could throw salt at you," she said brightly, "that would make me feel better."

Blue looked wounded. "Durn, I was just trying to help."

"Try helping by bringing those boxes from the storeroom," she said.

He eased himself up, like a Texas oil derrick slowly hoisted to standing, planted his boots solidly on the hardwood floor, adjusted himself slightly with a shift of weight from one foot to the other, then moseyed off toward the stairs. She watched him walk away. He was, without a doubt, the best looking item in the shop.

Alone for a moment, without the presence of Blue to distract her, Rose opened her desk drawer and pulled out the black-and-white photograph of Virginia Louise. It was ridiculous, worrying about a child who must be an old woman by now. She calculated quickly . . . age five in 1941, counting back would have her born in 1936 . . . that would make her sixty-five, if she were still alive.

That might be so, Rose thought, *but you're still a child until I find out what became of you.* This was more than simply finding a picture of a child in an old album or a drawer. This child's photograph had been hidden. The reason for such secrecy, for such an act of deliberate concealment, intrigued Rose.

It might have been the baffling memories of her own childhood that made her want to find an answer to the mystery of Virginia Louise, when she'd never been able to find answers for herself. Rose's mother had brought her to Carmel when she was eight, the only time she'd ever met the two great-aunts who'd owned this shop. The reason for her visit, and the feeling of fear that Rose had always connected to it, somehow reminded her of why a five-year-old little girl's photograph had been put where no one would ever find it — fear, and hiding from something or someone.

Until now, Rose thought, determined to unravel this more than fifty-year-old mystery. *An antique,* she realized, amused at the thought. Learning about this girl would be just like researching the history of an old and valuable possession. Not much different than appraising an antique, discovering its background, finding its maker. In this case, the maker was most likely the person who had hidden the photograph between the frame and the backing of the mirror.

She began with the purchase order. Each antique in the shop had either a purchase order or a consignment agreement on file. The scroll mirror had been inventory of the shop, not a consignment item. She knew that much from the tag. Consignment items had green tags, shop inventory tags were white. The tag dangling from the broken mirror had been white.

Blue, lugging two heavy cardboard boxes, came back downstairs as Rose finished typing *scroll mirror* into the inventory file, clicked *search,* and waited for information about the piece to appear on screen.

Blue carried the boxes to behind Rose's desk. "You want me to go through these boxes?" he asked, casting a meaningful glance at the file on the monitor. "Looks like you're all tied up with something else."

"I'll get to them," Rose said, a little too defensively. "I want to check who owned the mirror, that's all. Anything wrong with that?"

"Nope." Blue was a man of few words. He didn't have to talk. The set of his mouth and the slight shake of his head said it all.

"What?" asked Rose.

"I didn't say one thing."

"Yes, but you were thinking plenty. I want to know to whom to give the picture back," she said, defending her actions.

Blue made no comment.

"I'm not obsessing over this," she debated his silence.

"Didn't say you were."

"Well, I'm not."

He shrugged.

"Don't you have work to do?" Her tone was chilly.

A wise man, as well as good looking, Blue didn't need to be told twice. He was out of there. "Shelves," he said. "I have shelves to sort."

Where to start? For a moment, the thought of beginning this search seemed overwhelming to Rose. She turned back to the computer monitor. Under the heading OWNER, she read — The estate of Mrs. Julia O'Neil, Carmel, CA. There was a phone number beside the name. Without giving herself enough time to feel foolish and back out, Rose punched in the numbers on the phone. She glanced in Blue's direction, but he was keeping busy elsewhere.

The conversation was brief. The estate agent, Elaine Parks, provided Rose with little information.

"She died this year?" Rose asked.

"Three months ago."

"She was a widow?"

"Her husband predeceased her by four years."

"Did they have children?"

"No, that's why the State asked me to dispose of her property."

"Oh, right. Is there anything else you could tell me about her?"

A pause. "What did you want to know?"

"I'm not sure. Do you know Mrs. O'Neil's maiden name?"

"Holland," replied the agent. "That's what I have listed, Julia M. Holland."

"Thanks," said Rose, and hung up. The name moved through the corridors of her mind, like a child's ball rolling down a long hallway, *Julia M. Holland.*

The door opened and three customers, tourists by the conversation they were having, wandered into the shop. "Do people really pay this much for old dishes?" asked one. "Would you take half price for this glass bowl?"

Rose answered their questions. Yes, people really did pay that much for old dishes. No, she would not accept half the listed price on the tag. When asked by them, she offered the suggestion of a nearby restaurant for lunch. She rationalized that she was doing her good deed for the day. After all, someone had to eat at the worst place in town.

A little later, one of her regulars, Mr. Gordon, stopped by to pick up a Santa Fe Railroad blanket for his collection. Mr. Gordon had been a train conductor for thirty-five years and now made it his hobby to find pieces of railroad memorabilia to remind him of those days. Whenever Rose had anything interesting from that category, she called him. Mr. Gordon was a bright spot in her day. He not only loved the blanket, but found a little railroad mug that had somehow missed her attention, and bought that, too.

From late morning through midafternoon, there was a steady stream of customers. A few were regulars, like Mr. Gordon, or Mrs. Carter, whose passion was for Stickley furniture, or Mrs. Webster, who collected children's porcelain nursery rhyme mugs. Rose kept a file on each of these customers, noting their special interests.

Whenever Mrs. Webster came in, she made a point to say hello to Griffin and give him a friendly scratch behind the ears. To Rose's amazement, the cat tolerated this affection without biting the hand that stroked him. At the moment, Mrs. Webster was calmly rubbing Griffin's tummy, which was the equivalent of playing Russian roulette.

"He'd never let me do that," remarked Rose. "If I tried touching his stomach with my bare hand, I'd pull back a bloody stump."

Mrs. Webster laughed, as if Rose had been kidding. "You've got to have the knack. He likes me, I guess, the sweetheart."

Rose kept her opinion of the "sweetheart" to herself. Like a mother receiving a compliment on her child, no matter how sullen and impossible he might be at home, she was glad other people saw nice qualities in him. He was cute, she had to admit.

Mrs. Webster bought the Spode nursery rhyme mug Rose had just put on the shelf two days before, and was tempted by a Carlton Walking Ware children's mug with feet. Mrs. Webster couldn't buy the walking mug at the same time, being on a limited retirement income, but she had Rose hold it for her.

By late afternoon, there were long breaks between customers. Rose took this opportunity to make a few more calls about the mystery photograph. She tried the Hall of Records in Carmel and Monterey, asking about a birth certificate for a baby girl born in 1936 to Julia Holland. That search turned up no records.

Next, Rose contacted local hospitals, both in Carmel and neighboring Monterey, asking if hospital records were kept that far back. One helpful clerk agreed to check on the name Julia Holland, but found only a single admission to Carmel Valley Hospital for anyone by that name, and it was in the surgical wing, not the maternity ward.

Blue stopped by her desk later, reminding Rose that it was past closing time. "You notice that it's dark outside?" He was less than subtle.

"Right," she said. "Time to go home."

"It's none of my business," Blue said, which is how he always began when he intended to give her unsolicited advice, "but don't you think you ought to forget about that picture? Seems to me you're getting worked up over it. Might be better if you forgot about it."

"I don't think so," Rose said. She wasn't ready to give up on Virginia Louise yet.

At home that evening, Rose searched online, working late into the night and into the small hours of the next morning. Her most exciting find was checking the name Virginia Louise against the birth year of 1936, both in Carmel and Monterey counties. She didn't locate a child born to Julia Holland, as she'd hoped, but she did find a baby girl born on November 7, 1936, to a Helen Lawrence (maiden name) and her husband, James Lundquist. The Lundquist's daughter was named Virginia Louise. Exhausted, but sure she was on the right path to finding answers to all her questions, Rose went to sleep that night feeling that she was on a journey, traveling back in time, and now had a destination. It wasn't until she awakened a few hours later that nagging doubts invaded her happy mood. *If Virginia Louise was the daughter of the Lundquists, why would Julia*

Holland bother to hide the child's photograph against a mirror backing?

"Your eyes look like a raccoon's," said Blue the next morning, giving his unsolicited opinion, as he was fond of doing.

"Thanks," said Rose, "I don't know what I'd do without your daily report on my faults and flaws."

"Always happy to oblige," said Blue. A big, slow smile stretched his mouth from cheek to cheek.

The phone rang, saving Blue from possible injury. To Rose's surprise, it was the estate agent she had spoken to the day before.

"After our conversation yesterday," said Elaine Parks, "I wondered if you might be interested in seeing the remaining household furnishings from Mrs. O'Neil's estate. There isn't much of any great value, which is why I didn't suggest that you come to the house in the first place," said the agent, "but most of it is still here if you'd be interested in coming over."

A small thrill of excitement flamed in her at the thought of moving closer to finding out about the hidden picture. "Yes, I'll come by right away."

"Oh," said Elaine, "I haven't had a chance to clear out the dresser drawers or throw away the junk, but if you don't mind seeing everything as is, I could meet you at the house at eleven."

"Please," Rose said, "don't throw anything out until I get there." The address Elaine Parks had given her was in Carmel Valley. Rose started to leave as soon as she got off the phone.

"Hey," complained Blue, "you just got here. Mrs. Carter expects me to deliver that Stickley writing desk and chair she bought yesterday. She'll be put out if I don't get them to her this morning."

"She'll wait," Rose called back to him as she hurried out the door. She had the rare satisfaction of seeing Blue look put out. Raccoon eyes, huh? A big, slow smile stretched her mouth from cheek to cheek.

Twenty minutes later, when Rose pulled up to the address Elaine Parks had given her, what she saw was a modest house that looked in need of a fresh coat of paint and a pair of hands to weed the overgrown flowerbeds. The front door opened and the estate agent stepped out.

"Hi, I'm Elaine. Come in," she said warmly, holding open the door and giving Rose her first glimpse into the house.

"I took you at your word," said Elaine, showing Rose one of the drawers bulging with papers. "I'm afraid Mrs. O'Neil hadn't gone through these in a long time."

"Is it all for sale?" Rose asked.

"All?" asked Elaine. "You mean the entire contents of the house?"

"Yes, everything."

"I don't know that some of it is worth selling," Elaine said honestly, "but it all has to go."

"I'll take it all," said Rose, aware of a vein at the base of her throat beating wildly.

"But, you haven't even seen the other rooms," Elaine said.

"I don't need to," said Rose. "I'll give you five hundred dollars for it all, but I want everything exactly as it is. Nothing is to be thrown out."

Elaine Parks stepped back, assessing this situation. The old furniture in this house wasn't worth five hundred dollars. She'd be lucky to sell half of it. The rest would have to go to charity or be junked. *Have I missed something?* she wondered. She glanced around the room again. No, there was nothing of any real value. This stuff was the bad kind of old, worn out, tired looking, and virtually worthless. And yet, it troubled Elaine that an antique dealer was willing to make an offer on it all without even looking at the other rooms.

"There is the jewelry. I couldn't let you have all the furniture and the jewelry for that amount," she said, taking a risk. If she could get another fifty out of this woman, that could go right into her pocket. No one would have to know.

"I'll give you one thousand dollars for the entire lot," said Rose, "but that's it."

"We have a deal," Elaine said, and closed her mouth before she could gasp in surprise.

"Got any trash bags?" asked Rose.

Elaine found a whole box of Hefty Bags. While Rose dumped the contents of drawer after drawer into the bags, Elaine was busy, too, planning where she'd spend the money.

"I'll send my assistant over this afternoon to pick up the furniture," Rose said. She left the house with trash bags full of papers, which she stuffed into her car's trunk, backseat, and passenger seat. A little voice in Rose's head kept muttering all the way back into town. *Have you lost your mind? A thousand dollars for some out of style, beat-up old furniture! This is nuts. This is totally, totally nuts.*

It may have been nuts, as her raving and ranting good sense was telling her, but it was also the most daring thing Rose had done in months. The moment had taken her and she had simply gone for it. If the whole thing amounted to nothing more than some used furniture with heaps of grocery lists, bills and receipts, and plain old junk, then it was a risk Rose had determined to take. Besides, she wouldn't have to haul all that furniture back to the shop by herself; there was Blue.

Sorting through the contents of the bags proved to be no easy task. With Blue delivering Mrs. Carter's furniture, Rose was the only one available to help customers. It was Thursday, and the approaching weekend had brought in more vacationers. By the time Blue returned with the O'Neil estate furniture Rose had just bought, it was closing time. Frustrated, she shoved the bags against the wall behind her desk and sat down at the computer to enter the furniture into the shop inventory.

"You could do this in the morning," Blue pointed out.

"With all the customers coming in, I haven't had time to do anything," she said. "I'd better do it right now."

"I'll stay with you," he offered.

"No, you go home."

"I oughtn't to leave you here alone," he argued.

"As well meaning as that is," she said, "I'm looking forward to a little quiet time."

Blue looked unsure. "I don't know. You might get into trouble here on your own."

She gave him a look that convinced him. "Go home."

He quit arguing.

Two hours later, Rose was knuckle-deep at work on the keyboard, typing in particulars of each piece of furniture purchased from the Julia O'Neil estate. It would have been easier if most of the furniture had been from one manufacturer or time period. Instead, the furniture was a collection from many different styles, but each had to be researched and appraised individually.

A highboy chest of drawers seemed to be the best of the lot. It wasn't much to look at, to an untrained eye, but was better quality than any of the other pieces. The dresser was walnut, with two short drawers at the top and three graduating drawers beneath, and four graduating drawers in the base. Inspecting it, Rose began to suspect the well-made highboy might be late eighteenth century.

The answer was in the workmanship. Rose pulled out the bottom drawer to check the construction, looking for how the sides were joined. When she turned it over, she saw a letter taped to the bottom of the drawer. The letter was addressed to Miss Julia Holland.

The envelope was yellowed with age, but did not tear as Rose slipped a sharp knife beneath the tape and cut it free. Aware that she was scarcely breathing, Rose pulled two sheets of folded paper from it and began to read.

Dear Julia,

James and I wanted to write to thank the woman who gave us our beautiful baby. We are so grateful to you for letting us adopt her. We have named her Virginia Louise. We were so sorry to hear of your emergency surgery following the baby's birth. It grieves us to know that now you cannot have other children of your own. Because of this, we want to suggest that we might arrange for you to see Virginia Louise once in a while. You have given us such a wonderful gift, a blessing in our lives. We hope to be able to return some of that blessing back to you. For your sake and for hers, we won't tell her who you are, but you could visit occasionally as a friend of the family.

The letter went on to say that they hoped Julia would remain in Carmel, now that she had come to live here, and was signed, *With our love, Helen and James Lundquist.*

Rose stared at the signature, knowing she had found the answers to her questions. The letter was dated November 12, 1936, only days after the baby's birth. It was clear to Rose now. Julia Holland had been Virginia Louise's birth mother. She had come to Carmel to have her baby, and because of the willingness of the Lundquists to let her see her child, had stayed. Later, she had married. The child had been Julia Holland's secret, one she kept even from her husband. That was why the photograph had been hidden against the mirror backing.

That night, Rose pored over the other papers in the plastic bags she'd carried to the shop. In none of them was there a mention of a daughter given up for adoption, but there were letters between Julia and her husband, Michael. The letters were a story of a childless couple, who although they grieved over this, loved each other.

It was late when Rose left the shop and drove home. Her thoughts were filled with lives she had come to know through letters, anniversary cards, receipts for medical bills, and one letter taped to the bottom of a drawer. At home in her own bed, she dreamed of them all: Julia Holland, Michael O'Neil, Helen and James Lundquist, and most of all, Virginia Louise.

Rose was late driving into town the next morning, having overslept, and careless when she put the cat into his carrier. The latch was loose. It was a warm, pretty day, and Rose put down the windows of the car to smell the salt air. She was headed downhill, had stopped at a four-way stop sign, when suddenly a large German shepherd that had been sitting at the curb beside his owner took that moment to lunge right at the passenger side window of Rose's car, ferociously barking at the cat.

The attack took Rose so much by surprise, she instinctively plastered herself back against her seat, away from the dog's head at the passenger window. Her leaning back made a perfect escape route for Griffin, who sprang from his carrier with the unfastened latch, shot straight across Rose, and leaped out the driver's window.

It happened in an instant. One second

the cat was on the seat beside her, and the next he was gone. Rose pulled over, parked, and searched everywhere for Griffin, but couldn't find him. She marched up and down the streets, with the cat carrier in one hand and his favorite toy in the other, hoping to lure him out of hiding if she found him. Nothing worked.

After two hours of hunting, Rose drove to the shop, hoping someone might have found Griffin and called to leave her a message. It wasn't until she got to the shop that she remembered Griffin hadn't been wearing his collar. She had brushed him the night before and the collar with its tag was still on the kitchen counter where she'd left it. No one would know where he belonged. No one could return him to her. He was lost.

Rose had just hung up from a call she'd placed to the animal shelter, letting them know that her cat was missing and that she would stop by that afternoon to check on any strays they might have picked up, when the door to the shop opened and in walked Mrs. Webster. Never in Rose's life had she been so glad to see a customer. Tucked under Mrs. Webster's arm, purring contentedly, was a butterscotch-colored cat.

"Griffin!"

Mrs. Webster handed him to Rose. "I spotted this little fellow wandering down the sidewalk as I was heading home," said Mrs. Webster. "There's no mistaking him. He wasn't the least bit afraid. I think he liked his adventure. He was poking his head into store windows like a real tourist."

Rose hugged Griffin and kissed him all over his furry little face. Griffin allowed this display of affection for only so long, then let it be known that he'd had enough by aiming a well-placed nip. Rose made sure the front door was closed, then put him down. He ambled off and found his favorite seat in the front window, in a spot that the sun had warmed to his liking.

"I can't thank you enough," Rose said.

"Oh, he was just a little lost," said Mrs. Webster. "All I did was find him and bring him back home."

"He didn't try to bite you?" Rose asked, amazed that Griffin had let the woman carry him for two blocks.

"No," said Mrs. Webster, "and he never once tried to get away."

Rose smiled at the image of this nice, gentle woman lugging a fifteen-pound tomcat cradled in the crook of her arm like a baby for two blocks. Then, she saw something that took the smile right off her face. Funny, she'd never noticed it before. It was there in plain sight, dangling from a thin chain on Mrs. Webster's wrist.

"That's a very pretty locket," said Rose. "So unusual. Where did you get it?"

"I've had it since I was a girl," said Mrs. Webster.

"May I look at it?"

Mrs. Webster held her hand closer. The design on the locket was a Celtic pattern Rose had seen only once before. She looked at the woman more closely, especially the eyes. *Yes,* Rose thought, *older, but there's no doubt.*

"Mrs. Webster, is your given name Virginia Louise?"

"No one has called me that since my parents died," said Mrs. Webster. "Everyone else calls me Gina."

"I have something I'd like to show you," said Rose.

The photograph was where she'd left it, still on her desk. Rose brought it over and showed it to Mrs. Webster.

"Why, that's a picture of me. I have one exactly like it in my album at home."

"Sit down," said Rose, offering Mrs. Webster a chair. "I have a long story to tell you."

When Rose had told it all, Gina Webster said, "It's incredible. I knew her. I thought she was one of my mother's friends. All those years, she never said a word about it, not even after my parents died. Now she's gone. She was always so kind to me. She gave me presents when I was little. I remember her so well," said Gina, her eyes misting up, "my mother."

A few days later, Gina Webster stopped by Two Sisters Antiques. She handed Rose a small velvet box. Within was the gold locket with the Celtic design. An accompanying note read: *This is for Griffin to wear on his collar so he will never be lost again. With my eternal thanks, Virginia Louise.*

"Are you sure you want to part with this?" Rose asked.

"I'm sure. If Griffin hadn't walked right up to me on the street that day, I might never have found out about my birth mother. I want to give this to him. Please let me."

Griffin's name and Rose's phone number and address had been engraved onto the back of the locket. Rose fastened the locket to his collar and slipped it around Griffin's neck. The gold locket hung like a bright jewel on the ruff of fur at his chest.

"You look handsome," Rose said, admiring him.

"He does look nice," Gina agreed, petting the cat's head.

So much had happened since Rose had shown Gina the photograph and told her about Julia O'Neil. Gina bought all the pieces from her mother's estate, including the highboy dresser, which turned out to be a reproduction and not worth thousands after all, but meant even more than that to Gina. Rose gave Gina all the letters and documents that had belonged to her birth mother, along with the photograph. Together, they figured out that the Lundquists must have sent the photograph to Julia when their daughter was five years old, and that Julia, who had married that same year, must have hidden the picture inside the mirror to keep it from her husband.

They would never know why Julia hadn't taken the photograph out of the mirror frame after her husband died. Maybe she hadn't been strong enough to pull the heavy mirror off the wall and take it apart. Maybe her mind was becoming forgetful. Or, maybe she had simply left it where it had been all those years, out of respect for her husband's memory. Some things couldn't be answered.

The disposal of Julia O'Neil's remaining estate was being reconsidered by the estate agent now. With the letter from the Lundquists to support Gina's claim, plus the hospital record of Julia Holland for "female problems" on the same day and at the same hospital where the Lundquists' baby had been born, Gina had a good chance of being declared the heir to her birth mother's estate. There was only the house and a little money in the bank, but mostly, there was the recognition at last that Gina was Julia's daughter.

"How do I ever thank you?" Gina had said to Rose. "What can I possibly say?"

"You don't need to say anything," said Rose, then remembered Gina's words when she'd returned Griffin. "You were just a little lost. All I did was find you and bring you back home."

Griffin, settling into the shop window, stretched lazily and draped one tufted paw over a blue silk scarf, and eased one back foot onto a yellow Wedgwood saucer. Comfortable at last, and wearing his shiny new locket, he settled down to the business of a serious nap.

"Did you know there's a cat messing up the display in your front window?" said a customer. "He's knocking things over."

Rose glanced at the display window and smiled. "It's all right," she told the customer, surely a tourist. "He owns the place."

Had He but Known

by Marlys Millhiser

Our cat, herein named Madame, is a joint venture. From a tiny kitten, she grew up in college, a gift to my daughter from a long-gone boyfriend. That's where she acquired her name and why I won't use it in this story. I suspect she was weaned on pizza and beer. Her strange infancy and childhood made our cat clever, fat, and mean. So mean that she flunked the kennel's cattery and must go to my daughter's and son-in-law's home when we leave town and stay with my husband and me when they do. Only family could appreciate this cat. She even bit our ninety-three-year-old grandma. Twice.

Everybody (except Grandma) loves her to death and for absolutely no good reason. So I decided to plunk her

down in history (her story, if you read it right) and see how she might deal with a time every bit as ornery as she.
— Marlys Millhiser

"That's the fattest cat I ever saw." James Frank peered at the animal splayed on a shelf of the back bar in P. J. Werley's Saloon.

"That's the *meanest* cat you ever saw." P.J. set a frothy glass of Zang's in front of James.

This was not your ordinary bar. It had a marble top and polished brass handrail with towels, to wipe the suds from your mustache, hanging evenly spaced along it. The footrail, to prop a boot on, was brass, too, and so were the spittoons every few feet on the floor in front of it. There were hard-boiled eggs and salty pickles and spicy sausages for nibbling while you drank. This was a first-class saloon for a dusty buffalo pit like Boulder, Colorado, for sure. Frank almost felt a pang for what would happen to it. "What kind of cat is he?"

"That, sir, is a she cat. The only 'she' allowed in here," P.J. said with pride and a wink. Not that there was much glory in that. Females weren't allowed in saloons, anyway, only brothels and dance halls.

An eight-mule-drawn wagon lumbered by on Pearl Street with a load of steam boiler and pipe, followed by another with six mules hauling riveted sheet iron pipe for drainage at the mines. Both on their way to the canyon mouth, they added dust billows to the saloon windows. The mules, straining against the wind at their heads as well as the burden at their tails, complained in a raucous clamor abrasive enough to make a man grit his teeth. The floor trembled beneath Frank's feet. The bottles on the back bar rattled around the she cat, but she just blinked back at James Frank.

The door opened to more dust and then closed again behind a big man, tall and broad. "P.J.?"

"Marshal?" The proprietor reached for a bottle of rye next to the she cat's head and she moaned low and dangerous — hissed, spat.

"What do you feed her, nails?" Frank, disappointed it wasn't the boy, spat, too, into the closest spittoon.

"Madame will eat chicken legs — cooked. Hard-boiled eggs. Chopped-up sausage. Buttered bread. Boiled beef. Pieces of apple now and again. Used to drink a little beer, but she's given that up, drinks cream instead. Likes to chew on wood, mice, and rats — raw."

Frank drained his glass. Zang's was an interesting beer. Not good, but interesting. "Wood."

"Keeps her teeth sharp as her nails." P.J. broke off the business end of a match and handed the beheaded stick to the fat feline who proceeded to shred it and, with a jerk of her head, sling the slivers out onto the shelf below.

"Why do you keep a mean cat in this public establishment, anyway?"

"Well now, that is a whole story in itself. Right, Marshal?"

"Oh yeah, meanest damn cat in town now that all the mountain lions been shot." The marshal had himself an egg, dipped in the small shallow bowl of salt provided, and studied Frank in the mirror of the back bar, as well he might. But he showed no sign of recognition. Funny how just a few simple changes cloaked a man from eyes that should know better. "Madame's a legend in this town."

"Madame — what? She a bohunk cat?" Frank played along and had an egg, too. The marshal made them look so good. Madame's chest and neck ruff were thick, fuzzy, sand-colored fur. The tiger stripes began with a few bars on her face, then grew closer together as they went back on her body to completely darken her tail. Her eyes were real blue, shiny blue. They widened big and then shrunk to slits for no reason.

"You haven't heard of Madame here, you must be traveling through on the railroad. Marshal James Tarbox. And you, sir?"

"We call him Jimmy," P.J. said.

Town marshals west of Kansas were pretty much all alike. Dumb. "Frank." They shook hands, exchanging a bit of egg yolk and salt. "James Frank. Nobody calls me Jimmy."

First thing Frank did when he came to a town was to check the Wanted posters. If he was shown with a mustache and sideburns, he shaved them. If he was shown clean-shaven, attached both with a special gum substance he ordered from the Sears Roebuck catalog.

When Madame inhabited a building, you never saw mice or rats or even grasshoppers, the bartender contended. "Just blood on the floor the next morning."

"Oh yeah, meanest damn — even burned down a whorehouse." The marshal of Boulder Township nodded, scratched his nose reflectively, and had himself another egg.

Frank stared at the cat. The cat blinked, lazy and slow. Frank winked back. "What'd she do, eat the wrong end of a match and cough it up in a puddle of kerosine?"

"Well, now that's a thought." P. J. Werley turned to look at the she cat but really watched James Frank in the back bar's mirror, too.

"Blood's all that cat's left on the floor come morning?" James Frank's mother had always been partial to cats on the hearth as well as in the barn. Made home homey was her contention.

"Does her business in the alley just like the gents."

Frank could remember the stink of the Gents out back very early this morning. The grumblings of stray burros roaming the alleys, dogs howling back at coyotes provoking chatter, and nervous dispatch squawks from chicken houses all over town. Whole lot of critters came out nights with James. Every now and then you'd hear one of them get squashed and eaten.

The door opened again to let in more dust and the hoot of a whistle and the grinding of tracks as the empty coal train roared down the canyon into town. It closed on a tall thin man with eyes so light and hard they looked nearly white. He walked into the first table inside the door and knocked over a chair. Three more and Frank's guest list would be complete. But it still wasn't the boy.

"Sheriff?" P. J. Werley looked at the bottles on the back bar, this time uncertainly. "How's the family?"

"Beer, I'll have a beer. I don't care what." The sheriff of Boulder County righted the furniture and removed his hat to swipe his brow with his sleeve. His limp was so profound it made you wonder if he'd lost a heel off one boot. "Make it strong."

"Strong . . ." P.J. and the other two men in the room exchanged glances. The she cat yawned and a remaining match sliver dripped to the shelf below.

"Zang's it is," the proprietor said with a shrug and poured a double shot of whisky into it.

"We were just explaining Madame to Mr. Frank here," Marshal Tarbox said. "You know, how she burned down Pearl's. How mean she is and everything."

"The cat," P.J. said helpfully. "This is Sheriff Trezise, Mr. Frank."

This side of Kansas, the only thing dumber than a town marshal was a county sheriff. Frank happened to know the sheriff's limp was due to a fall off a plodding livery horse. But now it was James and Sheriff Trezise staring at each other in the mirror of the back bar. The she cat blinked between them.

James Frank got this itchy prickle he always did when someone needed killing. A little over a year ago, he and a friend who lived here (and that's why Frank knew how the sheriff came by his limp) decided to rob the Mercantile Bank down the street from Werley's. Just when, as luck would have it, the respectable ladies of the community decided to burn down the whorehouses. They sent no cat to do it. This town was stupid. How could a respectable bank robber pass it by?

The door opened yet again. The wind gusts stirred up Pearl Street to grit so thick you could smell dirt and mule poop on the air that blew in with the short rotund man clinging to his hat. The marshal hurried to help him shut the door on it and then stayed behind to shoulder that door against a blast that hit the building like an explosion. The lazy she cat managed to look irritated. But when he drank in a slug of his doctored Zang's, the sheriff looked like he'd been shot.

"Doc?" P.J. said and drew another Zang's.

"Nasty out there. Worse in the alley out back." Doc reached for an egg and took a long thirsty drink. "What's that critter doing up there? Told you about vermin and microbes and such. Shouldn't mix with people."

"According to you, people shouldn't mix with people." The marshal rejoined them at the bar and told James Frank, "Don't ask Doctor Bonner about the French Disease."

"So what's the verdict?" the bartender asked.

"Well, she's dead." Most fat men have a big belly held up by a flat back. Doctor Bonner's middle was round all the way around him.

"I know that. I'm the one found her, Fred. Me and Madame, here."

"She was murdered."

"Know that, too." P. J. Werley had the thickest head of hair Frank had ever seen on a man, carefully trimmed sideburns, mustache, and beard to match. "Ain't often a person slits their own throat. So how come you didn't come in the back door?"

"Otto's got it blocked with that damn

wagon of his. I need a stogie." The doctor took his beer to the glass case on the end of the bar and selected a Pollock's Crown. P.J. snipped off the end and slid the ornate box of matches down the bar top. After some sucks to get it lit and several satisfied puffs, the good doctor raised the cigar in one hand and the Zang's in the other. "Best cures invented, gentlemen. Both do restore and elevate."

"What was a woman doing in the alley, anyway?" Frank wanted to know.

"Could have been drug there." Doc nodded, agreeing with himself.

"Could have been chased there." Marshal Jimmy squinted with the import of his thoughts.

"Could have been lured there." The bartender was cracking eggs, rolling them in his hands, and expertly removing the shells, leaving not a pock on the hard-boiled whites.

A very long but narrow place, Werley's Fine Drinking Establishment had a kitchen at the back, alongside it a shoulder-width hall that led to the alley and the Gents — a one holer that couldn't begin to accommodate a heavy beer night — making the alley an unseemly and nasty place for a lady at any time.

A permanent sign painted on the saloon's street window advertised tender boiled beef sandwiches, "finest in the state." While most places ground the tough but tasty meat, Werley's boiled it until it turned to strings, laced the boiling water with salt, pepper, onions, and strong coffee to make a gravy to mix with the meat, and served it on sliced store bread. The aroma alone brought in drinking customers and helped dispel the alley odor.

James Frank knew all this firsthand, as well as when the Chinaman in the kitchen came to work and left, and when eggs were delivered for boiling — most of the cooking here involved boiling for sure. The sandwiches and drink came at a hefty price. The lure was the trappings, the clientele — high toned by Boulder standards — and free bar food. The delicious odors of the nearly constant boiling of the beef encouraged all to buy sandwiches with their beer as well, continue drinking, no need to go home for supper. A man could brag, belch, eat, drink, curse, smoke, break wind, chew, and spit in peace and with his hat on. Life didn't get much better than that.

The cleaning man and floor scrubber worked in the mornings before and after the saloon opened. If someone was trying to polish tobacco spittle off the brass footrail and you were imbibing before noon, you moved aside as the man did his ragging in saloons anywhere.

The next gentleman to appear in this saloon did so from the hall to the back alley and all in black with an old-fashioned stovepipe hat. Otto Buchbeit, coroner and mortician, ordered a beef sandwich with his beer, and pretty soon everyone but the barkeep, including James Frank, was eating beef sandwiches, too. The strings caught in your teeth. Frank's guest list was complete, but for the boy.

James Frank had made it out of Boulder last year. Half the loot hadn't. All because of a boy whose beard probably needed shaving once a month and these men. They'd stolen half his stolen money. And the boy had stolen his partner's stolen horse with that money in the saddle bags, and his partner ended up dead.

The talk turned to the body in the alley. It was a Mrs. Fanny Strock. She ran a boardinghouse down by the railyards.

"Poor old Fanny was a hardworking woman," the marshal said. He had mustard sauce on his chin.

"Somebody needs hanging." Otto, the

coroner, dug for beef strings with a fingernail. "What's that cat doing up there?"

Doctor Bonner, beef juice running down
his chin onto his vest, chewed and swal-
lowed, took a puff on his cigar, and finished his beer. "Gentlemen, something
must be done about wicked assassins in
our society. And it must start right here in
the township of Boulder. And cats should
always be outdoors or in barns. Regular
caldron of germs."

"But Madame's a legend around the
town," James Frank reminded them. "From
what I hear, anyway." Something fishy
smelling about the feline. She hadn't been
here last spring.

"Here, here," Sheriff Trezise agreed and
offered his glass for a refill. "Who's Fanny
Strock?"

P. J. Werley, the only man neither drinking nor eating, poured whiskey into the
sheriff's refill of beer, too. "Landlady at
the Railman's Boarding Hotel on Water
Street, one who won't take in ranch hands
or miners. You still sleeping at the jail?"

"Jail's a lot tamer than my house." The
sheriff's wife had given birth to three sons
in one afternoon. Miraculously, all three
not only survived but vigorously thrived.
Concerned citizens worried more about

their father now, P.J. explained to the new-comer with the same proud tone he explained the fat feline on the back bar. The cat remained unimpressed but the sheriff was getting tiddly.

Fanny the landlady may have been hard-working, but she was an ugly witch with warts on her nose and even fatter than the cat. Not much of a loss as far as James Frank could see. Question was still, what she was doing out there last night while he was planting explosives about the building at the only time there wasn't someone cooking or scrubbing or polishing the damn place? Served her right for getting in the way.

Women had their place in this world, after men took their pleasure and after breeding and choring for offspring. But it was limited. Except for Frank's mother. She was a fine example of womanhood and her warts were barely noticeable. As a matter of fact, not so long ago Frank had shot a man who'd claimed otherwise. He'd died.

Old Fanny had been sort of staggery when she'd surprised him, as he remembered now and motioned for another Zang's. It was brewed in Denver but Boulder had a big distributing warehouse here to serve the county and the rich mining districts in the mountains to the west. Werley's had barrels stacked along the wall opposite the bar. P.J. didn't know it, but one of those barrels wasn't Zang's.

Point was, women shouldn't drink; that's why they were so against men doing it. She had no business being drunk in the alley. And it was odd, now that he thought about it, most women don't drink. And if they do get fat, they fill out on rich food, not beer. But she'd served his purpose like a gift. Got all these people together for him. He'd planned to kill the cook to get their attention. But there she was, warts and all, old fat Fanny. More likely to draw these men in than a Chinaman for sure. Would she draw the boy? He, more than the others, was responsible for stealing James Frank's stolen money.

"I never heard of no Fanny Strock," the sheriff of Boulder County insisted. "Thought it was Mrs. Monday who wouldn't take in cowhands because of the way they stink. She oughta meet my brood."

James Frank ordered another sandwich, didn't figure he'd have to pay for it. And another Zang's, too. That he could get other places, but it would soon be the end of the salty, tasty, stringy beef sandwiches. He'd heard of a place in Dodge that had tried to make them like this, but there was a secret to the recipe that would die with Werley's. Right soon, too.

Frank also didn't worry about getting away in time even with a belly full of beef and beer. It was such a wonderfully simple scheme, even a drunk or a female couldn't botch it.

"We told you about old Fanny," the marshal told the sheriff carefully. "Rememmmber?" He winked a quick one that James caught but wasn't sure Sheriff Trezise had.

"We all told you about old Fanny." Doctor Bonner added a deliberate raise of the brows.

That's when James Frank began to suspect that things might have gone wrong. But the cat hissed and bristled, and Frank was distracted by something in the mirror of the back bar that couldn't be. Apparently only he and Madame noticed the figure sort of float by. "Thought you don't allow females in this saloon."

"We don't." The hairy proprietor rolled another egg and skinned it.

"No ladies in a respectable saloon. Bad luck for business. Like on ships at shee."

The sheriff drained his glass. "Thashure good beer."

James turned around ever so casually to rest his elbows on the bar, then raise his glass to his lips. He and the cat had seen her drift by in front of the barrels along the back wall, the cat straight on and he in the mirror. Nobody else noticed.

Where had she gone? Frank had investigated the place carefully to set this up. Her only way out was the front door, which hadn't opened because the sound of the grit-laden wind alone would have signaled that.

Seemed sort of odd, now that his doubts were raised, that the only people here were the ones he wanted to be here. It wouldn't have bothered him to dispatch a few bystanders while he was at it.

She'd had warts on her nose, the floating figure. And she wasn't James's mother. Her head sat funny, as well it should considering her throat was slit. And she was a whole lot thinner dead than she'd been alive. He didn't know what was happening, just that it was time to light the fuse. One central fuse that would light the rest. And it would take only one match.

He heard the clank of falling bottles behind him and the exclamations of the other men as the she cat left her perch to leap to the bar top close to one of Frank's elbows and from there to the floor in front of him. Madame was too fat for grace and sounded a short grunt and a long plunk with each landing. She headed for the tallest stack of beer barrels and began sniffing around like a dog.

He was about to shoot the cat to make his enemies nervous when she flushed the boy from behind the barrels of Zang's. James decided he'd spare her for now for making his party complete.

Frank was the only man armed in the saloon. The marshal and the sheriff carried rifles when chasing bank robbers, but couldn't hit anything. Neither could sit a horse. Frank had been chased by some of the best posses in the West, even the Pinkertons, who were not that good. But this was the only time he'd been chased by horse and buggy. He'd had no trouble getting away, only problem was he'd spooked his own horse. James rarely laughed and the animal didn't know what to make of the sound.

These men and the boy had led the posse. He'd seen them often in this establishment while he and his partner were sizing up the town. He decided Werley's was a good place to assemble and destroy them all together before he robbed the Mercantile again for old time's sake and to get back the other half of his stolen money.

"There was no cat at Pearl's before it burned," James Frank said in the voice that had made braver men than these blanche. He ought to know, he'd robbed Pearl's, too. This had to be the dumbest town in the West, named its main thoroughfare after the madam of a whorehouse. Had it been so dark in the alley, he'd just thought he'd slit old Fanny's throat? That's when he noticed the rounded edge of something metal sticking out of a corner behind the kegs.

Frank should have been warned then just what was afoot but instead picked up a free match off the bar and strolled to the barrels to see what he could see and do what he'd planned to do for some months now. The kid had been a tad too close to the area Frank did not want exposed.

"You should be in school, son," P.J. told the boy.

"Well, I'm not and I'll have a Zang's, barkeep." The kid brushed rudely against Frank's side as he strutted over to the bar, his hat at a tilt. A slight boy who would never have made much of a man, anyway.

"Come on, P.J." The marshal belched

like a buffalo on spring grass. "How many of us were still in school at his age? We were all out working. Except Doc, here, of course."

"Drinking beer at Werley's is not work and not for . . ." Doctor Frederick Bonner had turned mean at the sight of the kid and he spat out the last word, ". . . boys."

James Frank bent down pretending to stroke the cat, intending to light the fuse instead, and discovered her chewing on it. She bit him with the speed and sting of a coiled snake when he slapped her away. Well, it would be the animal's last bite of anything for sure.

Just as the fuse took fire, he noticed the crumpled cloth stuffed into a crevice between wall and barrels. It was much the color of the dress worn by Fanny in the alley. He noticed too that the wide tube of riveted sheet iron in the corner, a cut off version of the drainage pipe those mules had just hauled up Pearl Street toward the canyon, had suspenders hanging down its side.

James Frank stood quickly, to find the arrangement of his victims altered, their expressions, too. Except for that of the sheriff, who raised his glass for a refill.

The boy with his beer in one hand and

his egg in the other stalled in the act of watching. The hulking marshal blocked the door to the street, and the doctor, proprietor, and coroner, the hall to the alley. The cat spit pieces of fuse or Frank's hand with a shake of her head. James Frank went for his Iver Johnson and nobody ducked.

That's when he began to think the hairy bartender had been doctoring his beer, too. That's when he noticed the boy had warts on his nose. That's when he realized the boy had cloaked himself as Fanny Strock out in the alley and then that he'd even cloaked himself as a boy.

That's when the boy dropped his egg and shot James Frank with his own Iver Johnson.

Frank started toward the kid with the half notion of luring the marshal away from the street door but went down before he got there. Wouldn't be time now to fight his way out even if he could fight. James Frank had not planned to die with his enemies.

"You are an outrage," Doctor Frederick Bonner told the boy and turned over the fallen man. "Drinking beer, shooting robbers." Next it would be cigars. His antipathy to the cocksure hero knew no bounds. But he couldn't explain why to his friends. Fred Bonner once married into this strutting pretender's family and knew his own early indiscretions could be gleefully disclosed to a town in which he'd found due respect for his professional services as a physician.

"Stopped him, didn't I?" The outrage handed the revolver to the sheriff and reached for another egg, Madame swiftly making the one dropped to the floor disappear. "I'd be careful. Man's not dead, you know."

"What do you mean outrage? He saved the saloon." P.J. drew the kid another beer. "On the house, boy. And, Jimmy, I thought you were going to ruin everything with that remark about the cat burning Pearl's. Embellishment's not smart when you're lying and he noticed it. He was in town when the ladies burned the bordellos."

"Lad's earned every penny for figuring out what this outlaw was up to. And then for shooting him." The coroner set his jaw and handed Bonner a bar rag to help sop up the robber's blood so he could examine the wound.

"Doc, you're the one who suggested Frank would move fast and we better find out what he was up to. This young fellow was in town and he'd helped us before. And he dreamed up the whole scheme. And it worked," Marshal Tarbox insisted. "Not just any man will wear a disguise that makes him look like a woman, no matter his age and for no amount of money."

The outlaw made mumbling sounds and Doc leaned closer. "Says we should all run away because the place is going to explode. But would we please take him with us."

"You sure you found all the fuses and dynamite, son?" P.J. asked. This, after all, was his saloon and living.

"Don't have to, just disconnected the one he was going to light. Wouldn't surprise me if some of those barrels aren't beer, though. You might do a more thorough search before you open up shop to the public."

This time the doctor made the mumbling sounds. He'd been against the use of this affront to humanity for any purpose, let alone one so important, but by the time he got wind of it, plans were already underway. God meant for women to earn their keep by selflessly and tirelessly succoring and sustaining others, making them comfortable, serving as a model of propriety and restraint against the baser instincts of men. Not drinking beer in saloons and shooting bank robbers.

"Frank's wanted all over the country." The marshal looked around the barrels, probably for anything that might still be sizzling and need stomping out, but apparently found none. "How'd you make him think your throat was slit?"

"Catsup sauce." The cocky pretender, who went under a variety of names, lifted a condiment bottle off the bar while letting neck and head go loose and wobbly like it was fixing to fall to the floor, making a choking, expiring sound, tongue hanging long and straggly. "Helped that it was dark out there in the alley and that he didn't decide to shoot me instead. Old Jacob cut holes in a piece of pipe that fell off a wagon in front of his blacksmith shop and cut it in half for me. A body shield of sorts. Holes were for the suspenders." The sham man pulled the sheet-iron contraption out from behind the kegs along the wall and staggered some with its weight. "Stole the dress off Mrs. Monday's clothesline."

Everyone but Doc laughed at that. Mrs. Monday and her two daughters were the largest women in all the county, maybe the state. At least they knew their place in the order of the universe.

"I still don't understand how you managed the slit throat," Otto Buchbeit, coroner and mortician, said. "Sheet-iron hanging from suspenders wouldn't protect your neck."

Lennora, the imposter, stripped the warts from her nose and stepped behind the barrels to pick up the neck brace that filled out Fanny Strock's high collar, held it up to show off the fact it had a sheet-iron liner. "Had to hike up the pipe when he came at me to close the gap between this and it."

"Well, it worked. And here's the fee agreed upon. Town's grateful." The cat scratched on the door to the street. The marshal went to open it, then turned back to the doctor and the man on the floor. "Now what's he saying?"

"He's calling for his mother."

"How'd you have time to do all this? Wasn't that much of it," P.J. said. The cook had seen the man hanging around the alley the last two nights and described him so well they remembered the robber and managed to outwit him.

"Jacob lined the soft rubber neck piece from one of those horrible braces females wear to correct posture. Wouldn't have been believable in daylight and without my special sounds. Took a chance, gentlemen. No time to plan else."

"I know that's what he was using to cut fuses with, but what'd you plan if he pulled out his pistol instead of a knife?" the barkeep wanted to know.

"Considered falling on him. Hard and real fast." The shameless fake staggered across the room with the metal contraption. "Too heavy to take with me. I leave it as a souvenir of the first woman allowed in this saloon, who wasn't a cat or Mrs. Werley. But the suspenders belong to Jacob Faus."

This brought laughter from everyone but the doctor and the fallen bank robber again. The latter gurgled again.

"What'd he say now?"

Doc leaned over his patient once more and put an ear to his mouth. "Said the same thing as last time."

"Sounded to me like he said, 'the lad's a she,'" P.J. said.

"Probably talking about the cat. What's all this malarkey about that cat, anyway?" Otto, the coroner, wanted to know.

"Yeah, whose cat was that?" Lennora lifted the armored disguise to a table top in front of the window.

"Showed up over a week ago. Kind of

took a fancy to her. Good mouser and you got to admit she did keep that outlaw distracted till you all got here."

"Where'd she go?" Lennora Poole took off her hat and dark hair to scratch at her scalp through blond hair cut to about an inch all over her head.

"Shat a lady?" The sheriff squinted as if it were dark at night before he slid casually to the floor to join the bank robber.

"She's no lady, gentlemen." Doctor Frederick Bonner stood to stare bullets at the lad who wasn't. But who'd get credit for saving them all, anyway, and Werley's, too. The impostor supported two men who took care of an aunt with the forgetting disease. It was scandalous. She should be the one changing her aunt's diapers for godsake and the men earning the living. "She's Len . . . she's a damned disgrace and a traitor to her gender."

Lennora's grin stretched so wide it exposed two missing molars on one side of her mouth. Doc had pulled one of them just last spring.

The other men in Werley's blinked like the fat germ-laden cat as the impish grin transformed to sweet shyness, a modest hint of seduction before the hat and wig returned and the cocky lad belched his beer and sauntered out to the street door jostling a nicely rounded bag of coins. Nearly half his sparse young beard appeared to have rubbed off one cheek.

Madame headed west out of town toward the canyon mouth, sniffing up the air of freedom and challenge and tomorrows. With her stomach filled, her senses searched for a spot of sun, a nap before sunset. But all urges lay in dormant preparation for the studied pounce and capture of the hunt when it grew dark enough to see clearly, the struggle of the live night meal before she squashed and ate it.

The she cat paused to stare down an approaching dog. When he veered to the other side of the road, she belched. Then, with her ears back, she waddled off into the wind and the dust and the scent of mule.

Crystal's Big Night

by Ed Gorman

Seventeen years ago, a few years before my wife, Carol, quit teaching and started writing novels full-time, a janitor came to her and said that some kids were throwing rocks at this tiny, terrified kitten. He'd broken up their *Lord of the Flies* fun but wasn't sure what to do with this mostly pure white little animal.

Carol took the kitten home, of course. The poor little thing could not stop trembling. We took her to the vet. Crystal, as my then-six-year-old-stepson named her, was suffering so many maladies the vet said he doubted that she'd live much longer than a few days. Well, she lived seventeen more years, finally succumbing a month ago to the heart

215

disease that had steadily weakened her over the past four years.

I've mourned many pets over the years, but Crystal was special. She was as cute and slight as a Disney kitten and far needier than any cat we'd ever had. She saw Carol, and I mean this literally, as her mother. We nicknamed her "the Velcro Kitty" because she was one indivisible with Carol.

So, Crystal, this story is not only about you, it's dedicated to you, sweet girl. At least a couple times a day I go looking for you only to remember that you're gone.

As for the war-on-the-homefront theme, I've been threatening to write such a novel for years. This is sort of a warm-up, I guess.

As Charles Schulz pointed out just before his death, very little has been written about the homefront as it really was during the war. Not everybody was dedicated to helping our troops by supporting the war effort. War profiteers come in all sizes, from munitions manufacturers to the muggers who preyed on our servicemen.

— Ed Gorman

1

The nighttime rallies in Milwaukee. The sounds of Third Reich anthems. The brilliantly lit stage. The Hitlerian salute. He had never attended anything so exciting. So deeply moving. So true. He was playing a role in history — this American who was just another piece of Depression flotsam until he'd discovered the German-Americans loyal to the old country.

But the movement had enemies. From FDR on down, there were attempts to stop these rallies and fund-raisers in Milwaukee and other cities, where the proceedings were usually begun with the reading of telegrams from such Third Reich stalwarts as Goebbels and occasionally Hitler himself. The German-American Bund. There was nothing more thrilling than to stand in a stadium filled with thousands of other like-minded German-Americans.

Why did people persist in seeing this as an affront to America? The people at these rallies only wanted their countrymen to understand that America had no business getting into a European war. Spilling fine American Christian blood. If only they would be more open-minded and try to understand that Hitler was a wise and good man and not the monster the press was portraying him to be.

The press.

Everybody knew what that meant. Jews. And it wasn't only in the press. It was in the motion pictures. It was in the radio shows. It was in many of the books people read. The dishonest and sinister way the Jews looked at everything. They would try to take over the world someday. And that's all that Hitler was trying to prevent. And he needed the power to do it. He would not be accessing other countries if it wasn't necessary to his ultimate defense of the white world. The pure world. The superior world.

He would help any way he could. He was only a single man, but there were enough like him to help the Reich in America once war was declared.

He would help in any way he could. . . .

2

In July 1943, Chicago was a city of eyes. Eyes that watched the skies for enemy planes. Eyes that read posters admonishing STAY ON THE JOB TILL EVERY MURDERING JAP IS WIPED OUT. And eyes that observed a new form of humanity walking the streets — returning soldiers who were missing vital parts of their bodies.

Jim Culhane was getting used to it. The stares. They weren't unfriendly. Just curious. He'd stare at a man missing a left arm, too.

Besides, there were a lot of other men being stared at. There was a war on, in case you hadn't heard. He was one of the lucky ones, and he knew it. He'd left a lot of good friends in the jungles of the Bataan. Friends scraped together and shipped back in boxes when Uncle Sam got the time.

Jim had been the youngest homicide detective on the Chicago police force before the war had come along. He wouldn't be a cop ever again.

That fact alone had given him some problems with accepting his lot. At first he'd felt anger, bitterness, depression, despair. He had to live through this before he could make his peace with himself. Visiting the military hospital close by helped. He saw men far worse off than himself. He used his old skills as a detective to find relatives of whom the injured men had lost track.

"Hey, hi, Lieutenant Culhane."

Jill Tolliver was her name. Twelve years old. Dressed in her Girl Scout uniform five days out of seven. Always collecting books and scrap metal and scrap rubber for the war effort, which she'd haul away in her rumbling red wagon. Pretty little thing with big blue eyes and a somewhat troubled smile. Her father was Army, same as Culhane had been, somewhere in Europe. She'd told Culhane that she said prayers for her dad an even dozen times a day.

"I saw a Nazi spy, Lieutenant Culhane."

Culhane laughed. "You're always seeing a Nazi spy, Jill."

The war had inspired both dread and fear in most kids. They tended to see spies everywhere.

"There were two of them, in fact."

He started to reach out and touch her head with his right arm. Then he realized he no longer had a right arm. It had been cleaved off. He'd been wounded, and then gangrene had set in.

He patted her on the head with his left hand and then took his keys from his pocket. He ran a small USO, one of many in the city. He always got here around nine on Saturday mornings to get ready for the night. Soldiers and sailors got awful lonesome on Saturday nights, far away from home and getting ready to ship over to a war from which they may never return.

Tonight was a special night. The movie star Ronald Reagan was visiting four different USOs in the city. This would be one of them.

"Were they wearing uniforms?" he said, inserting his key in the back door of the place. This was a big empty store, about a quarter of the size of a football field, which USO money had turned into a large snack bar, a dance hall, and enough second-hand furnishings to create little pockets of hominess.

She made a face. "Spies don't wear uniforms. They dress just like us so we don't notice them."

"Then how did *you* notice them?"

"Because I watched them go inside and they kept looking around like they were afraid of something."

"I see."

"My mom sent me to the store. That was how I saw them. I always take this alley as a short-cut." Then: "How old did you say I have to be before you'll let me in?"

He opened the door. He was getting good with his lone hand. Had taught himself to do everything with it. Shave, light a cigarette, even deal a poker hand. *The thing is not to give into self-pity,* one of the docs at re-hab had said to him. Best advice he'd ever gotten.

"At least sixteen, sweetie."

She sighed. "We saw this movie the other night where this girl goes to this USO and sings so well, this movie producer put her in a film."

He smiled. "Maybe that'll happen to you someday."

She made another face. "Maybe it would

if I could carry a tune in a bucket."

He laughed. "Well, see you. Thanks for the tip on the spies."

"They could still be inside there. You be careful, Lieutenant Culhane."

"I will. And you be careful, too."

Most of the work had been done yesterday afternoon. Posters of Ronald Reagan had been hung everywhere. So had extra red-white-and-blue crepe. There would be a live combo tonight, not just the usual records by Frankie and The Andrews Sisters and Glenn Miller. A college trio, true, not exactly pros, but he'd heard them and they were good.

The interior was dark, the only light coming through the parted drapes far up front. He spent twenty minutes inspecting everything. All the lights worked. All the refreshments and the food in the big refrigerator were ready to go. The small bandstand had been swept up, the piano tuned. There'd be some press tonight — when a movie star appeared at a small USO like this, the boys in Washington wanted all the public relations snapshots they could get — and he wanted to make an impression. He still had a kid brother in the war. Europe. Even though he could no longer fight, he wanted to help any way he could.

Troop morale was critical. At least three times a week, a lonesome soldier went into a crying jag here. Was scared about the war or missed his folks or girlfriend or had just had a little more to drink than he could handle. Culhane had developed some skills in dealing with boys like these. He'd been one of them himself, hadn't he?

He wasn't sure what the noise was. Or even where it came from.

He'd turned out all the lights after his inspection — with the war on, you conserved every kilowatt of power you could — and almost immediately after, the noise came. A kind of *thud*. Something falling against a wall or the floor was how his mind imagined it.

He went over to the small office area he used — a small desk, a filing cabinet, a couple of chairs — and grabbed a flashlight.

The first place he checked were the johns.

But nothing. He did note how clean they were. He wanted his entire USO to sparkle. A haven for lost soldiers.

The second place he checked was the storage area in back. Again, nothing. Looming stacks of cardboard boxes, supplies of various kinds, highlighted by sunlight through a small window high in the wall.

He heard the noise again just as he was leaving the storage area.

The closet on the west wall. He wished he had a gun. He hadn't grown up with guns. But his time in the service had made him comfortable with them.

He could call the police, have them come and check out the noise. But what if it was only an animal that had gotten trapped in there? Chicago was a city of great ethnic diversity, including that of raccoons.

Jill's words came back. About seeing two spies. Right. Spies in a USO. There was so much valuable war information here. Maybe they wanted to steal the recipe for chili dogs that Mrs. Freidman was so proud of. Or maybe Mrs. Gallagher's recipe for pineapple upside-down cake. There was something Herr Hitler had probably been losing sleep over.

By this time, Culhane had convinced himself that his unwanted visitors were raccoons. USO people found them everywhere in this draughty old building.

He walked over to the door and opened it. And the masked men leaped from the darkness inside.

Dark clothes. Dark gloves. Dark kerchiefs that covered the faces. Snap-brim hat pulled low over their eyes. A .45 in each right hand.

It happened quickly. Culhane was caught hard on the side of the head with the gun barrel. Then, as he was starting to fall, trying to grab the man with his one hand, his assailant planted a shoe tip in Culhane's groin followed by a concrete fist into his stomach. Culhane had just enough time to remember how good he used to be at street fighting. In his old Irish neighborhood you'd had to be. But those days had ended when his arm had been removed.

The gun came down on his head again and he was unconscious.

3

Why did he have to be so damned stubborn?
Sheila Courtney thought.

According to him, he had two perfect excuses not to marry her. One, he'd come from the working class. And two, he was missing an arm.

She thought about this as she sat at a stop light, a slender red-headed young woman the local gossip columnists frequently compared to a starlet named Rita Hayworth. In addition to looks, she had poise, intelligence, and a sort of kid-sister charm. Even though her parents were among the wealthiest people in Chicago, she wanted people to accept her as just an ordinary girl.

She hadn't always felt ordinary. She'd been a spoiled brat until she'd married Phil

Kane, who came from a family even wealthier than her own. "The ultimate society wedding" the gossip columnists all wrote. But something curious happened. Phil was, if anything, more vain, more spoiled, more bratty than she was. And the way she'd cheated on all her old boyfriends? Phil was a past master at cheating. (She even suspected that he'd slept with a conga dancer on their honeymoon cruise to Puerto Rico.) She began to see herself in Phil, and she was ashamed at the kind of human being she saw reflected. Then she got pregnant and the experience was a spiritual as well as a physical one. She gave up all her old ways for her unborn child. She became the perfect, selfless mother. Phil didn't seem interested. Her pregnancy, which at first had seemed to amuse him, ultimately frustrated him. She wasn't there for sex the way she'd once been. He turned more and more to his nightclub ladies. She found that she didn't care. She no longer loved him. She loved her child. Her child was all that mattered.

Four nights after she miscarried, she overdosed on sleeping pills. She didn't want to live. Phil was in Colorado, skiing with some starlet.

But she did live. And when she found

her legs again, she realized that she had changed completely. No hairshirt; no undying desire to spend time in a convent. But a deep longing for meaning and peace in her life. And values. For the very first time, she understood what was important and what was not important. The socialite's life amused and sickened her. She wanted no part of it.

Then the war came. Gasoline rationing — only three gallons a week. Turning in used silk and nylons to be used for everything such as parachutes, glider towropes, and powder bags for artillery.

The signs everywhere:

SCRAP DRIVES
1 shovel=4 hand grenades
1 lawn mower=6 three-inch shells
1 radiator=17 .30-caliber rifles
1 tire=12 gas masks

She worked twenty hours a week volunteering at a nearby military hospital and five nights a week at the USO. She'd met Jim Culhane at the USO four months ago. He was a decent, gently humorous man who'd spent endless hours trying to improve the lot of the soldiers who passed through this particular USO. Now, if he'd only marry her. She knew he loved her. But his pride . . .

Next to her, a sailor in an ancient Ford roadster, complete with rumble seat, honked the horn and waved at her. Two years ago, before the war had started, she wouldn't have responded so readily to this kind of flirtation. But she waved back. The war had changed girls of every social level. Girls in America were ready to give themselves to men as they never had before, which was one reason why the prudes were so much against USOs. They didn't want wartime romance, let alone wartime sex among unmarried young people, to happen. But there was no stopping it. When you realized that this soldier might be going off to his death, staying virginal no longer seemed so important.

She checked her wristwatch. Nine-thirty in the morning. He should be there by now. With Ronald Reagan coming tomorrow night. He wanted everything to be in great shape at the USO for the movie star's visit.

She gave her Chrysler convertible the gas, and then sped toward the USO.

4

"All right, Crystal. Where'd you'd put my wrist watch this time?" Mary Culhane asked the sweet-faced black-and-white cat sitting on top of her bureau. Mary always said that Crystal had a Disney face, as innocent and elegant and lovely as one of the creatures in a Walt Disney film. Even though Mary was eighteen, and a recent high school graduate, she preferred the world of make-believe romance such as Disney to the more realistic fare that seemed to be popular these days with moviegoers and book buyers. Give her a Faith Baldwin novel any day.

Mary lived with her brother Jim in a three-room apartment. She worked at night in an assembly plant where she was a truck mechanic, something she'd picked up from both her father and Jim. She made fifty-three cents an hour and wanted eighty, what male mechanics were getting. Even her boss admitted she was the best mechanic he had. "But I'm just afraid've how the men'd take it if they found out I was payin' you as much as them." She was determined to get what they got someday. She'd had trouble enough when she'd started there. She was a blond mop-head with a cute smile and a figure you couldn't hide even in greasy overalls. She made the men uneasy.

She was getting ready to run errands. Her six-nights-a-week shift didn't start till ten. Maybe she'd even see a movie.

If she could find her darned wristwatch.

"All right, Crystal, 'fess up. Where'd you take it?"

There'd been an old man living next door. No one locked their doors. Young Mrs. Simone Dennis, who had been hired as the landlady six months ago, explained that everything here was run "on the honor system." And everybody honored the honor system. Except Crystal. Crystal always got into other peoples' apartments. The cat was especially fond of bringing fountain pens, pocket combs, sticks of gum, and anything else that fit easily in her small mouth. She also took things from

Mary's apartment to other tenants.

Three weeks ago, the new tenant, a brusque young man named David Wayman, found himself missing a few trinkets. Crystal didn't amuse him. He'd hurled her out of his apartment one day. Good thing Mary was home. He'd hurt Crystal badly enough to make her limp for a few days.

Crystal was terrified of Wayman now. She hissed and cowered whenever she picked up his scent on the other side of the door as he was leaving for the day. But she also continued her errant pick-ups and deliveries. Sometime during the night, she'd picked up a cufflink belonging to Wayman and brought it back here. At least she'd left it out in the open. Sometimes, Crystal would hide things and not let you see them for days.

Mary suspected she'd find her wristwatch in Wayman's apartment. Wouldn't he be happy about that?

She wanted her watch. She'd just have to go down the hall and knock on Wayman's door and ask him politely if he'd look for it.

Simone Dennis was sweeping the hall. "Morning." She was a small, slight woman with a dark complexion and a very steady, amiable smile. She didn't gossip and seemed to like every one of her tenants. "Errands on Saturday, correct?"

"Correct. It's about the only time I have for myself anymore."

"This war." Simone Dennis shook her head. Then shrugged and moved off to sweep the staircase down.

A new voice said, "The prettiest gal in Chicago."

Mike Sheridan. A mass of curly red hair framing a dramatically handsome face. She had a crush on him but didn't know what to do about it. He seemed interested in her but at the bagel shop on the corner, he seemed interested in all the girls who streamed past his table, flirting and obviously hoping he'd ask them out. He'd injured his knee in high school football. He'd been designated 4-F. He worked in a pet store.

"Hi, Mike."

"Headed to the bagel shop?"

She walked back to him. He always smelled clean and male. She whispered. "Crystal's been at it again."

"What'd she drag into Wayman's this time?"

"My wristwatch."

"Wow. She's getting serious in her old age."

"Now I have to go ask Wayman if he'll look for it."

He frowned. Like the other people in the building, Sheridan had had a few run-ins with the surly Wayman.

"You want me to go with you?"

"Go with her where?"

The voice came from the west end of the hall. Wayman's apartment was at the far east end.

"Oh, hi, O'Banion," Sheridan said.

Ted O'Banion. Black Irish. That mixture of Spanish and Irish blood. He was trim and handsome in his Army uniform. He worked at the Army–Air Force base but lived in the city. He was always asking out Mary, but for some reason, she didn't accept. There was something about him . . . just some instinct, hunch. . . . Mike Sheridan was open, the boy next door. But there was something opaque about O'Banion.

"I'll be delighted to take the young lady wherever she wants to go," O'Banion said.

"She wants to go and talk to Wayman."

O'Banion laughed. "Well, that's one I'll let you handle. If you happen to remember last Friday night."

Everybody in the shabby apartment house remembered last Friday night.

O'Banion had come back from a round of bars more than a little drunk. He was a singer and a whistler when he drank. Actually had a pretty good voice. He'd come home around midnight. Singing a Bing Crosby tune called "Lila Claire." Apparently, he'd awakened Wayman, who'd come roaring out of his apartment, swinging wildly on O'Banion. O'Banion gleefully started throwing punches of his own.

Fortunately, both Jim and Sheridan were home. They separated the two men and sent them to their respective apartments.

O'Banion grinned. "I take it Crystal brought Herr Wayman another gift from you."

"My wristwatch."

"With your luck, Wayman's probably sold it by now."

He gave them a brisk mock salute and walked down the hall then down the stairs and outdoors.

"Well, I guess I may as well get it over with," Mary said.

"I'll go with you."

"I appreciate it."

She knocked on Wayman's door. Gently. She didn't want to wake him. He seemed to spend a lot of time napping. Nobody in the apartment house knew what he did for a living.

No answer.

"Mustn't be home," Sheridan said.

"I'll try one more time."

This time when she knocked, the door opened a fraction. Each apartment door had a lock on it but most people didn't lock their doors during daylight hours.

"You want to go in?" Sheridan said.

"When he's not home?"

"We could just take a quick look around for your watch."

Tempting as it was, she dreaded what would happen if Wayman ever found out. My God. No telling what a man as cold as he was would do.

"We'd better not."

"I'd stand guard. And let you know if I heard him coming." There was mischief in Sheridan's voice. He loved kicks. And this would definitely be a kick.

For him. Not for her.

"We'd better not, Mike."

He shook his head and grinned. "You're always spoiling my fun."

He glanced at his watch. "Well, I guess I'll hit that matinee after all. Don't tell anybody but I still hit all the Saturday afternoon serials. *Captain Midnight* and *The Shadow* today."

"Well, have a good time."

"Don't worry, I will."

Then he took the same path O'Banion had. The only difference being that he took the stairs two at a time. Just like an excited kid headed for a Saturday afternoon matinee.

5

"You should've been a doctor," Culhane said.

"Or at least a nurse."

Sheila had him sitting up at a small table. She had poured half a bottle of Coca-Cola down him along with three aspirins. She had also looked over his scalp carefully. Two bumps from being hit so hard. The skin wasn't cut on either. She checked his eyes carefully, too. No apparent concussion.

The USO was up to speed already, though it wasn't quite eleven a.m. Soldiers, sailors, Marines. With Negro and Hispanic men among them. Few of the USOs were integrated. When Culhane took this one over, he opened it up to everybody. While he didn't have any colored or Mexican friends, he figured that if a man wore a

239

uniform that entitled him to full privileges.

The Andrews Sisters were popular on the massive, bubble-stream jukebox in the corner. Their peppy harmonies soothed even a headache a gun barrel had brought on.

"Jill was right."

"Well," Sheila said, "why don't we split the difference?"

"Huh?"

"She was right that she saw two people in here. But that doesn't necessarily make them Nazi spies."

Burgers were frying on the grill. Girls and young women of every shape and size and color filled the low-ceilinged hall. Some servicemen came here to sit and read and have a bite to eat; some wanted to dance and meet women; some played cards and checkers and chess.

The romance of the uniform, as the national magazines constantly noted, was undeniable. It was a giddy, unreal time, wartime was, and while many married out of love, some married out of the romance of the time itself. And of course, as in all human enterprises, there were the predators. "Allotment Annies" they were called, women who married large numbers of servicemen under various names so they could collect the serviceman's military allotment while they were overseas. One girl claimed to have married fourteen different sailors in four different cities. She was collecting more than $800 a month, a fortune, when they nabbed her. Not that the serviceman always cared — they were scared and just looking for friendship. And if that friendship cost them their allotment, so be it. At least they'd have the illusion that somebody back home cared about them.

In the scuffle with his assailant, Culhane had torn both his shirt and trousers. He needed to go home. He lighted a Lucky Strike. Took a deep drag. "Think I could talk you into giving me a ride home so I can change?"

"Shouldn't you call the police first?"

"And tell them what? I didn't get a look at the guy. And he was probably nothing more than a thief, like you said. I'll let Shanahan know about it tonight."

Shanahan was a neighborhood cop who always stopped in for a Coke on his nightly rounds.

"Top up or top down?"

"The fresh air'll do me good."

"I'm glad you said that. It's a perfect day for a drive in a convertible, if we had the gas to spare."

Meat only twice a week. No more joyrides. Blackouts that brought everything to a halt. Irritating sometimes. But nothing compared to what the boys overseas were going through.

The car attracted stares. As did the driver. Culhane was used to it by now. She was a beauty, and so was her car. The car meant nothing to him. But the girl did. He loved her and wished he didn't. A working-class ex-cop with one good arm wasn't exactly a match for an elegant socialite. He knew that love was supposed to conquer all. At least in the movies. But as a guy who'd been raised in a troubled home, he knew how difficult marriage was between equals, let alone by people at opposite ends of the social scale.

"You want to wait or come up?" he said when Sheila pulled up to the curb.

"I'd like to say hi to Mary."

He wished Mary didn't like Sheila so damned much. She was always giving him unsubtle hints that he should send his pride packing and marry the girl. In fact, the two got along so well, they were always whispering and giggling about things, like little schoolgirls. He secretly found this sweet but wouldn't admit it to himself. He was corny enough as it was. A guy could get only so corny before capsizing.

The apartment house was its usual Saturday maelstrom of people running up and down the stairs of the three floors, doors opening and slamming shut, radios, phonographs, the occasional piano and trumpet, little kids and big kids and adult kids, smells of food and beer and cigarette smoke and aftershave and perfume. "Saturday Night Is the Loneliest Night of the Week" young Frankie Sinatra was always singing. But you sure couldn't prove it by this apartment house.

"She may not be home," Culhane said on the way up the stairs. "She runs her errands on Saturday."

He took out his key and started to insert. But the door was open an inch. And somehow he knew something was wrong. It was an unreasonable response — the apartment door being open during daylight hours was nothing new — but the open door made some kind of kinetic mental connection.

He said, "Wait here."

She grabbed his arm. "What's wrong, Jim?"

"Just wait here."

Given the nature of his parents' marriage — they'd both been drunks — Culhane had been both Mary's brother and ersatz father. Maybe that was why he knew instinctively that something was wrong.

He pushed the door inward and followed it.

Everything that was so familiar now looked alien. A stranger's apartment. Seeing it for the first time.

"Mary!" he called.

Maybe she was out running errands. Maybe she was downstairs visiting one of the neighbors. Maybe she was at the bagel shop wooing Mike Sheridan, her latest crush.

But he knew better.

And when he walked in the bedroom, he knew why he knew better.

He wasn't aware of the animal noise he made. But Sheila was as she hurried to his side. A noise that was a mixture of unutterable loss and unutterable rage.

"Oh, my God," she said, looking at young Mary tossed so carelessly across her bed. Somebody had smashed in half her head.

6

Two cops — one Irish, one Czech — questioned Culhane for an hour downstairs in the landlady's apartment. They were both too big, too loud, their cheap suits covered with traces of cigarette ash. The Slav had a little catsup on his Hawaiian necktie. The first team this was not. They obviously didn't remember Culhane from his cop days. And this was just as well. He would never have associated with this kind of cop.

Kremecek said, "Your sister have a lot of boyfriends, did she?"

"What the hell's that supposed to mean?"

"Was she a good-time girl?"

"Just because I've only got one arm doesn't mean I can't punch your face in."

"Hey, I'm a cop. You can't talk to me that way. You vets think you're so damned tough. Try walkin' into a colored bar on Saturday night sometime."

Flannery said, "All he means, Mr. Culhane, was did she have any friends of the male persuasion who got jealous from time to time?"

Friends of the male persuasion. These two were unreal. They took turns playing good cop–bad cop. Now it was the Irishman's turn to be the sympathetic one.

"She wasn't a good-time girl, whatever the hell that is, and she didn't have a boyfriend, jealous or otherwise. You know how it is in those war plants. They pull fifteen hour days sometimes. And then they come home and fall into bed. Alone, Detective Kremecek. Alone. At least that's what Mary did."

There hadn't been time for sufficient tears or rage. It was funny. He was carrying on coldly, as if Mary's murder hadn't affected him at all. But Sheila knew. She'd held him in her arms while they waited for the cops. She'd felt his entire body tremble. She'd heard the loving words he'd whispered to poor Mary; and the savage words he'd addressed to her unknown killer.

"What about the people in the apartment?" Flannery said.

"What about them?"

"Any romance there?"

"She has — had — a crush on a guy named Sheridan."

"They ever go out?"

"Not that I know of."

"You know anything about this Sheridan?"

Culhane shrugged. "Seems like a nice guy. Same with O'Banion. He's Army. Lives on the same floor. Then there's Wayman —"

"What's his story?"

"Couldn't tell you. Stays to himself. Isn't very friendly. Our cat, Crystal, got in his apartment once and he didn't like it. He threw Crystal pretty hard against the hallway wall."

Flannery said, "Maybe we've got our man."

"He seems to be a jerk," Culhane said. "But that doesn't mean he killed my sister."

"You don't seem very interested in finding her killer," Kremecek said, as if he'd just had a vision. "How'd *you* get along with her?"

"I didn't kill her, Kremecek. I loved her and she loved me."

"Now I remember you," Flannery said.

"Youngest man ever made detective. You were two years ahead of me in the academy."

"He was a detective?" Kremecek said. "Why the hell didn't you say so, bub? I wouldn'ta hard-assed you the way I did."

"Gee, thanks."

Kremecek glowered at the sarcasm.

"You know the drill, then, Culhane," Flannery said. "You'll have to find someplace else to stay tonight."

Culhane nodded.

"In the meantime, you think of anything, be sure and call us."

"I will."

"I shouldn't've made that crack about vets," Kremecek said.

He looked sort of hangdog as he spoke. Hard to hate a man whose face so clearly reflected his feelings.

"No problem," Culhane said.

And put out his hand.

A lot of the men who stayed behind, most for valid reasons, felt guilty about not serving. So they got defensive and started seeing vets as the enemy. Ten times a day Kremececk was likely asked why he wasn't serving in the Pacific or Europe. And ten times a day, Kremecek's masculine ego would suffer as a result.

He also shook hands with Flannery.

"I'll leave word with you when I find out where I'm staying," Culhane said.

"Appreciate that."

He was just leaving the landlady's apartment when he saw Sheridan and O'Banion on the front porch.

He went outside.

They'd already offered him their condolences — twice, in fact — and now were talking about Mary and all the cute and kind things she'd done for both of them.

"She was some gal," O'Banion said.

"She sure was," Sheridan agreed.

But Culhane had just one thing on his mind. "Either of you see Wayman lately?"

"Not since last night," O'Banion said. "I got home early. I heard 'Amos 'n' Andy' on his radio when I walked past his door."

"Either of you know much about him?"

They both shook their heads.

"That's what the cops wanted to know," Sheridan said. He smiled. "I said all we knew was that little Crystal annoyed the hell out of him."

Crystal. Culhane hadn't thought of her since finding Mary dead.

"I'm going to check on Crystal right now," Culhane said.

"You don't have to," O'Banion said. "I

saw her cowering in the corner when all the official folks came in. I stashed her in my apartment. Then I went and got her food bowl and her water."

"Thanks, I appreciate it."

"Say, speaking of Crystal, that reminds me," Sheridan said.

"What?" Culhane said.

"When I was talking to Mary this morning she said she was afraid Crystal had dragged her wristwatch over to Wayman's."

Culhane couldn't help smiling. "That damned cat. She'd haul off furniture if she had half a chance." But he meant it affectionately. He was as goofy about the little black-and-white thing as Mary had been.

"I was wondering —" Sheridan started to say. Then stopped himself.

"Wondering what?" Culhane said.

"Oh, maybe I'd better not say it."

"No, go ahead."

"I was just wondering if maybe Wayman found the watch and got mad and stormed over to your apartment and —"

"As soon as you mentioned Crystal and the watch," O'Banion said, "that's what I was wondering, too."

Culhane would've responded, but that was when he glanced down the block to the corner and saw David Wayman standing there.

Wayman was watching them. Even from here you could see that he was anxious, his body all sharp, tense angles. As soon as he realized that Culhane had seen him, he turned around and began walking fast in the opposite direction.

Culhane was down the steps and on the sidewalk before his startled neighbors had any idea where he was headed.

You ran differently when you had only one arm. Culhane's body balanced itself in a way he wasn't quite used to yet.

The hot summer streets were crowded. The block ahead was one of small shops. Wayman didn't have a hard time vanishing.

Culhane kept running, running into people, bumping off them, attracting stares and curses.

But he didn't have to go far, didn't have to go long, before he realized that he was never going to find Wayman.

Not at this particular moment.

But soon, he promised himself. Very soon.

7

They had listened to the radio until well past midnight. Both of them drank more than they should have. Every once in a while, Sheila saw Culhane's eyes glisten as they talked about Mary. She went into the kitchen at one point to make them melted cheese sandwiches. The phone rang. He took it in the living room. The call didn't last long.

"Listen, Culhane. It's Wayman. We need to meet."

Culhane froze. It almost seemed like a joke. Why would Wayman call him? Then he explained. Quickly. Raggedly. Then: "I got to go. Something's up." And then he said something that sounded like "the hun."

The hun? Who was the hun?

But by then, Wayman had hung up.

When she came back and asked him about it, he said it was Flannery. She had the sense he was lying to her. She wondered why.

The radio news detailed the manhunt for Wayman. Police had searched his apartment and found a box filled with pro-Nazi materials, illegal since the start of the war. At first, Culhane hadn't told the police about the man he'd struggled with at the USO. But now that seemed relevant. He phoned Flannery around ten that night and gave him all the details.

Sheila put him to bed, giving him two aspirin to stave off the worst of the hangover he'd likely have. Then she slipped in next to him. He was already asleep. Snoring lightly. She drifted off, too. Her apartment was on the fifth floor. Quiet.

She'd never slept well, so she woke when he did. The luminous face of the clock read 3:18.

He tried to sneak out tippy-toe but she raised up and said, "You're going somewhere."

"Bathroom."

"You always take your shoes to the bathroom?"

He laughed. "Very observant."

253

"You going to tell me about it? It's about that phone call, isn't it?"

"You really *are* observant."

She lighted them both cigarettes. He came back to the bed, sat on the edge, took the cigarette. She looked elegant in her white silk sleeping gown. The moonlight made it ghostly pale.

"You're a bad liar. I could tell you were hiding something from me."

"You won't believe who called."

"Who?"

"David Wayman."

"My God. Does he want to turn himself in?"

"No. He wants me to know the truth. Or what he claims is the truth, anyway."

"And that would be what?"

Culhane inhaled deeply, enjoying the taste and bite of the Phillip Morris she'd given him. "He claims he isn't a Nazi. Said he had a young sister who got sucked into that whole movement. And then she wanted out. But they killed her. He said he pretended to be a Nazi sympathizer so he could find who'd killed her."

"That's what he wanted to tell you?"

"That and something else."

"Like who killed your sister?"

"Maybe. He got spooked by something.

254

Said he'd meet me in this little greasy spoon not to far from where we live. Four-thirty a.m., he said."

"Shouldn't you tell Flannery?"

"Too much red tape. They'd be all over Wayman. And I'd never find out what he wants to tell me. They might even kill him before he got a chance to talk to anybody."

She exhaled, the stream of smoke as icy white as her gown in the moonlight. "What if you figure out that he killed your sister?"

"Yeah, I've thought about that."

"Why don't you leave your gun behind?"

"This time of night, I'll need it."

"I'm just scared you'll —"

His kiss hushed her. They held each other for a time and then he eased away from her.

"Now I have to go into the bathroom and put my shoes on."

She jabbed him playfully in the side. "Wise guy."

8

As Culhane made his way to his old neighborhood in the back of a taxi, Crystal slept on the window ledge of Culhane's apartment. Now that the police were gone, she'd taken the opportunity to return to her former abode. She liked the way the wind soothed her in the hot night. Her fur wasn't made for summer heat.

She was sleeping well, even though the window itself was closed. The cops had done it. She wanted to get inside to her hiding place and check out the stash of goodies she'd put there lately. Nobody knew where the stash was, either. Crystal was a clever feline.

But somewhere in the city, there was a person looking for one of the pieces in Crystal's personal hidey-place of goodies.

Looking desperately.

9

The owner of the greasy spoon might not have been all that deft as restauranteur, cook, or toilet cleaner, but at least he had a sense of humor. He called his place "The Greasy Spoon."

The place was empty.

A skinny guy with lesions on his arms, neck, and face shuffled up to where Culhane sat at the counter.

"You want somethin'?"

"Love and understanding," Culhane said. "Same thing everybody else wants."

"All we got is coffee, and that ain't too good."

"It'll have to do."

"Those're pretty good duds you're wearing. You must be a cop, huh?"

Culhane patted his empty arm. "How

many one-armed cops you seen before?"

"Guess that's a good point."

The linoleum-covered counter was sticky with the residue of a million swipes of a filthy wash cloth. Flies dive-bombed the lone piece of pie sitting out half a counter down. The counter guy kept hacking up phlegm. Culhane was glad he wasn't eating anything.

He sipped his coffee and smoked two cigarettes. The spidery counterman played a dirge by Duke Ellington. The music filled the long, narrow, shadowy café. It wasn't what Culhane needed to hear, even though the Duke was his favorite jazz artist. Made him think too much about Mary. And what a loss her death was.

A minute after the song ended, the gunshot sounded. Gunshots, actually. Plural.

Culhane jerked up from his seat. "You hear that?"

"Yeah. I hear it every night. It usually just comes earlier is all."

Culhane threw some change on the counter and ran out.

"Ain't nothin' special," the counterman said. "Just somebody dead is all."

Streaks of gray in the nighttime sky. And nothing, absolutely nothing, moving, not even the merest breeze. Low-power street lights casting deep shadows, hiding the daytime ugliness of the deadbeat little shops. Cars like hunched, waiting animals at the curb. A myriad of posters and signs tacked up to every surface available. All admonishing people to do their part for the war. And over everything, the stench of poverty — garbage, filth, the inexplicable but definitely real stink of despair — and then, his first sight of the man lying facedown in the street.

The blond man.

The husky blond man.

David Wayman.

"So he called you?"

"That's right."

"How'd he know where you were?"

"He probably took a chance. He's seen Sheila at my place plenty of times."

"So he called you and told you to meet him here."

"Yes."

"But he didn't say why."

"He told me about his sister."

"But not about your sister?"

"He didn't have time. I think he was going to but something spooked him. He just mumbled the word *hun* or something like that."

"*Hun* as in *kraut?*"

"I suppose so. At least that's what it sounded like."

"Any idea what spooked him?"

"I just assumed it was a person. Somebody seeing him in the phone booth."

"So he said he wasn't really a Nazi, huh?"

"That's what he said."

"He ever show you any of the Nazi propaganda he had in his apartment?"

"No."

"Well, if he wasn't a Nazi, he sure knew how to fake it pretty good."

The greasy spoon's breakfast business was just starting. Cops, ambulance, onlookers had all come and gone. The press was still here. They were waiting their turn with Culhane. Right now, Flannery had him in the back booth, shooting questions.

"Tonight's your big night."

"Yeah, I know. Some big night with Mary dead." Culhane made a face.

"I better let you go. You'll need some sleep. You've got the mayor and Ronald Reagan tonight."

"I'd better call a cab."

"No need to. Your girl got hold of me. She's parked outside. I'll have more questions for you but they can wait. The big thing is we got the man who killed your sister."

"I don't think you did."

"Then you believe what Wayman said?"

"Yeah," Culhane said. "I do."

10

He got three hours' sleep. Sheila had breakfast waiting for him. He drank four cups of coffee and smoked five cigarettes.

The shower he took was ice cold. He had a full day ahead of him. Ronald Reagan and the mayor would be visiting several USO sites, but his site was where the press would gather. The USO wanted to spotlight its neighborhood facilities, not just its more glamorous Loop site.

Sheila went to work with him. The kids were already there hanging crepe paper, dusting, polishing, and straightening. Food was being prepared. Microphones were checked on the bandstand. They wanted to hear Reagan good and loud. They'd all seen his movies. Great actor, no. But a handsome and affable screen performer who just about everybody liked. The jukebox was packed with a lot of big band "jump" tunes so the atmosphere was almost festive.

The Army security force got there mid-afternoon, five grim-faced men who had probably escorted one too many celebrities, seen one too many USOs. All in Army khaki. All toting big holstered guns and helmets that read MP.

They spent two hours checking out everything. Attic, main floor, basement. One of them even went up on the roof. Two or three USOs had been burned down in the east. Nazis were the suspected culprits. These men were going to make sure it didn't happen here.

The sergeant in charge came over and talked to Culhane. "Anything suspicious happen here lately?"

Culhane told him about the intruder.

"Strange. Have to be damned hard-up to break into a USO."

"Yeah. And then my sister was murdered."

The beefy sergeant's green eyes narrowed. "Tell me about it."

Sergeant Hertz his name was. He fired questions at Culhane even faster than Flannery had. He focused on the people at the apartment house.

"You know anything about this O'Banion or this Sheridan?"

"Not really."

"O'Banion's Army."

"Yeah? Where's he work?"

Culhane told him.

"How about Sheridan?"

"He works in a pet store."

"Tell me about Wayman."

When Culhane finished, Hertz said, "They travel in pairs a lot. Saboteurs."

"Like nuns, huh?" Culhane smiled.

Hertz didn't smile. "I'm going to check these two. See if we've got anything on them. Meanwhile, my men will be here from now till the place closes tonight."

"I appreciate your help."

"You'll like him."

"Reagan?"

"Yeah. Some of these celebrities, well, they're kind've jerks. He's just a regular guy. No big demands, nothing like that. Plus he gets out and dances with all the gals. They sure like that." For the first time, he smiled. He had a nice one. "Rest of their life, they'll be able to say they danced with a movie star."

By four o'clock, the place was crowded. WACs and WAVEs were out in force, mingling with their male counterparts. A few of the more adventurous were even dancing already.

Sheila came over and slid her arm around Culhane's waist. "I have fun just watching *them* have fun."

He squeezed her with his one arm. "Yeah, me, too."

"You don't *look* like you're having fun. If I may be so bold."

He sighed. "I just keep thinking about what that Sergeant Hertz said. About saboteurs working in pairs."

"You think there's somebody at the apartment house who —"

"He asked me about Sheridan and O'Banion and I realized I don't know anything about them."

"Gosh, it's hard to imagine either one of them —"

One of the USO girls came up. Sweater, short pleated skirt, bobby sox, saddle-shoes. Button-cute. "There's a phone call for you, Jim."

Flannery was on the phone. "Just wanted to tell you we're through with your apartment. Wrapped everything up about twenty minutes ago. One of our guys found your cat's hidey-hole."

"Yeah? Where?"

"That high shelf in Mary's closet. Way

down at the far end there's a hole, like a mouse hole. The shelf is so wide you can't see the hole unless you're practically standing on top of it. Your sister kept her clothes hamper right inside the closet. The cat used it to jump up on the shelf."

"Find anything interesting?"

"Not interesting to us. Just some receipts and a cufflink. And a pocket comb."

"The cufflink belonged to Wayman. It's one of the things Crystal took from him."

"Well, anyway, you're free to go in there if you want."

"Yeah. I need some shirts and things. I appreciate the call."

"The captain's satisfied that Wayman was the killer."

"Good for the captain," Culhane said. He decided not to tell him about his conversation with Sergeant Hertz.

After they hung up, Culhane walked back to Sheila and asked if he could use her car to go pick up some things at his apartment.

"Of course. But I'd be happy to go with you."

He shrugged. "Maybe it'd be better if I went alone."

She touched his arm. "Sure, Jim."

The USO was filling up quickly. "I'll see you in a while."

Early evening shadows softened the harshness of the old neighborhood. The melancholy sound of kids playing in the dusk took Jim back to his own boyhood. The kid sister was always there with him. She could bat well, run fast, even do pretty well when the football game got a little rough. Then she could turn around and put on some girl stuff and put half the boys into a kind of trance. They sure did make stumbling, giggling, grinning, blushing, stammering fools of themselves when little Mary Culhane prettied herself up.

Hun.

The same word over and over.

Hun.

What had Wayman been trying to tell him, anyway?

He parked curbside.

Young Jill was there. "Did you hear *Captain Midnight* tonight?"

"Afraid I didn't."

"He really gave it to those Nazis."

"Good for him. We need all the help we can get."

"I told you there were Nazi spies in the USO."

"And you know what I forgot to do?"

"What?" She squinted up at him in the dying daylight.

He reached deep into his pocket. "Give you a nice new quarter for warning me about them." He handed her the quarter. "Thanks for the tip."

"Wow. Thanks yourself."

"Be sure and spend it wisely."

"Oh, I will."

"On something sensible."

"Yeah, I will."

He grinned. "Don't spend more than twenty-four cents of it at Mr. Fleischmann's candy store."

"Now I can get the new *Captain Midnight* comic." Then, "Your landlady had a sister visiting her this afternoon."

"That's nice. Maybe that'll put her in a better mood."

"She is kinda cranky."

"You just noticed that, huh?"

He hadn't been expecting a *physical* reaction to coming into the apartment house again. His stomach muscles tensed, sweat sheened his face, and there was a faint twitching in his hand. Anger-melancholy-dread . . . he wasn't sure which feeling dominated him, they seemed to shift so effortlessly among themselves.

He looked up the stairs. They were Daliesque, endless stairs leading to a field of infinite darkness. Then he realized that for the very first time ever, the apartment house was virtually silent. No chatter. No radio. No banging about in kitchen or living room. Faint thrum and thrust of electrical currents; faint creak and cry of the ancient house settling. Scent of dust and spectral perfume; rose-colored dusk dying in the small high window on the wall to his right.

He went up the stairs one slow step at a time. So many times he'd climbed these stairs; so many times Mary had stood at the top of them, all kid-sister grin and kid-sister smart-mouth remark, that damned tousled hair of hers all over that sweet face.

No more. Never again.

That was what you had to get used to with this dying business. That it was final. Final. It took the human being many weeks and months to accept this. And maybe a part of you never really *did* accept it, that notion of finality, of extinction.

Tears glistened in his eyes, caught in his throat.

An even deeper darkness as he reached the second floor. The dust forced him to sneeze. Damned allergies. The sound was so loud in the silence it was almost profane.

All four apartment doors were dark. He made his way to his own. Took out his key. Put it in the lock. Pushed open the door. Reached around and clipped on the light.

Familiar and alien at the same time — the same feeling he'd had the other day. A murder alters a place forever. At least to someone who has lived there. He thought of a hundred goofy moments with Mary. She'd loved Betty Hutton and was always imitating her. His tastes were a little coarser. He liked Judy Canova, who, unlike the more elegant if frenzied Hutton, was pure B-movie corn. She made the Ritz Brothers look like Noel Coward.

He needed a drink and had one.

He went through every room but Mary's. He'd need a second drink before he could spend any time in there.

He was standing in the middle of the kitchen when he heard a familiar sound and turned to see Crystal padding into the room.

She jumped up on the kitchen table and held herself in eager tail-rigid anticipation of a scratch.

He did more the scratch her. He set his drink down and picked her up. In some way it was like holding Mary again, she and Crystal had been so inseparable.

After he'd held her a few minutes, he saw the small pile of things Flannery's cops had found in Crystal's lair.

He smiled. Mary would've laughed so hard about finding Crystal's hiding place.

Crystal meowed. Hungry, no doubt.

He found cat food in the refrigerator, fed her.

And as she was lustily eating, he looked idly through the contents of her secret cache.

Flannery had pretty much told him what he'd find so there were no surprises. Not at first, anyway.

But then he looked more closely at two small pieces of paper.

One was a receipt from a theatrical costume rental place. It simply said "Nun's outfit. $3.50."

The other was a pencil-drawn layout of a building interior.

It took a minute or so before he recognized the building the drawing described — his USO.

Then two other thoughts — Wayman had muttered *hun*. Or had he? Could he have muttered *nun* instead? But what was the significance of *nun?*

And who would draw the interior of the

USO. Then he remembered his run-in with the intruder.

A nun. An intruder. A floor plan for the USO.

And Jill had mentioned that Mrs. Dennis had a "sister" visiting her this afternoon. . . .

He turned the floor plan over. And saw, in faint cash register letters, CRITTERS Pet Shop.

Where Mike Sheridan worked.

Had it been Mike who'd leaped out at him in the USO that morning?

One way to find out about Sheridan was to pay a visit to his apartment. And he'd take the route Crystal would. The fire escape.

11

Sheila's feet were tired already. She'd danced around the floor seven times already — three sailors, four soldiers. A ballerina she wasn't. She was graceful enough when she walked, but when she danced . . .

While she was festive enough with her dancing partners, her mind ran film of Jim every thirty seconds or so. She had this sense of trouble. She wasn't sure why. What sort of trouble could he get into going back to his apartment?

The press was starting to push its way in now. There'd be a lot more in an hour or two, about the time Ronald Reagan was expected.

She finished dancing with a shy young soldier and started over to the canteen area. She was thirsty.

A large man stopped her. The MP helmet he wore marked him as official. His flat, intense face marked him as fierce. "Are you Miss Courtney?"

"Yes."

"I'd like to talk to you about Jim Culhane?"

Panic. A queasy feeling. "What about him? Is he all right?"

"I need to know where I can find him."

"You didn't answer my question. Is he all right?"

The big man sighed. "I hope so. That's what I'm trying to find out. I talked with him earlier —"

"Oh, you're Sergeant Hertz."

"Right."

"He said you had a good conversation."

"I told him I'd check up on some of the other people in his apartment house."

"Yes, he mentioned that."

"Well, I did it. And there's a problem."

"Oh?"

"He told me about this O'Banion. This so-called Army man who works at the base near here."

"What do you mean so-called?"

"The Army has no record of such a soldier. I called the base right away."

"But I've seen him in his uniform."

"Bogus. Has to be. Otherwise they'd have a record of him."

"Oh, Lord. Jim's over at the apartment house now."

"How long ago did he leave?"

"Forty-five minutes ago. Maybe a little longer. Let me call him."

But there was no answer.

"I'm going over there," Sheila said.

"You want somebody to go along?"

"Thanks. But I'll be all right."

She remembered then that Jim had her car. She borrowed one from one of the USO girls.

A mellow Glenn Miller ballad was playing as she left. She wanted to be on the dance floor with Jim.

12

When the light came on, Mike Sheridan stood in the door of his apartment and said, "You want to go through a long dialogue here, friend, or should I just tell you what happened?" He pointed the pistol right at Culhane's chest.

After finding the floor plan drawn on the back of the pet store receipt, Culhane snuck into Sheridan's apartment. He found two larger versions of the floor plan as well as two articles cut from the newspaper about Ronald Reagan coming to Jim's USO with the mayor and the press in tow.

"Somebody's going to dress up like a nun and assassinate Ronald Reagan. And or the mayor."

Sheridan said, "You're going to die for

the same reason your sister did. She made the mistake of going downstairs to ask Mrs. Dennis a question. When she didn't get any answer, she invited herself in to write Mrs. Dennis a note. And then she saw the three of us in Mrs. Dennis's bedroom."

"The three of you?"

Sheridan stood back to let the others into his apartment. O'Banion came first. No Army uniform now. Just a regular suit and tie.

Mrs. Dennis came next. At first he didn't recognize her. She was very convincing in her Mother Superior role.

A nun could move easily in the USO crowd. She could plant herself for a good shot then get out of her clothes quickly and vanish.

They travel in pairs, Sergeant Hertz had said.

Well, these folks improved on that equation. They traveled in a trio.

Hard to know why he hated them more. For killing poor Mary. Or selling out their country. He thought of all the Allied troops dying miserable deaths and then these three —

"You want to do the honors, O'Banion?" Sheridan said.

"My pleasure."

Tying up Culhane didn't take long. O'Banion laid him on the floor underneath the window.

"You'll be happy to know we're going to keep you alive for a little longer," Sheridan said. "In case we need a hostage."

Simone Dennis said, "I'd better get going."

Sheridan glanced at his watch. "Yeah. You both know the plan. Soon as it's done, you two head right back here. And then we head straight to the railroad station."

They were turning and about to leave when O'Banion said, "Oh, seems I forgot something."

"I was wondering," Sheridan said.

O'Banion, dapper, smiling, walked across the apartment floor to the window where Culhane lay.

"This is going to hurt, my friend," O'Banion said. "But at least it won't kill you."

He kicked Culhane hard in the side of the head.

Culhane tumbled into unconsciousness in only moments. The distant sounds of the trio saying their final words before the assassination and then — cold alien blackness.

Dreams and nightmares.

Pig-tailed Mary. Elegant Sheila.

Then the war in the Pacific. The screams. The sound and smell and sight of *ack-ack* gunfire in the night. A young soldier waking up and realizing he was blind — permanently, as it turned out — his shriek as loud as that of a predatory night bird swooping down on blood-throbbing prey.

Dreams and nightmares.

Mary sprawled in death. Mary's laughter on a spring night when she was going to her first high school dance. Mary sprawled in death . . .

Coldness. Darkness.

And then the slow return to semi-consciousness . . . holding in that purgatory that was not quite life and not quite death . . .

A sense of urgency.

The nun. The assassination.

He had to warn his people at the USO —

Sheila hurried from the car before the engine had quite quit throbbing. She'd let her mind play on the worst possible fates for Jim.

Dusty darkness greeted her in the vestibule of the apartment house. She didn't even bother to find the light switch for the stairway. She knew the route well enough.

Halfway up the steps, she heard voices. No, voice. Singular. Familiar but she couldn't place it. Then, Mike Sheridan. That was it.

She paused at the top of the steps. Jim's apartment was dark. At least, no light outlined the door the way it usually did when somebody was inside.

She crept on tiptoes down the hall to Jim's apartment. He seemed to be explaining something to somebody.

She was near the door when, three yards down, she saw the brilliant white coat of Crystal in the gloom.

Crystal came prancing up.

Sheila bent down and stroked her several times. Crystal reminded her of how much she'd loved Mary, loved Jim.

Behind his apartment door, Sheridan was saying: "Another few minutes your man Reagan'll be dead. Nobody'll suspect a nun. Simone came up with that one herself. She's a thinker, that one is."

Sheila tiptoed the last few steps to the door. But on her way, her weight found a board that didn't merely creak, it sang out.

And then the door was flung open and

there, in silhouette, stood Mike Sheridan, his gun aimed right at her chest.

"Now isn't this sweet?" he said. "A family reunion. Get in here. And right now."

What choice did she have?

She edged into the room. Sheridan looked nervous, belying the confident tone of his voice. He had to know that once Ronald Reagan was killed, there'd be no place for him and his friends to hide. The government would hunt them down till they found them. And execution would be swift.

But they weren't stupid people. Nor were their Nazi bosses. They likely had plans already set in motion for escaping this country. Maybe getting all the way to Germany. Or maybe South America. There were many Nazi sympathizers among government officials in the countries down there.

Jim was awake but he looked terrible. Blood was caked in his hair and on his forehead. It had trickled down his cheek in jagged ribbons. His eyes reflected pain and vague confusion. She wondered if he had a concussion. He'd been cinched up with professional skill. No way he was going to slip these bonds the way heroes always did in Saturday matinees.

Sheridan waved her over to stand by Jim.

"He'd tell you how much he loved you," Sheridan said, smiling. "But with a gag in his mouth that's kind've hard to do."

"Are you all right, Jim?" she asked.

He nodded slowly. The pain was even clearer now in his gaze. *Concussion for sure,* she thought.

"So we just wait?" she said.

"We just wait. Soon as I get the phone call giving me the all clear, you two get killed and I get picked up by Simone and O'Banion."

"I'm assuming those aren't their real names," Sheila said.

The smile again. "You're a smart one, you are."

Pressure. She surveyed the living room for anything she could pick up and throw. She had to warn the people at the USO — and she had to help them escape Sheridan.

Sort of tough to do when Sheridan held a gun on them.

The ashtray would be good.

Of all the things close by, the large, four-pointed glass ashtray would be the best weapon. It had weight. And if any of the points hit Sheridan at the right angle, it could do some damage. At the least, it would rattle him for a moment.

But the problem remained. Even though the ashtray was only a few inches away on the arm of the couch, how did she pick it up with Sheridan watching?

Sheridan started glancing at his wristwatch. She even saw an oily slick of sweat on his face.

"Getting nervous?" she said.

"Yeah. Are you?"

Her turn to smile. "How long are you going to wait for the phone call? Maybe it all went wrong and they won't call. Maybe the cops'll just show up to arrest you."

"Next time I hear anybody come in downstairs, you know what I'm gonna do? I'm gonna kill both of you on the spot. No waiting around."

She believed him. He was starting to get a little frantic. The slight twitch on the side of his left eye was an eloquent testament to that.

"Maybe instead of fitting in she'll stand out so much people'll get suspicious, you ever think of that?" Sheila said. "You don't see many nuns at USOs. Maybe that wasn't as good a disguise as you think."

"Why don't you shut up before I rough you up the way I did your friend on the floor?"

She glanced with true longing at the sharp-pointed glass ashtray. She could feel the heft of it in her hand. It would throw so nicely. So true.

She stared longer than she realized at the ashtray. As she started to turn back to Sheridan, the barrel of his gun came down hard against her temple.

She'd never been knocked unconscious before. She'd had swimming accidents, boating accident, horseback riding accidents, bicycle accidents. All the usual kid stuff. But she'd never been rendered unconscious because of them.

But he'd hit her so swiftly, so violently, that for a moment — a suspended moment, an unreal moment when there was nothing but pain — she felt her knees start to tremble and give, and her entire body start to sway, and she saw the screen of her vision fill with an inky sky pinpointed with glowing star-shaped dots. She was losing muscular control, too. No strength to enact the emergency measures her mind was sending to her body.

But she knew that if she passed out, there'd be no hope for any of them. Not the people at the USO. Not for Jim and herself.

She forced her body to find spine and

grit and renewed purpose. Her swaying stopped. Her knees locked in purposeful place. Her vision began to return.

"You're tougher than you look," Sheridan said. "You learn that in your fancy boarding school, did ya?"

A moment of triumph. She felt damned good about staying conscious and on her feet.

But there was the same old problem.

Yes, she could damage him with the ashtray, maybe even wrestle the gun away from him.

But how to get said ashtray to collide with said head?

And then she saw Crystal.

Serene Crystal. Just-walking-around-and-having-myself-a-very-nice-Saturday-night-thank-you-very-much Crystal.

Crystal had invited herself into a reasonably clean, well-lighted place. Indeed, the only well-lighted place in the whole apartment house at this particular time. Mr. Sheridan's apartment.

Crystal had always liked Mr. Sheridan. She didn't put all the same judgments on people that people did. If you petted her from time to time, she was your good and loyal friend. And if you also happened to feed her upon occasion, well, you had a friend for life, even if you lived to be 248 years old.

So when she saw Mr. Sheridan standing there, she did what she always did, she went up to him and nuzzled herself against his leg.

And Sheila, in wondrous and grateful disbelief, saw what happened then.

Now put yourself in Sheridan's place. You've spent weeks helping to devise this great plan for bumping off this actor at the nearby USO. Your Nazi bosses are on your back constantly with questions and concerns. Are you sure you can pull this off? Are you sure you've got everything in place? Are you sure she looks authentic in her nun's costume? Weeks of this crap. And so at the very last moment, (a) this Wayman guy proves to be not another fellow Nazi but a self-styled spy and (b) at the very, very *last* moment Jim Culhane shows up and damned near queers the whole thing — and would've if he'd been able to get to a phone.

And as if that's not enough, Culhane's very elegant lady friend comes out of nowhere, too.

And the phone call has not come.

And all the stuff the lovely Sheila is firing at you trying to undermine your self-confidence . . . well, it's taking its toll.

They *haven't* called to give you the all-clear, have they?

The cops *could* be on their way here to arrest you, couldn't they?

And maybe it *would* be wise, wouldn't it, to start thinking about your *own* escape plan, forget Simone and O'Banion? For all you know, they could be in the back of a patrol car. Or dead.

All this is roiling and boiling in your mind at the precise moment that you get this strange, unidentifiable *message* from the side of your right calf.

Now, at any other time, your mind would decipher all the information you're getting. Soft and furry; gentle purring sound; scent of tuna fish from most recent meal —

But not now.

You're holding a gun on this babe —

And you're wondering what the hell has happened to your co-conspirators in the death of Ronald Reagan —

And you're worried that maybe a cop car is presently wending its way toward you —

And then this damned cat — this cat you really *like* under most circumstances — the damned thing brushes up against you and you're wound so tight that you just go crazy.

Nothing big and bold. But you do give a little jump. And you do emit a little startled cry. And you do momentarily glance down to see Crystal looking up at you hoping for a pet or a scratch or at least a cheese-melt tuna fish sandwich —

And that gives Sheila (whom you've forgotten for the moment) all the time she needs to pick up that ashtray she's been staring at with almost sexual longing and to sail it unerringly at your head.

And so one moment you're standing there with the gun in your hand and the next moment you're somehow on the floor — these things can get so confusing sometimes, just how the hell did you end up on the floor, anyway? — and you watch, your head not only hurting but spinning and isn't that blood trickling down your forehead and dripping past your eye — you watch as she rushes to the phone and starts shouting into it to connect her with USO #19.

And then she's warning them about this nun — and then —

And Crystal is licking your face. Not the blood part. Crystal is too refined for that kind of thing. She licks the other part of your face.

Good old Crystal. Good old Sheridan.

Good old Sheila. And good old Culhane.
Good old Sheridan still can't figure out
how he got on the floor here. He saw this
ashtray flying at him, see, and then —

13

A week later, Culhane and Sheila were dancing to a new Peggy Lee ballad. Dorsey had discovered her one day right here in Chicago. Culhane liked her even more than he did Sinatra.

This was the first night the USO was back to normal. The press had been here every night since the averted assassination. The story was just too rich to be ignored. They must've interviewed everybody who'd passed within miles of the place the night Ronald Reagan came here. The nun and her pal had been arrested before they could even get close to the movie star. The press, of course, played it up as if he'd escaped with his life only moments before the diabolical plan had been put into action.

And Mary had been buried.

Culhane was pretty good until forty-eight hours after the funeral. That night, Sheila held him — lover-friend-son — until he passed from grief into weary sleep.

Now, he said, "Is it too late to change my mind about marriage?"

She laughed. "Is that a proposal?"

"I'm not that far along yet. But I think I will be in the next few months. Can you hang around that long?"

"Oh," she said, that great good face of hers girlish as anything in the gentle shadows where the soldiers and sailors danced with the ladies of the USO, "I expect that could be arranged."

Edelweiss

by Jane Haddam

Looking at her now, you'd never guess that Edelweiss was once an abandoned cat, dumped at the back door of the Naugy Doggy pet shop in Naugatuck, Connecticut, with the rest of a litter of kittens that nobody seemed to want. These days, she's fat, furry, and arrogant, and her dietary requirements resemble the main menu at the Golden Door spa. Unfortunately, she doesn't much like having her picture taken — she seems to think the camera flash is an unspeakable indignity — and she's iffy on small boys, especially the one in our house. Taking this picture required a whole role of film, the help of a few friends, and banishing my younger son to his room. When the photo session was over, she installed herself under my coffee table and refused to come out until the turkey in the oven was done. Maybe she should have her name changed to Greta Garbo.

— Jane Haddam

That morning, the air was hot and muggy and thick, the way it can be only in central Florida in the winter, and Miss Caroline Edgerton was taking her cat to work. Shelley Altman saw them coming out of Miss Edgerton's front door at seven forty-five in the morning, the earliest Shelley had ever seen Miss Edgerton head to work. By now, Shelley knew everything there was to know about "Miss Caroline," as the paperboy called her, right down to the size of her underwear and the pattern she preferred at Victoria's Secret. It was funny to think of Miss Edgerton shopping at Victoria's Secret. She was sixty if she was a day, and she was probably a virgin on top of it. Shelley hadn't found any birth control any of the last three times she'd searched the house. She'd been particularly looking for it, too, because Amanda absolutely insisted that that was one thing they needed to know. Was Miss Edgerton a virgin? Was she a lesbian? Was she anything at all besides a dried up old prune of a hag who had dedicated her life to making things miserable for girls who were younger than she was and prettier than she had ever been? It mattered, Amanda said, because the answers might change their minds about what they had decided to do. It was one thing to murder a woman who was nothing more than a waste of light and air. It was something else to murder a tragic victim of life's circumstances. Maybe Miss Edgerton had once had a lover who had died in a war — Vietnam or World War II, whichever. Maybe Miss Edgerton had always wished and hoped for a lover but had been too poor or too ugly to get one. Maybe Miss Edgerton was pining right now for some young man at her office, who would never look at her because she was far too old. Whatever it was, they had to find out, just in case it made her less than the best of candidates. It wasn't as if they were shy of people who deserved to be dead. Matahatchee was full of them. Amanda could name six right off the top of her head, and that was without going any farther afield than Main Street.

Out in the driveway next door, Miss Caroline Edgerton had put her cat very carefully into the cat carrier that she kept in the backseat for whenever she needed it. Her cat was named Edelweiss, because it was as purely white as some silly flower that grew in Switzerland, and it didn't like going into the carrier for any reason whatsoever. Shelley was always a little surprised that Miss Edgerton didn't take her cat to work *every* day. She surely lived with it like it was surgically attached when she was home. Sometimes, when Shelley looked into the windows at night, Miss Edgerton would be sitting in the big club chair in the living room with Edelweiss draped around her neck like a feather boa, the both of them watching something mind-numbingly boring on PBS. Shelley didn't care if Miss Edgerton was somebody who had had a tragic life. She hated Miss Edgerton with everything inside herself, much the way she also hated Mrs. Keller who taught English at school and Mrs. Partree who ran that youth group at the Methodist church. Shelley's parents went to the Methodist church. They made Shelley go with them. Twice a year they made Shelley go on a Bible retreat with the youth group, too. By now, Shelley had read through the really *good* parts of the Bible almost as often as she had watched *Natural Born Killers* — but only because she wasn't allowed to watch *Natural Born Killers* in the house.

Miss Edgerton had Edelweiss safely in

the cat carrier and the cat carrier safely on the floor of the backseat of the car. That was the safest place for Edelweiss to be if there was ever a car accident. Miss Edgerton came around front and got in behind the wheel. Her car was a trim little Volvo sedan, in navy blue, which matched her business suit today. Miss Edgerton always looked businesslike, even though she didn't work at anything any more important than being a secretary.

Shelley moved away from her bedroom window and sat down on her bed. Her school clothes were hung on her closet door. Her makeup was laid out on the vanity table in front of the beveled mirror that was supposed to be good for making sure you covered up your flaws and imperfections. Her fingernails were bright green. It seemed impossible to her that she should have to get up and go out and spend the day at Matahatchee High School, where she was only a sophomore and not considered very important by the other girls in her class. Amanda was important. Amanda was so important, she was already a varsity cheerleader, and secretary of the student council, and a member of the Key Club. Once a month at least, Amanda had her picture in the

Matahatchee Echo, which was the school newspaper. Amanda was a peer tutor. Amanda was an anger management peer counselor. Amanda sang in the choir at church. Sometimes, when Shelley thought about killing somebody, Amanda seemed to be the very best one to kill. Then Shelley would think about Miss Edgerton and change her mind. It was just that the waiting was making her crazy. It got to the point sometimes when she couldn't seem to make herself think. Now she got up and got her bright blue halter top off its hanger and started to put it on. She didn't know if she was glad to live in a place where it almost never got cold. She hated halter tops. They made her feel as if someone were about to scrape away her skin.

School made Shelley feel as if she were already dead. It took her forever to get dressed to go there, and then it took her forever to walk the six long blocks that got her to its front door. To pass the time, she went looking for Miss Caroline Edgerton on Main Street, through the front window in the offices of Carmeth, Brane and De-Voe, where she worked. Sometimes Miss Edgerton sat at the front desk there and answered the phone for hours. When she had the cat with her, the cat sat on the desk near the phone and looked up every time it rang. Sometimes the cat draped itself over the phone, as if it were a chicken and the phone was its egg. When it was like that and the phone rang, Miss Edgerton would lift the cat gently so that she could pick up the phone. She was never angry or impatient with the cat. She was better to Edelweiss than most parents were to their children. She was certainly better to Edelweiss than Shelley's parents were to Shelley. This morning, though, neither Miss Edgerton nor the cat was anywhere to be seen. The woman behind the front desk was young and weighted down under a cascade of falls and hairpieces. Shelley went around the back to make sure Miss Edgerton's car was in the parking lot — it was, right next to the bright red Porsche that belonged to Mr. DeVoe — and then she went to school, thinking about palm trees as she went. Amanda came from New York state someplace. She'd never seen a palm tree in person until her parents had moved here when she was still in junior high. Palm trees were the first thing she and Shelley had talked about, in Shelley's backyard, on the day they met.

"They don't look like real trees at all," Amanda had said, and then she'd seen Miss Caroline Edgerton come out her back door to potter around in her yard.

Shelley went to her locker and stowed away most of her books in it. She brought books home every night, because if she didn't, her parents screamed at her, her mother especially. They gave her lectures about how she would never amount to anything, and how she'd end up like those homeless people who slept every night on Segovia Avenue. She brought the books home, and she laid them out across the desk in her bedroom, but that was all she did with them. If she had homework and knew about it, she ignored it. Mostly she didn't have homework, because if you weren't in the college track, the teachers didn't see any point in giving any. She did go to class. Not going was the surest way to get the principal to call your parents, and Shelley lived to make sure she wasn't bothered by her parents.

She got her English book — *Explorations in Literature*, a complete bore — and headed down the hall to her homeroom. She would have skipped homeroom if she could have. It was nothing but sitting in a sea of people who didn't want to talk to her and listening to announcements about things she wouldn't touch with a ten-foot pole. Chess Club. Glee Club. Future Teachers of America. Homeroom, though, was the one thing she could not skip, not ever. If you skipped that, you were counted absent for the entire day.

She was just adjusting the strap on her shoulder bag for the fiftieth time when she saw Amanda in the hall, and for the first few moments she didn't pay attention. Amanda didn't much like talking to her in school. Usually, they passed each other in the halls without even saying hello, and saved their conversations for after school, in their own bedrooms. Their houses were only across the street from each other. Shelley started to go on by and take her seat in Room 122, but Amanda snaked out her hand and grabbed her elbow.

"Go to the girls' room," Amanda said. "I'll meet you there."

Shelley hesitated. It really *wasn't* all right to miss homeroom, although having to go to the bathroom was usually a good enough excuse for being tardy. She looked through the window in the door at Miss Carroll, who was wearing a sleeveless dress and a Crucifix. She wore the Crucifix be-cause somebody's father objected to the school board that they had a "Satanist" teaching in Matahatchee, by which it turned out he meant Catholic. Shelley prodded at her hair. The school's air-conditioning was only half working. Her hair was full of sweat.

"Go ahead," Amanda said. "This is important."

Miss Carroll looked up and saw Shelley standing outside the door. Shelley made hand motions meant to explain that she was heading to the bathroom. Miss Carroll nodded. In Shelley's imaginary universe — the one where she and Amanda were masterminds, committing murder after murder, whenever they felt it was necessary — Miss Carroll was the second to go.

In the girls' room, Amanda was standing near the sinks, putting on lipstick. She put on makeup four or five times a day. Her hair never looked full of sweat. Today she was wearing the short little kick pleat skirt that was practically the uniform of the Key Club. If anybody wore one just like it who didn't belong, the Key Club girls ganged up on her on the athletic field and made sure it would never happen again.

Shelley put down her books on a corner of the sink. She didn't want to put on makeup. She didn't want to look in the mirror at all. Mirrors made it impossible to forget that she had acne running all across the ridge of her jaw.

"What is it?" she asked, folding her arms across her chest. "I thought I wasn't supposed to talk to you here. I thought it would compromise the operation."

"You aren't supposed to talk to me in public," Amanda said. "It *would* compromise the operation. If everybody knew we were friends, they'd guess right away."

"They'd guess about Miss Edgerton? Why? Why would our being friends mean we'd done something to —"

"Shh," Amanda said. She abandoned the lipstick for some kind of powder. When Shelley put on makeup, it seemed to clot up on her skin. In a few hours, she looked as if she were walking around with pieces of plaster clinging to her face. Amanda's makeup didn't even look like makeup. When Amanda's makeup had been on Amanda for a few hours, it just seemed to disappear.

"I don't think it has anything to do with Miss Edgerton," Shelley said. "I think that's just a big cover so that you don't have to talk to me in front of your popular friends. I mean, for God's sake. What is that? Amanda the supercheerleader."

Amanda had gone from powder to something for her eyebrows. "You could be popular, too, if you put in a little effort. I don't know what's wrong with you that you want to be by yourself all the time."

"I don't want to be by myself all the time. I want to be with you."

"Well, that wouldn't make much sense, under the circumstances. Especially today. Did you see her? She's here."

"Who's here?"

"Miss Edgerton," Amanda said. "Mr. DeVoe is here doing something or the other, and she's come with him. She brought her cat, too. It's in with Miss Lazio in the secretaries' place, you know, the big room in front of the principal's office. Anyway, she's here, and I hung around the office for a little and from what I heard, she's going to be here until noon."

"Why?"

"I don't know. Some legal thing having to do with the school, I'd guess. Mr. DeVoe is a lawyer. She's a lawyer's secretary. What does it matter?"

"That's what I want to know," Shelley said. "What does it matter? Why should we care where she is or what she does?"

Amanda stopped putting on makeup.

"You must be joking. You know why we care."

"I meant why should we care where she is or what she does today?" Shelley said. "I'm not a complete idiot, Amanda. I know why we care in the long run. But what does it matter if she's here today?"

"Well," Amanda said. "I was thinking. It might be the perfect chance."

"The perfect chance for what?"

"For us to do what we want to do. Think about it. You live next door to her, right? She knows who you are?"

"Of course she does," Shelley said. "She knows who you are, too. You live right across the street."

"But she doesn't know me that well. We only moved here a couple of years ago. She's known you forever."

"So?"

"So, you could ask her for a ride. You could go out to the parking lot, and run into her, and ask her for a ride somewhere."

"Where?"

"I don't know." Amanda sounded impatient. "Make something up. Make somewhere up. How about out to Grandview Park?"

"It's a swamp," Shelley said.

"So?" Amanda said.

"Why would I want to go there? Why would she go out of her way to drive me out there? You aren't making any sense."

Amanda's makeup things were spread all across the stainless steel shelf under the face mirror above the sinks. She opened her bag under the shelf and swept all the jars and tubes and bottles out of sight. She looked angry, the way only Amanda could look angry — as if she had every right to expect you to do what she wanted you to do, and you were being evil to refuse her.

"Listen," Amanda said. "This was your idea as much as mine. You wanted this as much as I ever did. If you're not interested anymore, just tell me."

"Of course I'm interested," Shelley said.

"Well, then. I'm going to be out at Grandview Park at twelve thirty this afternoon. You ask Miss Edgerton for a ride and get her out there and meet me. I don't care what you tell her. Just be there. Or we can call the whole thing off."

"You couldn't do it without me," Shelley said. "If you tried, I'd know it was you. I could go to the police and say it was you."

"Meet me out there," Amanda said again. Then she tossed her hair against her back, picked up her shoulder bag, and flounced out of the girls' room. If the door hadn't been on an air hinge, she would have made it slam.

Once she was gone, Shelley took a look at herself in the mirror. There really was a line of acne along her jaw. Her cheeks really were as puffy and round as a chipmunk's. Everything the other girls said about her was true, except that she wasn't actually stupid. If Amanda couldn't do it on her own, she couldn't, either, and she wanted to do it very much. She very certainly didn't want to give it up.

Still, for a while there that morning, Shelley did think she'd give it up. At least, she'd give it up for now, and lay low for a year or two, until she was old enough to get out of Matahatchee, and go someplace where nobody had ever heard of her or of Amanda Marsh. It was depressing to walk through school all day watching Amanda in the middle of crowds of people, all of them looking like they'd just stepped off the cover of *Seventeen* magazine. It was even more depressing to hear Amanda's name called out in homeroom for the honor roll the third time already this year. It seemed to Shelley that there should be some kind of balance. Pretty girls should be stupid girls. Not so pretty girls should be smart girls. That was the way it was in the movies, except that in the movies even the not-so-pretty girls were prettier than Shelley was, and they always blossomed into beautiful girls as soon as anybody paid any attention to them.

Shelley was not blossoming into beautiful, and by third period, she was already in trouble with three different teachers. She had forgotten her business math homework for the third time this week. She got caught talking in English class when the teacher was trying to read a poem. She got caught walking in the hall chewing gum, which had recently become verboten at Matahatchee High School, along with guns, knives, and charm bracelets. Charm bracelets were suspected of being vehicles for carrying gang symbols, although there had never been a gang of any kind at Matahatchee that anybody could remember. The trouble in English was stupid, too. The poem was this thing called "The Emperor of Ice Cream," and if anybody had ever been able to make sense out of it, Shelley would gladly eat cow dung. Holding the pink slips that meant she was due in the office during lunchtime to discuss the "appropriate discipline," wandering through the west wing corridor on the way to her study hall, Shelley found herself thinking about Miss Edgerton again. Miss Edgerton, who always wore the right thing at the right time. Miss Edgerton, who was always organized and polite. Miss Edgerton, whose car was always clean and whose clothes were always pressed. In some odd way that Shelley could not pin down, Miss Edgerton seemed to be at the root of all the trouble in the world, of all the trouble for people like Shelley. For some reason, she reminded Shelley of Amanda, all grown up.

It was the pink slips that decided it, in the end. Shelley had the pink slips and had to take them to the office. Miss Edgerton was in that very same office, doing some kind of work for the lawyer who was working for the Board of Education. Something. Shelley couldn't remember. She only knew that as she made her way toward the center of the building, she felt better than she had in hours. She felt light-headed and secure.

She'd expected to have to look around to find Miss Edgerton — in a back office, maybe, or closeted with the principal — but Miss Edgerton was right out front at a desk, next to Miss Lazio, and the cat was with her. Or rather, the cat was lying across a pile of papers, curled around a crystal paperweight that Shelley didn't remember ever seeing before. Maybe it belonged to Miss Edgerton, or the cat, and Miss Edgerton had brought it along to keep the cat happy. Miss Lazio was certainly happy. She reached across to Miss Edgerton's desk every once in a while to stroke Edelweiss's back, and Edelweiss curled around to nuzzle the fingers when they came close. It was, Shelley thought, completely nauseating. They treated that cat the way they should have treated a child, except that neither of them had children. They probably didn't even want them. Maybe Amanda was right. Maybe Miss Edgerton was a lesbian. Maybe Miss Lazio was her lover. Shelley seemed to be full of maybes today. It made no sense. She wished she could take off for the rest of the day and spend her time downtown, where there was nothing to do, but where nobody was watching her.

Miss Edgerton and Miss Lazio both looked up when she came into the office. Miss Lazio looked at the little clutch of pink slips with a frown. Miss Lazio was nowhere near as annoying as Miss Edgerton, because she was younger, and not so perfect. Her hair was forever falling out of the clips she used to try to hold it back.

"Well," she said, as Shelley pushed her way up to the counter that separated the desks from the waiting area. "You seem to have been busy today. Let me see what you've got."

She got out from behind her desk and came to where Shelley was standing. At the desk with the cat on it, Miss Edgerton sat still, staring. The cat was snaking around as if it were trying to rub itself rich. It was so white, it made everything near it look darker.

"I know you, don't I?" Miss Edgerton said finally. "You live next door to me."

"That's right," Shelley said.

Miss Lazio had gone through each of the pink slips. "I don't want you to think she's some kind of juvenile delinquent," she said. "These are all minor enough. They always are, with Shelley."

"That's right," Miss Edgerton said. "Shelley Altman. When you were younger, you used to play the piano."

"I gave it up in fifth grade," Shelley said.

"That's a pity. It's a fine talent, playing the piano. When I was younger, almost every girl learned. You should have had more ambition."

"I like your cat," Shelley said.

Miss Edgerton brightened, and put out a hand to let Edelweiss nuzzle against it. The two of them together looked like some kind of joke: the old maid and her cat. Miss Edgerton had long fingers with blunt, well-tended nails. Her nail polish was clear and uneventful. Shelley wondered, suddenly, which of the Victoria's Secret underwear sets she was wearing today.

"It can't be helped," Miss Lazio was saying. "Shelley? Are you listening. It can't be helped. We've got the curricular plan for next year to get out of this office today. I've got Caroline here to help us with the legal documents we have to file. There's just not going to be anybody free to talk to you about these until tomorrow. It would be different if you'd done something really serious. I could have sent you to Mr. Borden if you'd vandalized some property or threatened another student with bodily harm. But this —" Miss Lazio waved it all away with one hand. "This is barely worth talking about. You'll have to come back tomorrow and talk to somebody then."

"All right," Shelley said.

"I don't think it would have been better if she had vandalized property," Miss Edgerton said.

Miss Lazio brushed hair out of her face. "Just let it go," she said. "I'll charge these off on the book. You can forget all about them. Except the homework, of course, and that's up to your teacher. Why you girls don't do homework is more than I can understand. But then, I don't understand anything anymore, do I? We didn't have air-conditioning when I went to high school. We got hot, that was all, and we learned to live with it. They never learn to live with anything."

"I like your cat," Shelley said again.

Miss Edgerton smiled. Then she leaned over and picked up Edelweiss and laid her across her shoulder. The cat purred and stretched and yawned.

"I like my cat, too," Miss Edgerton said. "Nobody can be completely without sense if they truly love a cat."

Lunch was at eleven o'clock. Shelley didn't eat it. After she was finished in the office, she went down the corridor and out the side door, to the teachers' parking lot. She looked up and down the rows until she found Miss Edgerton's car. Then she walked through the planters until she was standing beside it. It had not changed since the last time she'd seen it. There was no reason why she should have expected it would. It was still dark blue, and it still had the cat carrier in the backseat. The carrier's door was propped open now, though, to make it easier for Miss Edgerton to get Edelweiss inside it when it was time to go. All the doors were locked, and the trunk was locked, too. Shelley tried it. Whatever she was going to do next, she wouldn't be able to hide in the backseat or the trunk until Miss Edgerton decided to go home.

She walked around the car a few times. She sat down on the concrete bumper that defined the parking space inside its two white border lines. The teachers' parking lot was full of these bumpers, although the student parking lot had none. Shelley had no idea what they were for. She didn't know how to drive, and it if was up to her mother, she never would.

She walked around the car again, and again, and again. She felt dizzy, but she didn't want to stop. She thought of going into Miss Edgerton's house when Miss Edgerton wasn't there, but the cat was. She'd been doing that long before Amanda had moved to Matahatchee and had come up with the idea of killing off Miss Edgerton, and not just Miss Edgerton, but lots of people, all the people who deserved to die. Shelley would have thought of it on her own, though, eventually, because when she was in Miss Edgerton's house and it was quiet and cool and dark, she sometimes imagined Miss Edgerton dead, on the floor, on the couch, stone cold and unable ever to come back to life again. Every once in a while, she even dreamed of it. She turned over in bed and there she was, in her head, in that house, with the body cold in the bathtub or the garage or someplace else out of the way. She sat down at the kitchen table, and Edelweiss came up to sit in her lap. She lay down in the big queen-size sleigh bed — why did Miss Edgerton have a bed that size, when she was the only one who ever slept in it? — and Edelweiss came to lay across her stomach. It was not stupid to love a cat, Shelley thought, if you loved it the right way. It was only stupid to treat a cat as a child. She was sure she would never treat Edelweiss as a child, if Edelweiss was her own. The only problem would be her parents, who did not like the idea of a pet in the house. They didn't like the idea of Edelweiss, either. When Edelweiss came across the yard to look for Shelley, Shelley's mother would shoo it back home. Cats bring lice, Shelley's mother always said. Then she gave Shelley a lecture on why it was more important, and more Christian, to love your fellow human beings instead of a cat.

The best thing, Shelley thought, would be to kill Miss Edgerton where nobody could see it and to hide the body where nobody could find it. That way, it could be months before someone came along to do something about the house, or the cat. She wouldn't even have to worry about the grass growing out of control. Miss Edgerton didn't have grass. She had pebbles in decorative colors, the way a lot of people did, so that they didn't have to look at brown and dying lawns during the long months of water rationing in the summer.

Shelley got up from where she was sitting, walked around the car again, and sat down again. When she put her hands into the thick warm air, she could feel Edelweiss's fur on her fingers. Buried in the white like that, her fingers looked as dark as sand.

It was ten minutes after twelve when Miss Edgerton came out of the building and headed for her car. Shelley was still there, in the parking lot, making no sense at all, and for a single frightened moment she thought that Miss Edgerton would not be alone. Mr. DaVoe would be with her, surely, or Miss Lazio would walk her out. That was the kind of thing adults did with each other. Shelley looked around, but the parking lot was deserted. So was the space at Miss Edgerton's back. There was only Miss Edgerton, carrying the cat.

"Miss Altman?" Miss Edgerton said.

Shelley had only been called "Miss Altman" before by teachers — school teachers or Sunday school teachers — and then because she was about to be in trouble. She blushed four shades of red and looked directly into Edelweiss's eyes. He looked miserable. He looked as if he knew what was about to happen to him. And why shouldn't he know? He'd probably been put in the car, and the cat carrier, often enough.

"I wasn't doing anything," Shelley said. "I was just — just —"

"Just what?"

"Just looking for somebody to give me a ride. Out to Grandview Park."

"Grandview Park?" Miss Edgerton blinked. She had her keys in one hand. She had Edelweiss in the other, tucked under her arm like a loaf of bread. She got the back passenger door open and reached for the cat carrier. "Why ever would you want to go to Grandview Park?"

If Edelweiss had been her own cat, Shelley would never have put her in the cat carrier. She wouldn't even put her in the car, if she didn't like to drive places. She stared stupidly as Miss Edgerton got Edelweiss into the carrier. Why ever would she want to go to Grandview Park?

"Shelley?" Miss Edgerton said. "Why do you want to go to Grandview Park?"

"Oh," Shelley said. "Well. My mother's there. For the afternoon. You know. She does nature stuff."

"Does she? I wasn't aware of that."

"Oh, yeah. She does. She always has. You know. Since college. She went to Agnes Scott, did you know that?"

"No." Edelweiss was hunched down in the carrier, making a noise like an angry purr. Shelley had to hold herself back from trying to rescue her.

"Well," Shelley said. "She did. Go to Agnes Scott. And now she does nature stuff. And she's out at Grandview and I'm supposed to meet her there. Except my ride isn't here."

"Who is your ride?" Miss Edgerton asked. "Possibly we could phone him." She reached into her bag and came out with a cell phone.

"I don't know her name," Shelley said

quickly. "It's somebody my mom knows at the Methodist church. I mean, I know her first name. It's Elizabeth. I just don't know her last one. If you see what I mean."

"I see that this seems to be a very disorganized undertaking," Miss Edgerton said. "Are you always this confused about your plans? Is your mother always this confused? She keeps such a nice house. I wouldn't have imagined she wasn't meticulous about her arrangements."

"There's never been any problem before," Shelley said, wondering when, exactly, this before was supposed to have taken place. The last time she'd been out to Grandview Park, she'd been ten years old and on a hike with the United Methodist Church's Girl Scout Troop. That was when her mother was still insisting that she belong to the Girl Scouts, before it turned out the Girl Scouts didn't have anything against atheists joining, or gays. Then Shelley's mother had gone on a long tirade about how she should have known it all along. Girl Scouts were always such tomboys. They hiked and tied knots. They were as masculine as lady wrestlers.

Miss Edgerton was standing by the side of her car. She had her keys in her hand. She had her jacket over her shoulders as if the day was a cool one instead of a lethally hot one. She squinted in the sun.

"I suppose there's no reason for me not to drop you off, if you have to go," she said. "But I do worry about what your mother is likely to say. I'm sure she doesn't want you driving around with strangers."

"You're not a stranger," Shelley said. "You live next door."

"Yes," Miss Edgerton said. Then she got in behind the wheel and popped the locks on the two doors that were still closed.

Shelley closed the door next to Edelweiss's cat carrier and opened the one to the front passenger seat. Behind her, she could hear the cat making that same low growl, miserable and angry. Shelley knew she would be miserable and angry, too, if somebody had put her in a cage.

It got too much to listen to after a while. Shelley could hear the low tortured growl over the sound of the Volvo's engine, even over the hum of National Public Radio, which seemed to have nothing else on it except people talking endlessly about things that didn't make much sense. All the radio stations Shelley had ever listened to either played music or Rush Limbaugh. When Rush Limbaugh talked, he sounded excited, not hushed and secretive like these people here. Shelley tried to concentrate on the conversation — about gardening, and whether it was better to grow vegetables or flowers — but finally she couldn't stand it anymore. She had to make Miss Edgerton stop.

"It's not as if I mean to make the cat suffer," Miss Edgerton said. "I put her in the back like that because it's the best place for her. She's safe there. If I put her up on the seat, she rocks the carrier until it falls over."

"It's all right," Shelley said. They had stopped near the curb on one of those long stretches of two lane road that were everywhere in this part of Florida. Palm trees lined the sidewalks on both sides, but nothing else did. Shelley looked around as she was getting the cat carrier out to put on her lap in the front seat, and there was nothing to see. The nearest house was blocks away, except you couldn't call it blocks because there weren't any blocks. The nearest gas station was half a mile down the road. She shut the back door and climbed into her seat with the cat carrier in her hands. She got her seat belt on and her arms around the carrier. She could put her fingers through the grille at the carrier's front, the little cage part. Edelweiss nipped at her, causing no pain.

"She really is quite all right in the back," Miss Edgerton said. "She doesn't like it, it's true, but we can't always like all the things we have to do. I'm sure you don't like all the things you have to do."

"She doesn't know any better," Shelley said, although that was not what she meant. Edelweiss seemed to her to know better than just about anybody.

Miss Edgerton got back on the road. It wasn't very far to Grandview Park, now. If Shelley had ignored the noise, the cat would not have had to suffer any longer than a few more minutes. Still, Shelley felt better. Edelweiss had stopped nipping her fingers and begun to nuzzle them. She had stopped making that noise that sounded like agony.

Grandview Park announced itself with a tall gate that was always open, with a latticework arch above it that spelled out its name in metal letters. Miss Edgerton turned the Volvo into the drive and went in for the five hundred or so feet that were possible before all traffic had to stop. It was not really a park. It was a "wilderness area," designated as such by the federal government, and set aside to remain completely undeveloped. Like the Everglades, its only purpose was to exist. Shelley got out of the car and looked around. There was no sign of Amanda she could see. There was no sign of anything except a narrow trail leading in through the Spanish moss and the high grass. Shelley shifted from one foot to the other, unsure what to do.

Miss Edgerton got out of the car. "Your mother doesn't seem to be here. There's no car parked anywhere I can see."

"It's probably parked around the other side."

"Let's go there, then."

"Oh, no," Shelley said. "That's not necessary. I know where she goes. It's easy enough to reach from here. It's just —"

"Yes?"

"Well, if you wouldn't mind, walking in with me? I get a little spooked by the stuff, you know. Bugs and things. And there are alligators."

"If there are alligators, you shouldn't go in at all."

"Oh, the alligators aren't roaming around loose. I mean, they are, but they live at the bottom of this clifflike thing, you know, and they never come out where they're going to bother you. My mother comes out here bird-watching and stuff all the time."

Shelley rubbed the side of her face. She had no idea what she was saying. The park could be crawling with alligators. There could be an alligator behind every bush. She really did not remember, in any detail, the last time she had been here, except that she had sat down on a path and cried when she found out they hadn't brought any Coke. She should have brought a different kind of coke. That would have been the best idea. She looked around. She wished she knew where Amanda was. She wondered if she could do this on her own, and then decided she had to. If she had closed her eyes at just that moment, she could have seen Miss Edgerton dead again, this time on the overgrown grass, with alligators coming toward her.

Miss Edgerton looked from one side of her to the other, and then up the path. There was nothing to see there. The trees were too thick. So was the grass. So was the Spanish moss. When you looked up the path, all you saw was darkness.

"We'll bring Edelweiss," Miss Edgerton said suddenly. "I don't like to leave her in the car very long in this heat. She'll get dehydrated. Bring me the carrier now, and show me the way your mother will have gone. We'll walk for a while, but if we don't find her soon we'll go back. I'm not going to have you wandering around a swamp in central Florida on your own."

Shelley snatched Edelweiss in the carrier and came around the side of the car. Miss Edgerton took the carrier and nodded toward the path.

"You lead," Miss Edgerton said. "You're the one who knows where we're going. And call out. Maybe your mother will hear us and show us some mercy."

"Right," Shelley said, looking back at Edelweiss in the carrier. All she could see were the eyes in white fir, eyes as black as the asphalt pebbles that sucked up onto the road every year in the worst heat of the summer.

She turned toward the path and started in, her stomach turning, her head full of fuzz. Now that the moment was here, she could barely think at all. She needed Amanda to be here, and Amanda was not. Amanda would know what to do. As it was, all Shelley could manage was to walk steadily forward, into the trees, into the brush, and to imagine, as she had always imagined. For some reason, though, she couldn't seem to imagine Miss Edgerton dead — she couldn't imagine Miss Edgerton at all. It was as if Miss Edgerton had never existed. All Shelley could concentrate on was the light on Edelweiss's face as she let her out of the cat carrier and into the daylight. You shouldn't keep an animal caged, Shelley thought, you really shouldn't. Not even to ride in a car. If there was no way for Edelweiss to be safe in a car without a carrier, then she and Edelweiss would walk everywhere they went. They would start by walking home, as soon as Miss Edgerton was dead.

You shouldn't keep an animal caged, Shelley told herself virtuously, one more time. And then something hit her hard, on the back of the head.

Farther back on the path, Miss Edgerton stopped and put the cat carrier down next to her feet. She had seen the poker arch and Shelley's body fall, but she hadn't witnessed the details of the wound, and she had no intention of doing so. That was why she had her helpers in the first place. She needed someone to handle the messy parts, and she had never much cared for the sight of blood. Now she waited patiently while Amanda walked farther up the path and threw the poker into the brush. Then she came back into view, stripping off her white cotton gloves. There was a time when women everywhere wore white cotton gloves as automatically as they wore panties, but those days were dead and gone, and Miss Edgerton knew it.

"Well," she said.

"She wasn't paying any attention," Amanda said.

"They never do," Miss Edgerton said. "They get distracted by the cat. I'd better give you a lift home, or people will start wondering where you are."

She turned around and went back down the path, toward her car. She did not look back at Amanda, and would not have, no matter what she thought the girl was doing. She got to the car and put the cat carrier in the backseat, where it belonged. She got behind the wheel and waited. Amanda would want to look at the body, to prod it, to make sure of it. She'd only been at this six months, and this was only her third adventure.

Miss Edgerton could remember when *she* had only been at this for six months — but that was decades ago, and she had been younger then.

Going to the Dogs

by Maxine O'Callaghan

Growing up, I was always a cat person. But when my son John was nine, he desperately wanted a dog. I gave in, reluctantly, and ever since I have definitely, once and for all, become a dog person. Regardless of the popular opinion of the intelligence of cats, I've come to believe that dogs are smarter, and no one can challenge their loyalty and unconditional love.

Much as I love dogs, however, my life isn't set up to have one full-time right now. No problem. I am part-time caretaker of my son's two big mutts, and spend enough time with them so they are mine, too. They just don't live in my house.

Molly is the youngest, an overgrown

goofball with boundless energy. Wear black around her and you learn just how much she sheds. Mocha is, indeed, part wolf, with lots of stamina. She runs along with John on his mountain bike. Once they did twenty miles across the Santa Ana Mountains. She took a short nap and was ready to go again. She is also amazingly smart. The incidents I use in my story to illustrate her intelligence are true. One pitch-black night, she led my son to safety down a mountain trail, and the incident with the stepping stones happened with me, just the way I describe.

Just wait until she sees her name and picture in this collection. She'll demand extra dog biscuits for sure.

— Maxine O'Callaghan

Forget what you've heard about private investigators. I've been one for a while now, and trust me, I'll take good old routine work to danger and drama any day in the week. And with more and more companies hiring their own in-house investigators, you take what you can get. Which was why I was driving out to Rancho Santa Margarita on a Monday afternoon to meet with a new client who sounded like she just wanted me to do some well-paid house-sitting.

"It's nothing I can put my finger on," she had said over the phone. "I'm probably being silly, but I live alone, and I'd feel better if somebody was here the next few days when I'm at work."

"Have there been burglaries in your neighborhood?" I asked hopefully.

Routine is one thing. Being totally bored is something else.

"I don't think so," she said.

"Maybe you have a stalker."

"Well —"

"You have any problems with ex-boyfriends? An ex-husband?"

"No. Listen, Ms. West, I rather not talk about it on the phone, and I can't leave the house, so if you could just come out here . . ."

She said her name was Susan Logan and gave me her address. Always cautious, I did a cursory background check but turned up nothing worse on Ms. Logan than a small claims judgment of $200 to a neighbor for "destruction of ten prize rose bushes." At any rate, turning her down was not an option because she had the one qualification that guaranteed my services: She was ready and willing to pay me a sizable retainer and my expenses.

It was all blue skies and sunshine that afternoon in late May, the kind of perfection that builders have used since the twenties to lure people out to Southern California. Their sales pitch had worked so well in Orange County that tracts of homes and condos are piled up against the foothills of the Santa Ana Mountains, stopped only by the Cleveland National Forest. At least until the developers figure out how to sneak across that boundary.

This is where Susan Logan lived, precariously close to brushy hillsides already frying in the sun, on a street that belonged in an early Spielberg movie. The houses had white stucco, red tile roofs, and more driveway than landscaping. Hers was a small one-story, dwarfed by a three-car garage. I parked and got out.

I didn't see any rose gardens on the block, so maybe the neighbor never replanted. I could, however, make a good guess at how the bushes were destroyed because inside Ms. Logan's house, dogs barked loudly — at least two of them — announcing my arrival. And why was she worrying about being away during the day with a couple of big, noisy animals on the premises? Maybe there was more to this than she'd let on, and less boring, too.

Now, I like dogs just fine, but experience has taught me to be wary. Too many paranoid people out there with neurotic Rottweilers and inbred pit bulls. Besides, I'm a little paranoid myself, enough to be packing when I'm meeting strangers. So I was happy to have my little Beretta mini-automatic tucked into the pocket of my black denim skirt.

The frenzied barking turned up a notch as a woman cracked the door, which was secured with a heavy chain. She had fine red hair that framed a round face and a generous dusting of freckles on pale skin. A light blue tank top was tucked into white shorts and revealed more of the cinnamon blotches on her neck and shoulders. I guessed she was my age, maybe late thirties.

Well, okay, forty, if you must know, and I suppose she was, too.

One of the dogs poked a big blocky head around her, some kind of mixed breed, blond and furry. The other hung back, and I only got a glimpse of it.

"Ms. Logan?" I said, raising my voice to be heard. "I'm Delilah West. Could you put the dogs somewhere —"

But Susan was already undoing the chain and opening the door, saying, "Oh, don't worry. They're friendly."

She broke off to grab the collar of the huge blond fluffball, who barked wildly and lunged against the restraint, yanking her owner around. Susan was maybe five-two, a hundred and five pounds, but she wrestled the animal to a draw. I guessed the dog was golden retriever, most likely mixed with a Tasmanian devil.

"Molly, down," Susan yelled. "Stop it. No jumping. Sit!"

Molly ignored the commands, but the other dog, who had hung back to eye me cautiously, obeyed, adding a couple of deep "Woofs," to the bedlam. This one looked like there was a lot of malamute or husky mixed with something that gave it short hair and floppy ears to go along with a lean body, long legs, and those watchful amber eyes.

"Sorry," Susan said as Molly struggled to get to me. "She just loves people. Be nice, Molly. SIT!"

The dog finally planted its big butt and gave me one of those silly, tongue-lolling grins that disarm even the most wary, so I extended a hand and got it covered in slurpy dog kisses.

"Good girl," Susan said, releasing the collar and leaving me to fend off the beast and collect a fallout of blond fur on my black skirt. "I'm so glad you like dogs. Thanks for coming, Ms. West."

"Delilah."

"Delilah," she repeated. "Let's go sit down."

A sunny kitchen was off to the left, with a breakfast bar separating it from the rest of the living space. She led the way into what is called a great room, which just means, I guess, you use it for everything: eating, watching TV, entertaining guests. Through sliding glass doors, I could see a patio, a small yard with a high fence, and a weedy lawn.

Molly flew ahead of us. Rather than going around a sectional sofa that served as a divider from the dining area, she leaped over it in a huge bound, with more fur swirling in the air.

When the other dog hung back, Susan said, "You come too, Mocha," and it trailed at a cautious distance, all stealth and grace, with what I'd swear was a look of disdain for the rambunctious Molly.

I have a friend who once took some of her dog's fur with her when she picked out a chair, matching the color so the dog hair wouldn't show. The room looked like Susan may have done that. Carpet, sofa, and one easy chair were all done in light tans, shading toward yellow. I looked around and decided that unless she had a stash of jewelry or bearer bonds someplace in the house, no respectable burglar would risk being mauled just to steal the TV and low-end stereo. Which left me to wonder just what I was doing here.

Susan sat on the sofa with Molly beside her, ran a distracted hand through her hair, said, "I should be at work, but I knew I'd be too worried to concentrate."

I chose the chair that was safely against the wall. Mocha laid down where she could observe all of us, folding her legs gracefully and laying her head on her paws.

"Why don't you tell me what the problem is," I said.

"I keep seeing this big van," Susan said. "Dark gray — sort of anonymous, you know? It creeped me out. I've stopped taking the girls for a walk, and I stayed home from work today."

"Did you recognize the driver? Or maybe get the plate number?"

"No, the windows were tinted, and I never got a look at the license plate."

"Can't imagine why," I said, picturing Molly on a leash as she took another flying leap from the sofa over the coffee table and made a playful dive at Mocha. "Have you filed a report with the police?"

"No. To tell you the truth, I don't think they'd take me seriously."

"But if you suspect somebody is stalking you —"

"It's not me who's being stalked, not exactly," she said.

"Not you," I said. "Then who, exactly?"

But she was looking down at Mocha who had lifted her head and seemed to know something I didn't. I may be a little slow, but I suddenly realized just how low I'd fallen on the job scale.

Susan Logan didn't plan to hire me as a house sitter. She wanted a bodyguard for her dogs.

"Okay," I said. "So what are you afraid of? We're talking what? Dognapping?"

Susan nodded. "They want her back."

"Her — Mocha? You didn't steal this dog —"

"No," she said. "Of course not. I found her. But I'm sure she ran away, and — well, I just won't let them take her, not if I can help it. That van scares her. When they show up, she just bolts for home."

Molly came back to jump up beside

Susan, snuggle close, and give her an anxious look. Sunlight spilled in through the patio doors, and it was warm enough in the room, but Susan wrapped her arms around her body like she was cold.

"Define *they*," I said.

"I think, maybe — the government, or some kind of research facility." She paused, with a flush of pink showing in the pale skin. "I don't know how to explain this without sounding like a kook —"

"Try," I said.

"About a month ago, I took Molly to the park, and there was this dog under some bushes. She came right away, wouldn't leave my side."

Susan brought the dog home. It was too late to call the animal shelter that night and then it was the weekend, and by Monday she'd talked herself into doing nothing. "I thought her colors looked like mocha chip ice cream, and once I gave her a name, I couldn't give her up."

"Any signs she was abused?" I asked.

"Nothing obvious. I knew I should take her to the vet to see if she had a chip — a microchip," she explained. "They put them in an animal's neck for identification. Molly has one."

I said, "You got attached to her and didn't want to give her up."

"Yes, but it's more than that. Mocha is — different. At first I thought it was because she must have a lot of wolf in her. You can see that in the legs and the eyes."

"Okay," I said. Just my luck to find a paying client who turns out to be totally Looney Tunes.

"Look, I know it sounds crazy, but it's true. She's so smart. I'm sure she understands what I say to her."

I looked over at Mocha. Her head came up off her paws and she watched me intently.

"Uh-huh," I said, "if you say so."

"You'll see for yourself," Susan said. "You will take the job, won't you? Just until Friday, until I can figure something out."

Well, not like I had anything else to do. I could watch old *Rockford* reruns, gain a few pounds, catch up on my sleep, and get paid for it.

"Sure," I said. "Why not?"

Odd thing was, I couldn't tell who looked more relieved, Susan or the dog. It was definitely Mocha who sighed before she laid her head back on her paws and closed her eyes.

★ ★ ★

For the next three days, I arrived a few minutes before Susan left for work and stayed until she returned home. Susan had both cable and one of those small satellite dishes. Five hundred channels, proving only that absolutely anything ever committed to film or video can be recycled.

I vegged out.

Molly bounced off the walls.

Mocha did the laundry, cooked up some gourmet meals, and balanced my checkbook.

Yeah, right.

What she really did was lie with her head on her paws and watch me. After three days of this the look in her eyes was intense and I'd swear it was touched with a little scorn, like she was thinking, "Some private investigator you are, lady. Do something."

Or maybe I was going bonkers with inactivity.

I even, briefly, considered another assignment offered by my old pal, Charlie Colfax. Old ex-pal, I should say. We'd had a serious falling-out, and I figured he must be desperate for help if he was calling me. I reluctantly told him, "No, thanks," even though it meant more money, because he needed me right away.

That third day I kept jumping up and going to the window, hoping to get a peek at a dark van prowling the neighborhood. I noted a couple of Realtors cruising up in their Mercedes to show a house down the street with a for sale sign on the lawn. I saw plenty of women and kids in over-sized SUVs. I counted delivery vehicles from FedEx, UPS, and the U.S. Postal Service.

No mysterious vans.

And — okay, I confess. Mostly what I did was go through Susan Logan's stuff.

Well, what do you expect? Like the story goes, you can't hang out with a scorpion and not expect it to sting you. You don't hire a private eye and not expect us to snoop. In both cases, it's our nature.

If I was looking for some darker side to my client, some clear proof that she should be shipped off to the loony bin, I didn't find it. Instead, I just proved that she was a nice, ordinary woman with family on the East Coast and very few notations in her appointment book other than vet appointments and the occasional visit to her dentist. She paid her bills on time, spent too much on fancy lingerie, and gave small amounts of money on a regular basis to at least ten wildlife and humane funds.

One other thing I found out: She couldn't afford me.

Instead of waiting, keys in hand to make my getaway, when she got home that evening, I said, "We need to talk."

"What happened? Did you see the van?" She took a quick look at the dogs like she was counting noses.

"No," I said. "I just think it's time we reassess the situation, see where we stand."

"Oh. . . ." She brushed back her red hair and gave me a tired, wry smile. "Can it wait five minutes? I can take bad news better if I change my clothes and hear it over a beer."

Molly bounced off after Susan, but Mocha stayed to watch me reproachfully as I took a couple of Bud Lights from the refrigerator.

"What?" I said. "I never told her it was bad news."

Great.

Three days and now I was defending myself to a dog.

In faded jeans, a pink tank top, and bare feet, Susan sat on the sectional with an arm around Molly and a look on her face that said she was expecting the worst. She drank from the bottle and said, "You agreed to stay through tomorrow. You're not going to bail on me, are you? I'm setting it up so I can telecommute. I'm just waiting for the okay."

"So that's your solution? And then what? You'll spend all your time locked up here with the dogs? How about going to the supermarket? Or the drug store?"

"You can buy almost anything online and have it delivered. I'll manage. What else can I do?"

"You can let me do my job," I said. "You know, you're making some big assumptions here. You're jumping at shadows and suspecting the worst. What we need to do is find out if somebody really is trying to take your dog and, if they are, deal with it."

Mocha had been following the conversation, looking from one of us to the other. Now she came over and stood right in front of Susan and gave her one of those intense stares.

"Look," I said, trying to tone down the sarcasm. "Mocha approves."

Susan patted the dog, finished her beer, and said, "She saved my life, you know. Or at least saved me from a bad fall and Lord knows what kind of injuries."

I knew I was in for one of those miraculous dog stories, the kind you hear on Animal Planet, and I was right. This was shortly after she found Mocha, before she got so spooked she didn't leave the house with the dogs.

"We went for a hike," she said. "Up Holy Jim Canyon. It's nice because I can take the dogs off their leashes. Not many people on the trail, all of them coming down. That should've been a clue how late it was. It was stupid of me. I'd just lost track of the time that afternoon."

So there she was, a couple of miles up in the mountains, and darkness coming fast. No jacket, and it started getting chilly as the sun slid behind the high canyon walls. Worse, no flashlight. She just had a fanny pack with some dog biscuits, a packet of sunflower seeds, and a bottle of water.

"It got so black," she said. "There was no moon, just starlight."

The rocky trail was along a creek, a beautiful walk when you could see what you were doing, damn dangerous when you couldn't. The dogs stayed close, Mocha in front and a subdued Molly close behind.

"All I could do was inch along," Susan said. "I was terrified. I was about ready to stop, cuddle up with these guys, and try to stay warm until the sun came up, then Mocha took over."

Susan said it took her a minute to realize what the dog was doing. Mocha stopped right in front of her, a big furry barrier. Then, staying close, she deliberately stepped down off a big rock — a huge drop-off that would surely have resulted in an injury for Susan.

"Once could have been coincidence," Susan said. "But she did it again, and it dawned on me what was going on. I put the leash on her, and she led me down that trail."

"Maybe she has guide dog training," I said, impressed more than I wanted to let on.

"Maybe, but it was more than some obedience thing. Don't you see? It was her idea. I'm telling you — I've been around dogs all my life, and I've never seen one like Mocha."

"Yeah, okay," I said, not willing to argue, especially with Mocha giving me her stare-down look. "Any possibility you're right, even more reason to find out who's in that van."

After I left Susan's that day, I cruised around the neighborhood for a while, hoping I'd spot our suspicious vehicle, but no such luck. I keep a few clothes in my van, so I parked, put on a Lakers shirt and cap, added some oversized sunglasses, and jogged back to her house. For the first time since she got scared and stopped going out, Susan came out with the dogs and set off on a walk, with me staying a block or so behind.

At that point, of course, I was sure that Susan was blowing her fears out of proportion just the way she was leaping to conclusions about the dog. I figured at best the dark gray van was being driven by some soccer mom, following Susan's dog-walking route. At worst, I'd be mediating an ownership dispute and hoping she didn't wind up back in small claims court.

Nothing unusual happened, except I got some much-needed exercise.

After a long boring Friday, we repeated this exercise with the same results. On Saturday I was back in the morning in a rented Jeep with my assistant, Danny Thu. We brought along Danny's bike, a cooler for water bottles, a thermos of coffee, and several changes of hats and shirts. Well, okay, I also brought Cheetos and some Snickers bars. It would be another long day.

Danny does marathon biking, like from L.A. to San Diego, so cruising around Susan's neighborhood for hours was no problem. I switched off between driving around in the Jeep, jogging, and leisurely strolling. Surveillance is not fun and gets old in a hurry. To be accurate, we were combining countersurveillance with protection. We trolled for a stake-out around Susan's place while she was inside. She alerted me by cell phone when she planned to walk the dogs so we could be close by.

Saturday went by and most of Sunday. I was getting sick of junk food and all I could think about was going home, putting up my feet, and sitting there for about a year. After trailing Susan and the dogs on one more walk, that's where I was headed.

Susan called on the cell, and I called Danny. "Pick them up in five minutes."

"On it," he said.

He rang me back as soon as they were out the door. Susan followed a set route, heading for the park about five blocks away. I prowled back and forth, arriving a minute before she did.

The park had two levels. The lower one was a grassy soccer field. The upper provided swings, slides, benches, and picnic tables. Kids played an impromptu game in the soccer field. More kids were having a good time on the playground. Parents sat on the benches and at the tables, keeping an eye on their broods.

There was a small parking lot between the two areas. As I idled past, I noted the lot was full and counted nine vehicles, including one compact and one van — white, not dark gray. I wish I could say I had a flash of intuition then, but the truth is I was thinking the thing was a bust and that Susan needed a good shrink instead of a private eye. I was also thinking that maybe I'd turn around and pull into the small lot and park because the white van was backing out of a space.

I could see Danny coasting down past the playground. Susan and the two dogs were ahead of him, and she was having some trouble managing the dogs as she angled across the asphalt lot. I assumed the problem was Molly, unruly as usual, and was glad to note that the white van had stopped to let them go in front of it.

Forget flashes of intuition. This was a bolt of knowing, because I saw that it was Mocha struggling to get free and head for home. Danny must have sensed something was wrong, too. He put on a burst of speed as I slammed on the brakes and left the

Jeep in the middle of the street, yelling at Susan. She stopped but she and the dogs had already crossed in front of the white van.

Danny arrived then, tried to get to her, but the driver of the van goosed the accelerator. He clipped the bike's front wheel and sent Danny flying off. Then he slammed on the brakes. Susan was screaming bloody murder. I could see parents on the playground hurrying toward their kids, not knowing what was going down, as I ran into the parking lot yelling Danny's name.

"I'm okay," he said. "Stop them."

I was running toward the front of the van. I saw a sliding side door open on the passenger side, and a man leaped out. I thought about the Beretta in a holster clipped to my jeans but no way was I going to even take it out, not with the playground right there, so I just charged, still yelling, as the guy shoved Susan aside and grabbed Mocha. The dog snarled and snapped, but he wore gloves and what looked like a padded jacket, a big man who picked her up and threw her in the van.

The instant he was inside with the dog, the van peeled out, coming right at me. I had to jump aside to keep from being hit.

Danny came limping over. Susan sat on the grass bordering the asphalt, holding on to a scared and subdued Molly.

"I should never have listened to you." Tears streamed down Susan's face. "You never believed me, and now God knows what's going to happen to my poor baby."

"You're right," I said. "I'm sorry, but I'm going to get her back."

"How?" Danny said. "I didn't get the plate. I think there was mud on it."

"Doesn't matter," I said. "I know who was driving the van."

I'd once punched Charlie Colfax in the nose, and, believe me, you don't forget a face you've punched out. So, even though I'd only gotten a glimpse of the van driver, I had no doubt it was Charlie. And now I understood the only reason he'd called to offer me a job was to lure me away from Susan's place.

The Colfax Agency wasn't answering their phone on a late Sunday afternoon. I sent a numeric page, then left a message on voice mail, threatening dire consequences if he didn't meet us at his office.

"You think he'll show up?" Danny asked. He had cleaned up a scraped knee and insisted on coming along.

"If he doesn't, I know where he lives," I said.

Charlie had office space in Triangle Square in Costa Mesa, upscale compared to my digs in Santa Ana, but a far cry from the luxury suite he once had in the Newport Center. Then, the Colfax Agency was the largest private investigation firm in Orange County, one of the largest in California. Not anymore. Long story, but Charlie blames me for putting his business on the skids, and I'd like to think he's right.

No lights on in the office and nobody answered my pounding on the door. I was wondering about what kind of security he had and if I could pick the lock, when my cell phone rang.

"Sorry I couldn't get back to you right away," Charlie said. "What's up?"

"Like you don't know," I said, picturing him, a short fireplug of a man. I hoped he was picturing my fist aimed at his nose. "I saw you, Charlie. Come over here so we can talk."

"Look," he said, "I've got dinner plans. I bet you've got better things to do, too. We were both hired by a couple of crazy pet owners. What say we just chalk it up?"

"What say I give you one chance to get

351

your butt over here with the dog?"

"Or else what?"

I'm not above a good lie when necessary, so I said, "I dropped Danny at the hospital. How about a hit-and-run charge to start? And then when you're in jail, how about I spend my every waking moment tracking down your client?"

"Danny's not really hurt, is he?"

"The clock's ticking," I said.

"All right," he said. I could hear the suppressed anger in his voice, and figured he'd try to find a way to pay me back at some point. Just then I didn't care. He said, "Probably won't be tonight, but I'll see what I can do."

From past experience, I knew he'd have somebody checking emergency rooms and be on the phone with his attorney. Eels could learn a thing or two from Charlie, so I figured he'd never be charged for hitting Danny. I just hoped my other threat would give him pause, because he does know how tenacious I can be. Still, this wasn't a whole lot to offer Susan, and I didn't blame her for hanging up on me when I called to say we'd have to wait and see.

Danny has a cadre of friends from his computer classes at the University of California, Irvine, who can unearth almost anything ever committed to electronic media and were animal lovers, one and all. He promised to meet me early the next morning and rally the troops.

I didn't sleep all that well anyway, so I was at the office by six thirty a.m. No cars in the parking lot. Even too early for Harry, the janitor, to be there.

There are a few scrubby bushes next to a cement wall that separates our lot from the one next door. I saw something move in the shrubs just as I got out of my van. A dog, coming out to me, but stopped short because it was tethered to a bush.

It was Mocha. By the time I ran over and hunkered down beside her she was so happy to see me she was doing some Molly-type leaps and yelps. There was a note attached to her collar that said: She's all yours as long as you don't do any digging.

I recognized Charlie's scrawl. He never returned my calls. Susan was adamant that I not try to find out who his client was. She still firmly believes in the whole government research thing. There's no proof, of course, except for what could be a deep scratch — or maybe a small incision on Mocha's head — that Susan swears wasn't there before. This was probably done to remove the ID chip, although Susan will never believe that.

As for me, I'm not a believer in conspiracies, super dogs, or the Easter Bunny. Still, I do keep remembering an incident that happened on that last Friday when I was dogsitting.

The sprinklers in Susan's backyard were on an automatic timer, but there had been a power outage during the night — nothing new for California these days — that screwed up the timer clock. So the sprinklers came on around noon and ran much longer than normal. Molly had long since dug up the bushes in a planting area around the patio. Naturally, not being in a dog-owner mode, I didn't realize the consequences of this water and dirt combination until I opened the patio door and the dogs ran out.

"Hey! Stay out of the mud!" I yelled, already knowing this was a futile order as Molly galloped through the planting area, muck flying.

But Mocha stopped on the patio, turned and looked at me. There were two square concrete blocks in the dirt for stepping stones over to the grass. She very deliberately used the stones to cross the mud.

Then, five minutes later when she made the return trip, she stopped on the edge of the lawn, gave me a "watch this" look, and carefully stepped back across to the patio on the stones.

Now and then, thinking back to that moment, I remember what Susan said about the incident on the trail, and I know she was right. What the dog did was not a response to a verbal command.

That second trip back to the patio was definitely Mocha's own idea.

The Accomplice

by Gary Phillips

This was an intimidating task for me, writing a so-called cozy short story. My usual work is considered hardboiled and noirish. But a challenge is a challenge, and I had a blast doing it. 'Cause I figured what other chance would I get to feature the family's semi-useless mutt, Mitzy, in a pivotal role. Our kids really did find her as a pup years ago in the park where their then pre-school, Hilltop, was. As the happy abandoned pooch wandered over to us, my son took his thumb out of his mouth long enough to christen her Mitzy, and so it was. She's lame as a guard dog, can't catch mice or other vermin, though she is adept at sticking her snout in trash cans in search of treats. So what's not to love?

— Gary Phillips

Aubry Harris awoke with a blue jay singing merrily in his head. He blinked, and that hurt. It was also painful to turn his head in any direction; he was sweating alcohol in his boxers.

He swung a leg over the side of the bed, and his foot came down on something soft and fuzzy. He picked up a fur G-string and it flooded back to him. Cheri, no Charise . . . no, that wasn't quite it, either. She was an exotic performer, a stripper at the Polka-Dot Tiger near the airport. Outside, he could hear the morning traffic ooze by on the overpass, next to his less-than-luxurious apartment. Nightly his was a lullaby of car engines and the aroma of exhaust.

"Arghh," he growled, getting both of his legs onto the floor. The ache in his neck traveled the length of his spine and exploded into a thousand pinpricks in his lower back. Then the sensation reversed course and settled into the left side of his brain. He rubbed the heel of his palm on his forehead but it didn't help. Nothing was going to help except half a gallon of V8 Juice and scrambled eggs bathed in Louisiana hot sauce.

Harris rose wobbly to his feet, a prizefighter who'd gone one too many rounds. Scratching his belly, he shambled to the bathroom. Afterward, he Frankenstein-walked toward his kitchenette. On the way, he noticed the portable TV was lying on the floor. At first he figured the wild love-making he and Shari — no that wasn't her name, either — had engaged in had upset the box. He bent to pick it up and put it back on its plastic milk crate. Then he felt the loose duct tape underneath the set.

"Dammit," he swore. Harris groped then sank to a knee, upturning the TV set. His house piece was gone. The gun was an old-fashioned Smith & Wesson snub-nosed .38. It had been "acquired" from a home-boy's crib after a raid of his place for narcotics when he worked vice. Originally, the heater had been stolen by the gang member from a gun shop. It never hurt to have a cold piece, Harris had rationalized.

"Now what do I do?" He put the TV aside, and retrieved a bottle from the refrigerator. Listlessly, he poured some club soda into a foam cup left over from a Carl's Jr. He let the liquid mix with the residue of old coffee. He had to find what's her face and get that gun back. Why the hell had she snatched it? He drank more and tried to visualize the woman and what they'd done and said last night.

The phone rang. He grabbed the handset on the third jangle of his nerves. "Hello," he rasped.

"Hi, Aubry."

"Aunt Sarah."

"You okay? You sound a little under."

"Ah, just a bit," he coughed, his throat thick with nasal back drain. "What's up?" He wanted to sound cheery so she wouldn't be aware of his physical state. She knew he drank, but he knew it disappointed her to hear about his binges. Let alone him bringing home another woman who was in no way like his ex-wife, Claire. But since the divorce and the move to crappy quarters, his aunt had been great about taking care of his dog, and he was grateful.

"I was wondering, dear, if you had some free time?"

Uh-oh. "What is it, Aunt Sarah?"

A hesitation, her steady breathing getting louder as she built up to her request. "There's been a break-in at the senior center."

Despite himself, he made a sound. "What, somebody make off with the bingo cards?"

"Aubry," she scolded.

"Sorry. But I am a homicide cop, Aunt Sarah."

"So you're too much of a hotshot to see about this?"

"You know what I mean." How easily he slipped into that twelve-year-old whine. Man. But he had far more important matters to handle at the moment. "Was it phoned in to the division?"

"Not exactly."

"Huh." The blue jay was warbling inside his head again.

"What are we talking about, Aunt Sarah?" He could hear his dog's muffled barking on the other end.

"I, ah, well . . ."

"Aunt Sarah, could you get to it please?"

"Money," she whispered.

"What, the pensioners are selling bootleg Doan's Pills out the back door?" He almost laughed but it required too many muscles.

"Listen," she talked close to the handset. "You know good and well if you're retired and are drawing Social Security you're only allowed so much extra income or they start deducting that amount from your checks."

"Yes," he answered.

"Some of them work little extra jobs but are paid in cash so there's no trace of the money."

"Seems to me I could get a reward for turning you cheaters in."

"That's not funny, Aubry."

"So you desperados pooled some of your ill gotten gains to take care of busted windows and what have you."

"Right. There was about $4,000 in the kitty."

"See, crime pays."

"This is serious," she stressed. "Given the current administration in Washington, I'm afraid the IRS will come down on my friends if this gets out."

It was worth the discomfort to laugh. "Look, just because your candidate didn't win, again, I don't think you're on anybody's enemies list. I mean, your saving grace is you do like barbeque." He chuckled but had to stop as phlegm congealed in his chest.

"Hey," he said, and the dog could be heard barking again. "How's that semi-useless dog of mine?"

"She's good, she's out back probably chasing a lizard. I'd put the phone up to her but she'd just lick the receiver."

"Yeah, and wag her tail and shake her body at the same time," he remarked fondly.

"Can you help us?"

"I'd like to, Aunt Sarah, but I've got urgent business to take care of." He had to find that woman and that gun before some bad, bad thing went down.

She sighed. "I see."

"You know" — he brightened — "you're good with people. You've stuck your nose where it didn't belong plenty of times."

"Thanks."

"You know what I mean. You worked in a free clinic back in the Free Speech days in Berkeley, been a social worker, run a tenants' rights organization."

"I don't know." Mitzy barked again.

Now she was being coy, but he'd go along. He needed to keep her distracted while he tried to find the woman and his gat. Niggling at the back of his head was a name. It wasn't hers, it was the name of the clown he knew she was gunning for. That much was clear to him from last night.

"Aubry," she'd said sweetly, as she unbuckled his pants. He wasn't clear on his response, but it was probably somewhere between a grunt and a mumble. He did remember leaning forward from his sitting position groping for the beautiful, nubile young vision.

"How many guns do you have?" She'd

been wiggling out of her Versace jeans and did one of those fake little girls voices sure to turn on a twisted hump like him. He couldn't dredge anything else up, but he must have told her or pointed at the TV. Yeah, at that point he would have done anything with the promise of making love to —

"Aubry," his aunt said sharply, interrupting his lewd reminiscing. "Have you been listening to me?"

"Yes," he coughed again. "You're going to go over to the senior center and talk to a few of the regulars, and will give me a call in a couple of hours."

"Okay," she answered.

He hadn't heard a friggin' word of hers, but what the hell else was she going to do to get moving on the old timers' loot caper? "Buzz me on my cell."

"I will. I think this might prove interesting, Aubry."

"Yes, I'm sure it will. But you confine your investigation to the center, no roaming around, right? If somebody happened to see one of these pants saggin' knuckleheads hanging around last night, that's my department."

"I got it," she said impatiently. "You know it's not like I haven't faced danger before. Back when I was on the Freedom Rides through the South in the sixties, those rednecks and night riders did their damndest to turn us around, and they didn't. We stuck to our guns, so to speak."

"I know, and I'm proud of you for that," he responded. "But that was a long time ago and you've lost a step or two."

"You not getting any younger yourself."

He patted his rumbling gut. "Ain't that the truth. Talk soon."

"All right." She hung up, humming. She could tell that her nephew had been boozing the night before and she hoped that was the least of his sins. Sarah Hutson wasn't what you'd call a holiness woman, but she did subscribe to the adage about reaping what you sowed. And since the break-up of his marriage, she was very concerned that he was dulling the pain with expensive scotch mixed with hoochie mamas as the kids say. Well, she'd talk with him, but she knew she had to be tactful about it, not confront him and make him defensive. Her nephew had been head-strong since she didn't know when. She smiled at the memory of her late brother, his father.

She went to the back door and opened it. Mitzy was looking up into one of her grapefruit trees, barking at a squirrel. Nearby was a small patch of freshly turned earth. She'd been busy burying one of her chew toys again. One of them, in the shape of a gun — an ex-cop Aubry knew owned a pet supplies store — was also lying about.

"Come on, girl, let's take a walk."

Mitzy gave the squirrel a few more yelps then bounded inside. The black dog was middle-aged, the offspring of a chow and Labrador. Her tongue, attesting to the chow side of her heritage, was splotched with dark spots. She was medium-sized, about fifty-two pounds with hair that needed trimming and some grey sprouting around her snout. Her tail curved up and over the rear end of her body, and one of her favorite activities was to lie on her side in the sun rolling back and forth as she warmed her belly.

Sarah Hutson's nephew had found the dog as a pup wandering across a baseball diamond in a neighborhood park. The body of a cholo stretched out crucifixion-like over third base with twenty-seven knife wounds in him was the reason Harris had been summoned to the field.

As the cops and techs went about their job, the dog sat on its haunches and watched, its head slightly cocked. After doing what they could at the crime scene, and loading the body for transport to the coroner, Harris was walking away, the dog following him.

"Unless you suddenly learned how to speak human so you can tell me what you saw," he'd joked then, "you're not much use to me, you know that?" But he'd made the mistake of stopping and squatting to scratch the playful pup behind its ear. The dog responded and nibbled at his hand with its sharp new teeth.

"Okay, runt, go find your mother." But Harris knew the dog had been abandoned, though by accident or choice, by canine or owner's will, he couldn't say. Sometimes when the litter is too big, people will get rid of a few of the babies because it is just too many mouths to feed or clean up after. Hell, he'd seen people do all kinds of crazy shit with their own kids if they got to be too much of a burden or they couldn't provide for them. Such behavior was not always out of malice or selfishness, but could be the kind of sacrifice you made for love of the innocents.

The young dog, a female he could now tell, was on its back, its gangly legs and paws wrapped around his hand and wrist as he gently squeezed the animal. He laughed and he realized it had been some time since anything had made him genuinely do so for the joy and not the usual reflexive morbidity that was symbolic of the mental defense mechanisms of his work. Like when one of the patrolmen turned from the pin-cushioned gang member and opined, "One beef tenderloin homeboy coming up." The gathered had chuckled softly at the tasteless reference.

And the pup was cute.

Sarah Hutson smiled, recalling the story. She and the dog, on one of those retractable leashes, made their way up the flagstone path to the Brookside Senior Center. "Let's go around this way, girl." Aunt Sarah tugged on the dog as she dug her snout in the hedges lining the walkway. Mitzy offered token resistance, then, tail wagging and head moving, she went along.

In the rear of the building was a parking lot area bordered in by a low cinder block wall. A shuffleboard court had been painted on the black top, and there was talk of erecting a putting green, too. Beyond the wall stretched a line of single family homes reflecting the moderate income neighborhood the center abutted. But it was the rear fire safety door that was of immediate interest to her. Mr. Stovall was already busy working on the steel jamb and lock.

"Eric, how are you?" she greeted him. Mitzy sniffed at his legs, wagging her tail.

"Doing okay, Sarah." Stovall was the Center's unofficial handyman. He was in his late sixties and had retired from the printing business. The Center received city funds and attention, but repairs had to be processed through a central office, and this included forms and waiting. It had proven much more efficient to impose upon the mechanically inclined Stovall to handle a broken window or leaking pipe. The cost of such materials another use of the secret slush fund.

"So how'd they get it?" Aunt Sarah got closer, peering at the area around the lock where she could see gouges. Mitzy sniffed at the oily wrenches and sockets in Stovall's toolbox.

"The old-fashioned way," he grunted as he pried at the partially smashed lock guard with a large blade screwdriver to loosen it. He'd already taken out the screws. "Whoever it was used a heavy duty pry bar and stuck it between the door and jamb and wrenched this rascal open."

She shook a finger at the decal of Gladiator Security stuck on the door ironically near the violated lock. "Why didn't the alarm go off?"

A wan smile appeared then retreated from Stovall's craggy face. "I've got to get finished here, okay?"

She frowned but didn't pursue more inquiries with him. No sense half-stepping, as her comrades in the Black Panthers used to say. It was time to go to the source. "Thanks, Eric."

"No problem."

Sarah Hutson guided Mitzy away and back around front and into the Center. There was a hallway that led to the large activities room where lunch was also served each day. To her right were stairs leading up to the classroom spaces on the second story. A flyer taped to the wall to her left announced the square dance this coming Thursday night. Also to her left was a large glass pane behind which was a small receptionist's area used for storage. Deeper into the space was the door that let into Olivia Kelley's office. Her door was open, and Hutson could see the Center's director was on the phone. She tied Mitzy's leash to a chair in the storage area and waited. The dog panted and looked around and spied a trash can underneath the desk. She began poking in the receptacle, tail wagging.

"Do you have a moment?" Hutson asked as the other woman hung up the phone.

"Sure, Sarah, come on in." The large solid woman waved a hand at her cramped quarters. Aside from her gray industrial desk piled on one side with file folders and an over-stuffed letter caddy, there was her banker's chair, a bulletin board with a blizzard of papers on it, boxes of photocopy paper in a corner, another chair, and the plaster bust of Paul Robeson set atop a dented file cabinet.

"I know this might sound odd," Hutson began as she sat down. "But how did the thief know the alarm company bill hadn't been paid?"

Olivia Kelly clasped one large hand over the knuckles on the other. "Mr. Stovall should learn to keep his own counsel."

"He does, Olivia. I guessed that was the case since the robber had been so blatant at gaining entry."

"It's not a question of malfeasance."

"Oh, that never crossed my mind."

The director let her long fingers spread out, palms up, on her desktop. "Last week I got into a, shall we say, sharp discussion with that absolute imbecile Clevont Williamson over him increasing his rates without any prior notice."

"Williamson is the man who owns the alarm company the Center subscribed to?"

"Yes," she drawled. "His sister attends my church and everything had been fine for the three years we've been using them. Or rather," she quickly added, "until the last two months or so."

"What happened then?"

Mitzy peered around the corner, a Jack in the Box hamburger wrapper in her mouth. She then ducked her head back and could be heard gnawing on her find.

Both women laughed softly. Olivia Kelly went on. "Maybe it's the downturn in the economy or, well, I shouldn't say, but I do hear Williamson likes the ponies."

"And they've been running again." Hutson didn't bet extravagantly, but followed the horses enough to feel comfortable wagering to place at the track occasionally. Plus the serving staff was in the United Food and Commercial Workers Union, and she'd once been an organizer for them years ago. She justified to herself that by patronizing the racetrack, she was contributing to worker security. And maybe making a buck or two on a nag's nose to invoke Damon Runyon.

"Anyway," the director was saying, "I understand his losses were up, and like any business, big or small, he sought to pass his bad judgments on to the consumer. I told him I didn't appreciate his shenanigans last week after getting a fax from him announcing his unjustified price increase." An uncomfortable look momentarily scrunched her face. "You've got me gossiping here, Sarah. What would my pastor say?"

"Could be you're doing the Lord's work, Olivia." Mitzy barked but it was her happy one. She must have discovered a morsel of cheese or meat on the wrapper she was chewing on.

"Really," the other woman answered dubiously. She was ready to get back to her work.

"This is how we find out who really did the break-in. If it really was someone from the outside."

Olivia Kelly let a hearty burst of laughter escape from her ample body. "You're going to be the urban version of Jessica Fletcher? So it's an inside job, Sarah? Then why bust up the door's lock?"

"To make it look like it was a random crime. The slush fund was the only thing taken, right?"

Kelly shook her head. "No, the thief also swiped a Palm Pilot and one of those digital cameras."

"But all stuff out of this office or the front area," Hutson pointed out. "And I bet the robber didn't have to tear up the place looking for our cash reserves."

"But if you broke in, where would you look?" Kelly countered. "It's only logical they'd come into the office first.

"And given the amount of people who traffic here, it's not exactly a state secret that we had the cash on hand."

"That's true. But I'm sure this was all to make it look like it was one of the neighborhood wannabes or panhandlers did the stealing."

The director's shoulders rose and fell. "We'll see," she said, smiling. "Thanks for your time."

She got up and started to reach for Mitzy's leash. "One more thing, Olivia."

"Now you're doing Columbo," she said, snapping her fingers.

"Who else knew about the alarm situation?"

"Only me. In fact, I have a bid from another company I was going to act on today."

"But someone could have easily overheard you talking to Mr. Williamson, isn't that right? You keep your office door open most of the time, and your voice does carry."

"Okay," she nodded, not committing to anything.

Hutson gathered Mitzy from her trash exploration and went back into the hallway. Some folks were arriving for the weekly computer class held in the upstairs classroom.

"Hello, Sarah, and you, too, pooch."

"Hi, Eli." Eli McAlister had worked as a brakeman for the Southern Pacific Railroad and the Santa Fe when the SP had been bought out. He patted Mitzy on the head as he moved past.

"Sarah," Jane Rodriguez greeted.

"Howdy." Rodriguez was still a looker in her late fifties, and worked part-time for the school board in the special education services.

"Been out to the casino lately?"

"Oh, not so much lately, I may get out there next month."

Sarah looked shrewdly at Mitzy who panted, her wet brown eyes returning the attention. She'd gone with Rodriguez and others on turnaround bus excursions to Indian casinos in the high desert. Hutson played the video slot machines but Rodriguez didn't fool around. She took up residence at the poker table. Maybe Rodriguez figured to settle her gambling debts with stolen lucre. Or maybe, she reasoned walking outside with the dog, it was Williamson all along. He knew the alarm system would be off. And he was around the Center enough to have knowledge of the money.

"We have another stop, girl. And you get to ride in the car this time."

Mitzy panted, and her tail whipped back and forth, the rear end of her body doing so also.

In Sarah Hutson's car, a well-worn 1989 Plymouth Gran Fury — the last year the model was made — with a rebuilt engine, Mitzy of course stuck her head out of the partially rolled down window on the passenger side to let the wind course over her snout and ruffle her ears. The companions pulled into a parking slot in front of Gladiator Security Detail. The facility was located in an industrial park of ubiquitous design near the nexus of three freeways and massive power lines. On the roof was a fifty-foot inflated figure of an ancient fighting man that looked, at least to Sarah Hutson, a lot like the late actor Woody Strode in *Spartacus*.

"Here we go." Hutson had the door open and Mitzy leaped out. She sniffed at the ground, her nose searching the new territory for the smell of previous dogs or something to eat.

Hutson clipped on the leash and walked her toward the smoked glass door. The door was locked but a buzz sounded and she pulled it open.

"Yes, can I help you?" The young woman at the front desk had a pierced eyebrow and nose, and a studded tongue. To the left was a set of swing doors. There was also a couch and one of those sawed-off cylinders that passed for a modern coffee table. She gave the dog a raised eyebrow.

Hutson asked for Williamson.

"Do you have an appointment?"

"No, but —" a gunshot cut her off.

"What the hell?" the young woman said, staring wide-eyed and openmouthed.

Mitzy barked and people yelled. The sound of things crashing and going bump against walls could be heard beyond the swing doors. Outside there was the screech of tires and the rending of metal against molded plastic.

Mitzy was shaking and barking and Sarah Hutson was in motion, ducking for cover. She'd been shot at once in the South doing voter registration work among sharecroppers and tenant farmers. Some crackers had let off some buckshot at a van she was riding in, peppering the side of the vehicle with their special greeting. The past collided with her present as she yanked on the terrified dog's leash to also get her behind the couch.

"Oh, Mitzy, please," she pleaded as the dark glass of the front door imploded and a body hurtled through the new opening.

"Better freeze, fool, 'fore I have to regulate." The receptionist produced a slim and efficient black Beretta Centurion.

"Aubry," Sarah Hutson exclaimed, on her hands and knees behind the couch. Mitzy was yipping and yapping, unsure of whether to run to her owner or go around in circles.

"Hold up, I'm a cop," her nephew announced. Bits of the door's safety glass tinkled from him as he thrust his badge at the woman brandishing the gat.

Mitzy peed on the floor and bolted out the busted glass front. The swing doors banged open forcefully and a man flew out, landing on his belly.

The gun-toting receptionist reflexively swung the piece toward this figure and Aubry Harris yelled an order.

"Drop it, lady."

The man on the floor was crawling toward the exit, and from inside the depths of the security company came the timeless strains of Tony Bennett. Momentarily, nobody moved, even the crawling man had stopped, craning a look behind him as Bennett crooned "God Bless the Child." Then a gunshot sounded from within, ceasing the recording.

"Get out of here," Harris hollered at his aunt. "And take La Femme Nikita with you." He jerked his gun at the now crouching receptionist. The crawling man had resumed his progress.

"Aubry, what's —" Sarah Hutson started to ask as her nephew he ran past her and into the depths of the facility.

"Get out," he repeated. Hutson and the receptionist joined the crawling man out front. They hunkered down behind a blue Navajo, peering around the corners of the large SUV.

"Who's shooting?" Sarah Hutson asked. She didn't see the dog.

"Don't know," the scared man answered. "I was rewiring an alarm box and all of a sudden there's shouting and cursing and shooting. I didn't ask the particulars, lady." He looked back at the building then the expanse of the rest of the industrial park. "If I were you two, I'd get the hell out of here." And with that, he was up and running around a corner.

"Chump," the young woman with the Beretta snarled contemptuously. "Don't worry, ma'am, they ain't gonna get us. You remind me of my grandmother."

"Thanks. But it's my nephew I'm worried about."

Backing out the entrance came a man with his hands out in front of him. His pants were down around his ankles and he wore loose boxer shorts with anchors on them.

He was vociferously shaking those hands as if warding off an attack. His opponent was soon apparent as a woman in hip-hugger jeans and platform shoes also stepped out. It was evident that she was the shooter. The .38 in her hand was very steady on the object of her wrath.

"You must take me for a fourteen-karat fool." She advanced on the retreating man.

"Naw, naw, baby, it ain't like that." He almost tripped over his pants down around his shoes.

"Then why don't you tell me what it was like?"

"Shayla," Aubry Harris called out, having

finally remembered her name and who she was. "Put that damned gun down. So far, you've just shot into the air and at a CD player. But you're about to make one big nasty mistake." He was on one knee in the doorway, his nine-millimeter held shooting-range fashion aimed at her back. His finger squeezed slowly down on the trigger.

"The only mistake I made was trusting this bastard."

"Baby, let's talk this over. This is all a mistake." He was backed up against the Navajo, sweating profusely. The receptionist and Sarah Hutson were crouched on the other side and the young woman was determined to use her gat.

"I'm gonna bag this chick," she promised through gritted teeth. The woman started to rise.

"Let the professionals handle this, miss." Sarah Hutson grabbed the woman's shoulders from behind and wrenched. The Beretta spasmed upward and let off two rounds. Mitzy, who'd been under the Fury, darted out and barked and growled at Shayla as the pleading man fainted. Later, he'd state he believed Shayla had an accomplice, and this one bushwhacked him from behind. Shayla kicked at Mitzy as the inflatable Gladiator deflated, having been wounded by the Beretta's bullets. Mitzy ran around her and nipped at her legs as Harris crept up quickly. The rubberized sword and arm of the giant fell across the angry woman, obscuring her vision momentarily. This gave Harris enough time to tackle her. As she hit the ground, her grip loosened on the gun and it slid across the asphalt. The two became tangled in the giant balloon's material.

Sirens punctuated the air and employees of Gladiator Security Detail, including terrified security guards, came outside as Aubry Harris, having gotten free, cuffed the maddened woman.

"You stick around, too, homegirl," he told the gun-happy receptionist. On the ground was his cold piece. Mitzy was on her haunches, happy that Harris and Aunt Sarah weren't hurt. She was right next to the incriminating weapon.

"Hey, Lil Kim," Harris said to the receptionist, "I've got a deal for you." He didn't wait for an answer and then addressed his dog. "Mitz, toy, toy," and pointed vigorously as the law arrived and his dog took off with her prize.

That weekend, Harris was over at his aunt's house for breakfast.

"I hope this has been a warning for you, Aubry." She pushed the plate of sausage links toward him. "Have some more."

"Oh yes," he admitted, "I know Shayla smelled the lonely on me, Aunt Sarah. But when you get dumped, you want to believe some hot chick still finds you, well, you know." He chewed his biscuit.

She sipped more coffee. "Only she knew you were a cop and played you, as the young folks say. Debbie, or Shayla as she goes by when she's gyrating on a pole, went home with you figuring that was the fastest way to get a hold of a gun to go after this —"

"Pete Hamilton," he finished. "He was an installer for Gladiator Security and was always looking to get rich quick. He falls for this line of b.s. put out by these guys who set up an office where he put in the alarms. They tell him they're gonna have so much money going through there, they'd have to buy wheelbarrows to take it out." He shook his head. "Some people are so gullible."

She didn't comment on his unintended ironic observation. "But it was really just a new version of the Ponzi scheme."

He dug at a piece of gristle between his front teeth with a fingernail. "Uh-huh. Get the suckers to buy in, and pay off the next round with that money while raking off healthy administrative fees. So of course Hamilton gets taken and his family members he convinced to go in on this. And in particular he's got a brother-in-law who's done hard time very bent out of shape about his lack of monetary return."

His aunt nibbled on some of her egg. "So in desperation he ripped off his girl-friend, Shayla's, tip box where she kept the bills you men slip into her G-string."

He nodded, a rueful grin on his face. "And he knocked over the senior center 'cause he knew the alarm was out and had heard from his grandmother who goes there about the slush fund. But one of the women who strips with Shayla had seen Hamilton sneaking out of the dressing room a week ago and she started to plan her revenge."

Aunt Sarah snorted. "And she caught him when he was in the rest room at work."

"Yep."

In exchange for Harris getting Olivia Kelly not to press charges, Pete Hamilton agreed to make restitution. He was going to have to work a lot of nights cleaning up the Polka-Dot Tiger as their part-time janitor. Shayla would also get paid back as long as she kept cool about where she got the gun.

Williamson would get the Senior Center contract back, at a slight but by no means unfair increase, as long as Harris was glowing in his report of how the receptionist had helped in the situation — even though her gun was unregistered. The D.A. was content to charge both women with misdemeanors as long as everyone was satisfied. Of course there was still the matter of what happened to the .38 that Shayla had used. She said she'd dropped it inside the Gladiator office, but it hadn't turned up yet.

"Hey, Mitz," Harris called. The dog was under the sink, her head in the trash as usual. She looked up and padded across the linoleum to him. He gave her a piece of sausage.

Hutson sighed. "Even making your sweet dog an accomplice in all this."

Harris scratched Mitzy at the base of her jaw. "Can I help it if she likes to bury guns? Anyway, I've learned my lesson, right? No more boozin' and chasing fast women."

His aunt reserved a comeback. "Did I understand you have a date tonight?"

Consternation puckered his lips. "Yep."

"Who is it?"

"Her name's Ginger."

"That's a nice, wait, isn't that the receptionist from the security company?"

"She's all right, Aunt Sarah."

"She's gun crazy."

"She's just high-strung."

"You like excitement too much."

"It runs in the family."

Mitzy barked in agreement.

Black Zak and the Heart Attack

by Noreen Ayres

What is more mysterious than a cat?

"One can never be sure," Helen Thomson writes, "watching two cats washing each other, whether it's affection, the taste, or a trial run for the jugular."

When Zak came to rule in his new abode, he was a mere fistful of fluff. His tail looked like a tiny spike with metal fillings at alert from proximity to a magnet.

I worried it would remain that pathetic spear. How could I face the neighbors? Eight months later, it's the length of a garden snake and communicates mood in its own magical semaphoric manner. Mood, I say? Barely repressed ferocity defines it all. I don't protect

Zak from the outdoors. I protect the outdoors from him.

Zak is a Wal-Mart cat. One evening as I left the store, two dopey heads bobbed up from a cardboard carton on a woman's lap; two dopey heads to go, she had said.

A friend named him for me. She had just been given a prescription for the famous mood leveler bearing a similar-sounding name. Oh, for an apt cat dose when Zak acts up, I threaten it's back to Wal-Mart. Does he listen? No.

He's also known as The Plumber. Mornings find a track throughout the house of dispersed drain covers, four-inch sink stoppers, and trails of unrolled toilet paper. Yet, he knows one leap into my lap with a throaty purring and I am his forever.

How can a creature of such perfect gravitational poise manage to keep us vastly superior two-legged beings emotionally off balance? The answer is simple: They have us. Cats quietly await taking over the world. Dogs, on the other hand, would rather play ball. God love 'em both, but hand me that prescription bottle over there, will you?

— Noreen Ayres

Black Zak sat on the railing soaking up a patch of autumn sun.

Twenty steps away under the wood canopy of The Chowder Inn, RuthEllen Morris tore open a new sack of cornmeal and grumbled at her helper, Smithy, "We'll never get rid of that cat now," she said.

"You know how many cats roam around here?"

"Too darn many, is what."

"That there is one fine feline. Smithy knows his kitties."

"You think."

"Once in a while I do," he said, "but I'll try and correct my ways."

A nanosecond-grin passed over Ruth-Ellen's face.

Eight months ago, Smithy came upon the kitten under the dock. The wee thing was bedraggled and bespotted with some kind of undercarriage oil, and between his tiny toes lodged globs of sand tar. Such a sorry beginning kept the furry thing from trusting anyone for long. Two friendly scratches behind an ear and he'd disappear like a shadow when the sun goes down.

"Fill the coffee urns yet?" RuthEllen asked over her shoulder.

"What I'm doing right now," Smithy said, "if you'd quit worrying about that cat and pay attention to what goes on around here."

He could talk to his boss that way, considering what she could afford to pay. In truth, he did all right for himself from a combination of his tightwad nature, Social Security, and a pension from the brick-layer's union. As for her sentiments about the cat, Smithy had twice spied her tossing tidbits to the stray herself.

"Where you want that crate of cod coming in?"

"Leave it outside," RuthEllen said. "No time to deal with that now."

"They're about to power-wash out there. They want all the outside stuff inside."

"Then put it inside," RuthEllen said, widening her eyes as if the solution was a no-brainer. She hefted a box of potatoes onto the sideboard, tumbled some into the sink, the stainless steel ringing from their onslaught, then took to scrubbing the spuds with a brush.

Smithy came forward, wiping his nose with the back of his wrist. "No room."

"Oh fer cryin' out loud," RuthEllen said. She shook water off her hands and dried them on her jeans.

"More canned stuff coming, too," Smithy said.

"I know what I ordered," RuthEllen said.

Opening the oversized pantry at the back of the store, she commenced to shoving around food boxes and jugs of cooking oil until she made room for the crate of onions and two bags of rock salt stacked outside the back door. She huffed and puffed until she came up with room on the lower shelf for the box of fresh cleaning rags that had also been outside a day too long, miracle they weren't stolen.

"See," she said, "plenty of room. Let's do the freezer."

"No room in there either."

"Those potatoes are growing eyes in the sink while you stand there and argue," she said.

Smithy stood by her as she opened the lid to the big horizontal freezer. His sleeve brushed hers when he reached in, saying, "I'll get this here." It amused him to know she'd pull away as if she saw a frozen shark come to life. In that reticence she had much in common with Zak the Cat.

"Okay, then," RuthEllen said, and strode back to her potatoes.

The way that woman kept the freezer you'd think harbor seals dined and nested there each night. Smithy unstacked the first two layers and re-stacked them, making much more room.

When he was done and came back around the wall into the main cooking/serving area, he saw Fred Gonzalez perched on a wooden stool in front of the serving bar watching RuthEllen cut up spuds. Fred with his knit cap riding his eyebrows; Fred with his eyes always on RuthEllen's hips. Saying, "It's in the paper. Want me bring it down?"

Fred owned a produce stand up on the street that T-ed into where The Chowder Inn and half a dozen other stores pegged onto the pier. Fred's three sons tended his stand, allowing him to wander over to RuthEllen's whenever he wanted to be a pest.

"You don't have to bring the paper down. I believe you," RuthEllen said, and hacked at her potatoes harder.

Her face was flushed. Last week she'd come from the doctor's reporting high blood pressure. Could lose a few pounds, she reported. Smithy said if she was any more good-looking she'd get arrested. She told him he didn't have to give an answer for everything she said, but a blush extended from her neck to her cheekbone.

Fred was still jawing when Smithy went

to get a rag to wipe down the inside and outside tables. On the rail outside sat Zak with his eyes shut as if dreaming of slow salmon. Nary a gull flutter caused him to stir. Customers with hot coffee and pastries from the shop next door passed by speaking softly, as if louder tones might disturb a touchy king at snooze.

"How do you like our hood ornament?" Smithy asked.

"Beautiful," a woman in the set of three said.

"Hey, BlackJack," Smithy said. "Hear that?"

Zak's amber eyes cracked open, then shut again.

"BlackJack?" RuthEllen called.

"Black Zak, BlackJack, whatever," said Smithy. "Black Art, Black Bart, the Black Sheep of Ocean Street."

"Don't get carried away," RuthEllen said, "or you might find out he's a Black Belt."

"Har-dee-har har," Smithy said.

Detouring, he gave kitty a quick ear scratch, timing it so his hand was gone by the time the cat would try to sucker-nip him. Back to working, he heard Fred again and wished he didn't.

"This whole place will change. Frisbee

pizza and rubber burgers. Cat-food tacos. Bean sprouts in glue — same thing you can get at the mall. In six months this place will look like a dance floor in Death Valley."

"That's pretty good, Fred."

"What's pretty good?"

"That speech. But I think you're worrying too much," RuthEllen said.

"Oh? Why you so mad, then?"

"What makes you think I'm mad?"

"That frown on your face."

"Please don't tell me to smile, Fred. I hate that."

"But, you're so —"

"Go ahead. Say it, Fred. Say it in front of a knife-wielding woman."

Fred Gonzales knew how to flirt about as well as Smithy knew how to sew a hoop skirt. Such a nerd. Why RuthEllen just didn't insult him for good and good-bye was a puzzle.

Fred continued. "Me, I'm going to have a talk with Albert."

"Albert?"

"Yah, Albert. Big Singapore company's coming in, what the paper says."

"Now let's see if I got this straight," RuthEllen said, directing silent music with her potato knife. "Big Singapore company's coming in, so you think because Albert's last name is Ling he has some pull."

Fred shrugged. "Can't hurt."

"Sometimes I think you'd try to catch raindrops in a fishnet, Freddie."

The man grinned like a boy every time RuthEllen called him Freddie.

"I've got an idea," Smithy said, coming up, but neither of the two asked what it was. "What you need to do is hold a meeting of all the lease holders. Set it up for tonight, impromptu."

"Impromp who?" asked Fred.

Smithy considered the man. "Spur of the moment," Smithy said.

"Might not be a bad idea," said RuthEllen. "I'm willing to have it here. Say, ten, ten-thirty. We can strategize."

"If all of us get together, those big guys won't dare come in."

"Don't be a dummy," RuthEllen said. "They can do whatever they damn well please. But we might be able to hold them off a while."

"Sock it to 'em, Ruthie!"

"Please don't call me Ruthie, Fred."

"Okay, dear."

"Don't call me dear, either."

Fred gazed stupidly after her a moment, then looked at Smithy and winked.

★ ★ ★

That night, Smithy kept the coffee coming and the free fish-balls, but that was all that he dispensed for free, following RuthEllen's orders. When the discussion started, he sat on a bench at the back, watching the way certain store owners postured and certain others sulked as if forced to be there; you'd think those last would have just gone on home.

John Ferguson said how he had always been a believer in progress. "My way of thinking — and no personal offense to anyone here — but if a shopkeeper can't manage any better than to be bought out, why then, 'Happy Trails to You', and that includes me."

"You're missing the point, John," said Stacey Segrim, a woman who owned a bead shop on the street. Her windows displayed driftwood with strings of beads draped over them. "This is not failure of any one store. This is Big Money wanting more money. They won't buy us out. What they'll do is hike leases sky-high. They don't care a recession's on. I say don't sign. Don't sign and don't budge. Like a homeowner's association."

"She's right," Mitchell Oolong said. "What do foreigners care about keeping the special nature of this area?" In Mitchell's veins coursed Pacific Islander blood, but he preferred his Italian side. He ran a pizzeria.

"May I remind you," said John, "we were all foreigners at one time?"

"Not me," Fred Gonzales said. "I was born here."

"Our parents or grandparents, Fred," John said, rolling his eyes.

Sam Bohannon, owner of a fish market, stood and said, "Listen, folks, not signing lease papers seems all well and good, like a union going on strike, huh? But think about it. Sooner or later, one month or three, we'll be evicted if we don't pay. I for one can't afford to go anywhere else. Anywhere you go there will be higher lease amounts, not to mention the sheer disruption of moving, the starting over. . . ." His words trailed away as he picked up his foam cup and headed off to the coffee urn.

"Somehow," young Stacey said, "we find a way to wag the dog, not the other way around."

RuthEllen had been quiet but now she spoke, asking if any one of them had actually met or talked to the new property owners. "How do we know this company's intentions? It's common practice to raise lease amounts at renewal time anyway, no matter who's holding papers. How much did yours go up two years ago, Harvey? Seems to me we may be panicking here."

Harvey, one of the sulkers who owned an antique shop on Ocean Street, merely twisted on the bench and shrugged.

RuthEllen said, "Let's send a spokesman."

"No good," Mitchell Oolong said. "The handwriting's on the wall."

"Mine won't be on any new lease," Stacey Segrim said.

Dan Burgess said, "Let's get an attorney on it."

"You want to give money to a lawyer," Stacey said, "when you already know what the outcome will be?" She held a twenty-six-year-old's hard certainty.

"Lawyers can be a great investment," he replied. As a tree-trimmer, Dan lost an arm to a wayward chainsaw when it hit a rock in a squirrel's nest. Aided by the artful prodding of a lawyer, Dan was able to open his souvenir shop with money from a reluctant insurance company.

"I say go along to get along," John continued. "Cooperate. Explain our position. Tell the new owners — Zang Limited, right? Tell these guys our goal of keeping this area unique. Who knows, they might even have a few new ideas to throw into the pot to pick up sales."

Dan Burgess lifted from his shirt pocket the rose-tinted glasses he wore during the day and handed them over to John. "Here, take these. They're better suited to you than me." Even the two sulkers laughed.

"Albert," RuthEllen said, "what's your opinion?" Albert, a quiet man who did a lot of body bobbing when he spoke.

"Good businessmen look to future."

"What about Wynona?" As if RuthEllen needed to ask. Wynona Ling could qualify for boot camp sergeant. Smithy had a wife like that once, back when he thought a seven-course meal was a six-pack and a toothpick. She turned out to be two shades meaner than the devil himself. Wynona Ling, a woman who towered over Albert, could easily be her sister.

"My wife say big company not hurt us. She home right now, our daughter visit, but she think like me, yes." Surely Albert rejoiced to have his helpmeet anywhere but occupying square footage within his hearing. His dear wife's bellows could be heard by passersby even with the shop door closed, more so lately.

The evening wore on, with John and

Dan proffering tales of how changes of fortune often worked out better than thought. Mitchell Oolong was coming around, and even Stacey was weakening though she confessed to thinking about moving to Hawaii anyway.

Then Wynona Ling showed up, bringing poppyseed lemon rolls and special herb tea. She wore a blue flowered dress and had her blonde hair loose instead of in its usual topknot, and she was sweetly subdued, serving everyone while the talk went on. It passed through Smithy's thoughts that Albert must have fed her a tranquilizer chased with some Far Eastern love potion. She sat next to Albert, every once in a while smoothing the recalcitrant stub of hair at his crown.

At a quarter to twelve, when the gatherers were beginning to stand and adjust jackets, Wynona spoke: "I have something for you to look at," she said. "It came to us first because our lease is up next month, earlier, I think, than all the rest of you." She didn't read the document she held, but summarized. It was an offer from Zang Ltd, to renew leases in one-year terms instead of three, with the inducement of a fifty-dollar a month decrease. Her audience was stunned. A landlord who gives up money? "A gesture of good will," she explained. "I spoke with Mister Chu, who clarified, because like you I wondered." She laughed then, like it was all a false scare, and urged everyone to look it over for themselves when their offer came in this week.

Smithy could read RuthEllen's look through a brick wall. She began picking up three paper cups at a time and gathering paper dishes. She stopped, looked at Wynona, and said, "You might as well feed that letter to the seagulls, Wynona, for all it's worth." But other store owners had had enough. They trundled off while Wynona offered a few more words to RuthEllen and RuthEllen went about her business, until the voice of the woman in the blue flowered dress began to get its familiar edge and Albert tugged her away.

Smithy helped clean up the last of the tables, then emptied the trash to the outside bins, and lowered and locked the rolling overhead barricades that enclosed the store. As RuthEllen was about to flip off the remaining light, Smithy held out a knit ski cap and said, "I guess Gonzales left this."

"Mm," she said, taking it distractedly and then spinning it toward the counter. It lit on a pickle jar.

"You okay?" Smithy asked her.

"Sure. Got a little headache is all."

"Want me to walk you to your car?"

"You're parked down the other way," she said. "But thanks for staying, Smithy. I appreciate it."

He stepped out ahead of her as she closed the door. They walked to the street together. Her gaze focused on something he couldn't see. "I'm not afraid of hard work," she said, "you know that."

"No argument on that score."

"But sometimes it feels like I'm holding back the tide with a teaspoon."

At the corner, the red hand glowed in the traffic box. Smithy stood with his hands in his pockets, saying, "Yeah, I know."

He did know, yes. The few times he ever mentioned his past it was in a jocular manner, making out to be a rolling-stone renegade. The facts were that in his time he had funneled through two trades, three businesses, four marriages, and a little flirting with the questionably legal. He at last came to feel the world was a pretty good place after all, and made a sort of wry and conservative peace with it overall.

But RuthEllen was not at that place yet. Smithy knew she had justification for her cloudy outlook. Five years ago she opened Chowder's, making it work as much to spite the husband who left her after she had a breast removed from cancer as anything else. The woman was pluck and gumption and plenty pretty at fifty-three. She had an uppity daughter in Silicon Valley and a son who'd chucked it all a decade ago and went to live in a power-free cabin somewhere in Alaska. RuthEllen was on her own. Perhaps she needed to be the one holdout in making nice with Zang Limited because any sign of caving in would signal the start of far worse concessions to fate and unfriendly circumstance.

The two said their see-you's on the sidewalk under the mist-shrouded street lamp, and then she went one way and he the other.

And in the morning when Smithy walked inside Chowder's and saw nothing set up, when he noticed no familiar coat on the brass hook and called RuthEllen's name without an answer, he knew he'd better hustle. He took hold of the handle to the large food pantry where the coffee was stored, and when he did so, Black Zak shot out, offering the only sighting of him within the restaurant proper at any time before. The cat flanked to the back door and curled in a C-shape in an effort to display his threatening size.

"Hold on, there, partner," Smithy said, slowly reaching for the handle to open the back door, and the felonious feline departed in a streak.

Now, how'd he get in here? Smithy wondered.

He glanced at the clock on the wall, the one with the image of a leaping swordfish in the center, and wondered if RuthEllen ran out of gas or decided, like Stacey, Hawaii looked a whole lot better than routine.

He filled the coffee filter baskets, flipped the switch for the water, and then, wanting the fresh half-and-half instead of that packaged chalk they call powdered milk, he opened the door to the walk-in cooler . . . and found her.

He brought thirty-six daffodils, all of them open.

"She can't have them in there," one nurse at the central station said.

"Sure, she can," Smithy told her, giving the nurse a bricklayer's stare, the face you present after laying brick for twenty-five years and your knees are gone and your rotator cuff has turned to pumice and grinds the nerves to sweet agony on cold mornings.

"On the windowsill, then," she said, "so they don't get knocked off."

He set the flowers on RuthEllen's bedside tray where she would see them if she should crack open an eye from inside the well of coma.

Emergency personnel thought an episode of vomiting triggered by a heart attack blocked her airway, causing brain damage. Later, the hospital resident said she suspected RuthEllen had had a stroke. Diagnosis might as well be multiple choice, it seemed to Smithy.

He studied her as she lay there, her face pallid, her lips bleached white. Even her ash-brown hair looked thinner. At her temple was a bump the size of a golf ball. "RuthEllen," Smithy said, but her eyes stayed shut all the same. He picked up the hand that held all compliance and no protest in it and said, "You hang in there. Smithy will take care of bidness, you betcha."

Smithson Tillett in his youth had been an angry man. In maturer days he'd tamped down tantrums but became instead a fool for spirit juice. Now he'd found a better path and would not turn back for provocation, yet a demonizing thing beyond the simple worry over the health and future of a good woman kept Smithy from sleeping. Early the next morning he caught up with the doctor making her rounds. He wanted to ask about that bump on RuthEllen's head, if that could have caused her coma.

"The injury to her temple indicates she did suffer a fall, though there is no fracture nor concussion."

Smithy said, "There was blood on the corner of a crate of oranges."

"Another cause of disorientation," the doctor said, "could come from having eaten tainted food."

"We don't have nothing like that at Chowder's," Smithy said, her remark close to a personal insult.

Unfazed, the doctor said, "We'll run tests to see if she suffered a severe bout of gastroenteritis. Frankly, her symptomology is a bit different from that expected following ingestion of paralytic shellfish biotoxins, but that would be my guess as of now."

Smithy didn't say that's why they call it medical practice, huh?, but it was wanting to jump out.

The doc went on: "We're having a very hard time getting her blood pressure to rise. And are you sure, sir, that Miss Morris did not eat any blue mussels prior to her incapacitation?"

"No, and she's got high blood pressure," Smithy said.

"Mm," the doctor said, not hearing him at all.

"It will be interesting if . . . when she awakens to see how potent her memory is." The doctor scrunched her brow, thinking.

"Ma'am?"

"Given an ingestion of blue mussel, which can carry what is known as amnesic toxins, short-term memory may be severely compromised."

Smithy was trying to hold on to the equanimity he was so proud to claim. "We don't serve mussels, and she's around seafood all day and is not inclined to eat it on off hours. Besides, I was with her all day, and —"

"Check with us tomorrow, I hope we've learned something by then."

Lady, you better sign up for a class in listening, Smithy thought.

Back at Chowder's, he hung a "Closed for Vacation/Come Back Soon" sign on the outside and went down to see Fred Gonzales. He asked Fred to step outside, out the back way so that it was just him and Fred in a cold, narrow passageway. Smithy maneuvered the man against the telephone pole and the trash can chained to it.

"I see you found your knit cap," Smithy said.

"Huh? Yes, I found it."

"It was on the pickle jar," Smithy said.

Gonzales looked beyond Smithy's shoulder for help from one of his sons. "So what? What the heck's the matter with you?"

"Let's see if we can put two and two together here. Maybe you see RuthEllen out in the parking lot, and you ask her to let you back in the store for your hat." Smithy yanked the cap off Freddie's head and tossed it away. He grabbed Fred's shirt, twisting it under his chin, while his right fist hung ready. "So, what'd you do, make a pass? I'll kick your butt till your teeth fall out your shorts."

"Hey!" One of Fred's son's applied a pincer-grip on the top of Smithy's shoulder, but Smithy's backhand sent him reeling. Fred squealed in pain as Smithy wrenched Fred's arm behind his back.

" 'Fess up, you little twerp."

Fred's other two sons stood staring in

the shadowed interior among the mounds of cabbage heads and apples.

"You hit her, didn't you?"

"Nothing, nothing," the terrified little man screamed.

Then the lights went out for Smithy, as Fred's oldest son whopped him at the base of the skull with a piece of cut rubber hose.

Fred wouldn't let his son call the cops. Instead, he lifted Smithy's head and gave him a drink of apple cider, which left him coughing. Smithy looked him in the eye and said, "That all the better you can do?"

"Hoy," Fred said, "I thought I was a dead man."

Freddie and his two sons helped Smithy up and stumbled him inside and sat him on the hardest, coldest chair ever built to torture man. Fred said, "Something come to me while you were out. I did go back to get my hat, that's right. But early this morning. The back door was open. I go in and there's Albert's wife at the sink, scrubbing her arm fierce like at the sink."

"Washing her arm?"

"Yeah. She says she scraped her arm on a nail. I say, I come to get my hat. She says, Go get it. I look around for RuthEllen, just stand there a minute. RuthEllen stepped out a minute, she says. She didn't seem like she was wanting to talk, so I left. But it's funny, don' you think?"

"I can't think nothin', you clobbering me like you did."

"Ouch," Freddie said, touching his own head as if he hurt. "I apologize, my fren', but you come at me like that, what's my boy to do?"

Smithy said, "Sorry, guy," and stuck out a hand and Fred put his in it.

This time when Smithy went back to the restaurant he snooped around like a detective. In the second sink was a milky brown liquid captured because the stopper was turned. The natural thing was to assume it was coffee, but Smithy had cleaned up well the night before. He put a finger to it and smelled, then licked it. Faintly onion but not quite. He got a teaspoon and dipped all he could into a clean salt shaker, took a paper napkin to soak up the rest and squeezed it in too, then screwed the cap on over a piece of tinfoil and stuck the shaker in his jacket pocket.

He went to the walk-in cooler and opened the door and just stood there, seeing in his mind's eye his poor RuthEllen sprawled there in her own vomit and excretion, her pupils unevenly wide but welcoming as death's door.

Before leaving, he shoved a hand into a sack of dry cat food he kept under the cooker in a place RuthEllen wouldn't see it. When he stepped out, there he was, Black Zak on the railing a few feet away. "Keeping an eye out, boy?" Smithy asked.

Still as stone.

"Okay, don't talk. Hold down the fort then, will ya? Back in a little while." Smithy set the handful of chow down on the deck near the wall of the building. That's when he spotted a broken piece of bowl behind a bucket. The ceramic was of a blue and white pattern. It still had moisture in it from contents. But what was it doing here, near a trash can they hardly ever used because it was too small? He stepped to the inset where it was lodged and tugged off the lid. Inside were more pieces of bowl. He'd seen that pattern before. When he looked up, trying to remember where, he saw Zak in his ready-to-flee mode, hair flared like the standing quills of a porcupine.

Smithy retrieved the shattered pieces, set them in a paper bag, then walked toward Albert Ling's to maybe buy an egg roll.

A bell tinkled when he shoved open the

door. Inside, he sat at the counter, placing the sack of broken china there. Two college kids had papers spread out on one of the tables. Empty cups and bits of fortune cookie poised on the one next to them. Wynona Ling looked through the cutout to the kitchen. "Hello, Smithy," she said. "Egg foo yong or omelet?"

"How about some tea?" Smithy said.

"You got it. Be right with you."

Smithy stepped over to the college-aged pair and said, "Howdy." The guy looked up with a mildly contemptuous question on his face. The girl kept her gaze on the odd man. Smithy laid a twenty on the table. "Get lost, will ya?" he said.

Slowly the boy slid papers together, stuffed them in a backpack, swiped up the bill, and headed for the door. The girl muttered a weak thank you as they left.

Wynona came out with a hot pot of tea, casting an eye to see if her customers left money or skipped. "This is yours," Smithy said, and handed her five bucks.

She set down the pot to shove the money in her apron pocket. "How's RuthEllen? Gee, what a deal. She's pretty young for a heart attack."

Smithy did not mention the doctor's dart game diagnosis, just said with assurance, "She'll be up and around soon, if I know RuthEllen."

Wynona's face played melodies of concern as she set a cup and saucer before him. "She did seem like she didn't feel well at the meeting."

"She was just tired."

"Oh?"

Smithy reached in the pocket of his coat to retrieve the shaker holding the tea-colored fluid. He unscrewed the cap, sniffed the contents, and offered the vial to Wynona's opinion. "You wouldn't know what this is, would you?"

Hesitantly, she took a whiff. "Why, no, Smithy," she said, all smiley. "What is it?"

"And you didn't happen to see Ruth-Ellen after the meeting, did you?"

"RuthEllen? Why, no. I mean, we all left about the same time, right?"

"I'm asking you."

"Well, I'm telling you." The old Wynona starting to come out.

"So you didn't maybe bring RuthEllen something to eat early in the morning or nothing like that?"

"Not I, nuh-uh." She glanced at the door.

"The lock's thrown."

"Pardon?"

Smithy set down the shaker and unfolded the sack with the pieces of bowl in it and slid them onto the counter. The small muscles in Wynona's face tightened ever so slightly.

"What's all that?"

"Well, now," Smithy said. "I figured you'd know. Since the pattern matches this here you use." Wynona remained silent. "I figure RuthEllen never made it home after the meeting. I figure she went back to the restaurant, or something called her back to the restaurant."

Wynona took to wiping off things on the counter that weren't there. Smithy grabbed her by the wrist. "What we got here?" he asked. She tried pulling away. "Bad scratch you got there, Wynona. You might want to watch it, see if it becomes infected."

"Infected?"

"Ever hear of cat-scratch fever?"

"No. What is it?"

"Oo, it's a bad one," he said, shaking his head. "I saw a kid sick with it once. He went into convulsions and bit his tongue bloody." Smithy released her. She threw herself back against the cupboards, rubbing the foot-long, fiery red scratch on her arm. "You fed her something, didn't you, Wynona? You came back to Chowder's and gave RuthEllen something. This bowl is from your kitchen. You tried to hide it this morning, but Fred saw you."

"I didn't go back. RuthEllen came over here. I wasn't quite done with putting things away here. She was still a little upset from the meeting, and she wanted to talk some more. I offered her some soup, and put it in there," she pointed to what was once a bowl, "and covered it with a plastic lid. She took it with her. If you found that over there, she must have dropped it."

Smithy gave her that bricklayer's stare. A sheen of perspiration glowed on her brow. "Why don't you tell me the rest of it," he said.

What came out was that Wynona's husband, Albert, owed money to the wrong kind of people, borrowed because the store was doing badly the last twelve months. Then he flew to Vegas. He flew to Reno thereafter, and there he gambled away that money and the money Wynona had saved for their daughter's wedding. He also sold family heirlooms and with the cash visited Indian casinos. As a last gasp, he asked an old friend associated with Zang Limited for help. Help was available if he agreed to persuade the oceanfront leaseholders to sign new leases. In a year or so the lease-holders would be sent packing and Zang would be free to tear down their shops and put up giant hotels. Wynona's world was coming apart. When RuthEllen's reactions foretold yet more obstacles, Wynona made her business neighbor some wild onion soup — roasted wild onion soup. Except another name for that wild onion is Death Cama. "I meant only to make her sick, but not this sick!"

"Just a little sick."

"Yes. Maybe with her history of cancer and all, maybe she would go along then, like the others."

"Quit her business. Not fight."

"Right. I'm sor—"

"You ought to take down all the mirrors in your house, Wynona."

"What? Why's that?"

"You're too ugly to walk by without them cracking six ways to Sunday."

Wynona Ling sat down at one of the tables, lowered her head to her arms, and cried. When she raised up, tears covered her face and her eyes were fiery red. She again looked in dismay at her arm. "Your cat," she said.

"My cat?"

"That black one. He scratched me when

I tried to put him out of the kitchen. Now, I'm the one who's going to get sick!"

Smithy could have told her not to sweat it, that adults don't get cat-scratch fever, but he didn't. He sure wouldn't want to deprive Wynona of something to worry her nights with while she was doing duty on the comfortable cot in county jail. He told Wynona maybe she should give the cops a call herself, tell them what she had done. Maybe they'd go easy on her. He trusted that she was so sure of her own cleverness and powers to persuade that she would. And, the witless thing, that's what she did.

That afternoon, on his way back to Chowder's he looked for Zak, but there was no sign of him. Still, he got out a round of salmon for him anyway and cracked the back door open and set it there, good kitty. Then Smithy went about sprucing up the place for whenever RuthEllen came free of her sleep and made it back. Or, maybe he'd just open up those barricades himself, get yakky Fred to come down and help so he could brag about it to RuthEllen.

Lost
and Found
by Jan Burke

Our dogs, Britches and Cappy, are much beloved mutts from the pound. Both are big dogs, more than seventy pounds each. They are each some sort of shepherd mix, but their personalities are quite distinct. My husband believes that Britches is a cross between Rasputin and a Zamboni. He is the hunter, the living motion detector whose deep bark unsettles those who dare to walk past our home. He loves to startle houseguests by barging into the bathroom at inconvenient moments. (We do warn them to lock the door.) If he ever learns to talk, I believe his first word will be "Charge!" There is never a bad time to play. There is never too much play.

Cappy, on the other hand, is a mix of

clown and gentleman. He is a talking dog, rather than a barker, liable to deliver a lecture on the Dog Bill of Rights if we spend too much of the morning reading in bed. At times, he is so finicky in his ways, we suspect he just may be a cat in a dog suit. He is always thinking. And ten thousand times more devious than Britches.

At least one of them is constantly at my feet when I write at home. They are also herders, and aware of every movement of their human sheep. We refer to them as the DBI — the Dog Bureau of Investigation.

When we were signing Britches out of the animal shelter, we learned that his file included the notation, "Owner was arrested." Although I eventually stopped worrying that some prison escapee might come up to me and shout, "You've got my dawg!" I've continued to wonder about his previous life, and "Lost and Found" gave me a chance to imagine one for him. I was also able to incorporate some of what I learned while researching the character Single, the cadaver dog in the Irene Kelly series.

— Jan Burke

I awoke from a rather pleasant dream in which I was running across the sky, chasing crows. Throughout the dream they had scattered silently before me, unable to caw their alarm, but just before I awakened, the beaks of the dream crows made clicking sounds.

Clicking sounds. I heard them now, and brought my head up. The room was dark, but apparently not dark enough for the ruffian. His nocturnal patrol had taken him down the hallway, and his nails snicked along the hardwood floor.

I sighed, stretched front and back, and checked on the humans. Sound asleep. I expected nothing else, but I know my duty to my pack.

The ruffian heard my approach — I saw his ears flick back — but he did not turn to look at me. He simply stared out at the moonlight, lunatic that he is.

I gracefully lowered myself onto a nearby rug. "You are impossibly rude," I said on a yawn.

"So you've told me," he said, still not looking at me. "Often."

"When an elder dog approaches . . ."

"Yeah, yeah, I know. I'm supposed to grovel and kiss your lips. Go back to bed, Captain."

He was failing to show proper deference,

but at least he had called me Captain. I was pleased by his use of my title from my long ago sea dog life. Some intuition about my pirate days had led our humans to name me "Cappy." Not the same, really, but remarkably close for two-leggers.

I watched the ruffian for a time. He seemed a little downcast. This concerned me. I'm not uncanine, after all — and as I said, I know my duty to my pack.

"What is it, Britches?" I asked, calling him the human's name for him.

He didn't answer.

"You're thinking of your last home, aren't you?"

He remained silent, but I saw the telltale flicker of those big ears of his. (I admit to a little jealousy. His stand upright.)

In our current dog's life, we had each been rescued from death row. Like many other five- to seven-month-old males, we had been incarcerated. If I hadn't been such an excellent spy (yet another life), I might have supposed that, like me, the ruffian's previous humans had tired of his adolescent antics. We dogs outgrow our cuddly puppyhood, and what do they do? Give us up before we complete the next phase. A little chewing, a little tunneling, and you're out of the pack, labeled as uncontrollable. I've seen the human adolescent, and really, we're nothing next to them, so I don't understand why the adults of their species find *us* so hard to live with.

The ruffian, though, had come from a troubled home. We had never discussed it, but in true spy-fashion, I had been hiding under the kitchen table when our humans were talking it over one day. "Owner was arrested," they said, speaking of a notation in Britches's file at the pound.

In addition to this unsavory bit of information, there were other indicators that his last owner was unworthy of a pack. The ruffian limped when he came to us, and for a time we thought he might be permanently lame. He was skin and bones. And wild to a fault.

Why the two-leggers thought I'd be pleased with him, I'm not sure. No more than I am sure why I took to the fellow straight-off.

He discussed nothing of his background with me, and of course, no honorable dog would press him to reveal anything he chose to keep secret.

So when he did not answer my question, I said nothing more, and merely watched him. His leg had healed, he had filled out — a bit too much, really — and his behavior, if not perfect, was much improved. Yet there was a restlessness in him.

I could have gone back to my comfy bed, but I stayed on the thin rug, to keep him company. A few minutes later, he surprised me by saying, "You know of Sherlock?"

"The Great Finder?" I asked. "Of course. Who hasn't heard of him. A great loss. But, well, I never have been able to understand what turned him into a criminal."

"He was no criminal!" the youngster said.

"Don't show your teeth at me, young whippersnapper. What do you know of a dog like Sherlock?"

"We were packmates, before I came here." He gave me an amused look. "You can't believe it, can you? But it's true. I was being trained as a cadaver dog, and by one of the greatest cadaver dogs that ever lived."

Now, whatever else might be said of Sherlock, this was true. His downfall had been preceded by many years of being a celebrity in our area. "You mean to say you were Rebecca Court's dog? When I heard that your owner had been arrested, I had no idea. . . ."

"You still don't."

"So why don't you tell me?" I said.

He sighed, a great heavy sigh, but then he began to speak in soft, low tones. Nothing our masters could hear, of course, but I shall never forget a word of it. This is what he said:

I first saw Becky Court not long after I was weaned. I was in a mutt's litter, but out of a well-known search bitch, and I had always heard that my father and mother met on a search. Becky never seemed to mind my mixed parentage. She came to our kennel during dinnertime, and threw a ball. The other pups continued to chow down, but I could not resist going after that ball. I quickly nabbed it, and looked back at her. She smiled. Here was a woman who loved to play with dogs, and I could see that she was pleased with my response. I saw something else, though — there was a sadness in her, one she hid from other humans, but which I perceived immediately. Of course, like any good dog, I wanted to comfort her. But it was more than that. She was a connector — one of those few two-leggers who can truly read us, and who are especially easy for a dog to read.

She quickly taught me to bring the ball

back to her, and to release it. She threw it again and again, and I would have continued to fetch it all night, for I soon wanted to do nothing more than please this two-legger who focused on me and praised me, and understood my desire to play. Only when I lay panting, tongue lolling did she stop, and when she walked away to talk to my mother's owner, I cried for her, more frantic at the possibility of losing that connection than for my own littermates.

She returned, though, and brought me home to Sherlock, a large dark shepherd, very deep in the chest. He put me in my place immediately. I did my best to test him, but any challenge of Sherlock was necessarily only a formality. He was powerful and wise, and I was no match for him.

Becky worked with me from the first, and I loved our lessons, which soon left me too tired to be issuing challenges. When he saw my devotion to Becky, as well as my ability to read her, Sherlock adopted me as his packmate. He showed me the way of things, and began to tell me of the training to come. I learned quickly, and now wanted to please both Becky and Sherlock. I quickly conquered basic obedience, and I was taken to the search group's training exercises. Every weekend I rode in Becky's truck, my own crate next to Sherlock's. They were proud of me, because at no more than seven months of age, I was showing promise as a finder. I never failed to find the pretend victim in the woods, and had already alerted to blood evidence. Once we were taken to a place where a body had been found not long before, and without being shown the location, I found my way to the dead one's scent in the soil.

"That might have disturbed a squeamish gent like you," he said, "but I was delighted. For me, nothing could be better. I was good at the work, and I was rewarded with a rousing game of fetch if I succeeded.

Sherlock told me of some of the training and tests to come. The shoes, for example. Becky had a trunk full of pairs of old shoes she had purchased over the years from thrift shops. She would take out one shoe of a pair, and I would be asked to find its mate by use of scent.

He told me of the sticks. Eleven people would handle a dozen sticks. The twelfth person would touch only one. I must find the stick that had the unique scent on it.

There would be many days in the woods, where Becky had hidden objects of human scent — teeth given to her by a dentist friend, a little blood-soak cloth, a small bit of bone donated to the group by the medical examiner, to help in training us.

I would be asked to climb ladders, crawl through small spaces, and achieve other feats of agility. I would learn about the things that might work for and against us. Strong wind and dryness would hinder us, while light breezes and moisture helped. We could be helped or hindered by familial scent, brought on when related people lived in the same household, ate similar food, used the same shampoos, laundered their clothes together. Plant life might hold scent, rain might wash it away.

There were law enforcement people in our group who would help us to have access to places others might not be allowed to go. One of them, a homicide detective named Bob Ross, had a retriever named Happy. We got along well with her, but our main interest in Bob was that he obviously loved Becky. A dog could read that a mile away. But Becky didn't seem to see it. He was a smart two-legger, though, and was making slow but steady progress in getting closer to her. Sherlock said that humans don't admire a fine nose and a big pair of ears, but I didn't think Becky noticed these things about Bob at all. I think she didn't trust most members of her species, but she should have figured out that she could trust Bob. A dog could read that a mile away, too.

Bob's connections helped the group to train. If someone died in the woods, after the body was removed, our group would be taken to the general area, and we dogs would be asked to find the place where the body had lain. Some of the death-scented soil would be taken by our trainers, and hidden in future training exercises. Wherever someone had been injured or died in a public place, I might be trained to locate that exact place, where the death scent would linger. I would be taken out in a boat on a lake on a still day, and learn to alert when I caught the scent of remains underwater.

I looked forward to all of this, but there were a great many I was not given a chance to try.

You might think that humans who spend so much time with us might be paid to do so. But they are volunteers, and buy all the special equipment they need on their own. Early on, I asked Sherlock why Becky was so dedicated to search work. He told me it was because of her sister.

Sherlock had heard the story from Nero, the first search dog Becky had trained. Nero had died before I joined the pack, but he, too, was a famous searcher. According to Nero, twelve years ago, Becky went camping with Lisa Court, her sister. They hiked into the mountains two weeks before Becky was to marry a man named Roger Moore — the trip was intended to be a chance for the two sisters to spend time together before Becky's wedding. Lisa had been opposed to the marriage, and during the trip, the young women argued about it. After one of these arguments, Lisa walked off from the camp, and never returned. Though there was a search, Lisa was not found.

Everyone tried to tell Becky that she was not to blame, but she remained haunted by Lisa's disappearance. She broke off her engagement to Roger Moore, and never married. She devoted all her time from that point on to search and rescue work, and eventually learned to train cadaver dogs as well.

I was grateful to Sherlock for this history, because it helped me to understand that unhappiness I had sensed in Becky.

We were pleasing to her, though, and she was as loyal to us as any dog.

One day, three visitors came to our door. Bob was there, and as always, we were happy to see him. But he didn't seem happy at all that day, and he seemed especially unhappy about the two men who were with him: Roger and Max. Becky seemed surprised that Bob would be in their company. If it had been Bob alone, we would have been free to nuzzle him and rub against him. But Becky told us to lie down and stay, and we knew that was because of Roger and Max.

Sherlock and I took an immediate dislike to Roger. He was handsome by human standards — they have no taste in these matters — but we could see that Becky did not want him there. Other dogs might have barked or growled, but we had been well-trained, and we did not voice an objection to his presence. We watched him closely, though.

We didn't feel any better about Max, who smelled of alcohol. It was clear that Becky was not overjoyed to see him. Nevertheless, she played the gracious hostess and invited them in. Max lurched his way to the couch. I wondered why Roger was there, but Sherlock told me that Max and

Roger were friends and business partners. Their business was modestly successful, but Sherlock told me that Becky had always made more money than anyone else in her family, a fact that made Max jealous of her. He didn't hide it well; he kept commenting on people who spent more on pets than family members.

"They are my family," she said.

Roger came near us.

"I'm raising dogs now," he said, eyeing Sherlock with open envy.

"So I've heard," Becky replied. "Don't get too close to him, he bites."

Bob raised his brows, and I nearly laughed at this falsehood, but Sherlock curled his lip convincingly.

Max was oblivious to this. "You two have so much in common," he said, his voice slurring. "Should have married Roger. Could marry him now . . ."

Bob shot him an angry look. "You might save that for another time," he said.

"If that's all you came to say, Max —" Becky began, standing.

But Roger interrupted. "Ignore him, Becky," he said softly, a kind of coaxing in his voice that made me all the more uneasy. He pretended to be angry with Max, but any dog could have read his body and seen that he was just putting on a show. "Max, really you surprise me," he said. "This is not the time to discuss such a thing. Sit down, Becky."

She stayed standing, eyeing him warily. Maybe she had read him, too.

"Becky," Bob said, "I'm sorry — I'm here officially."

"Officially? Is there a search? Why didn't you just page me?"

He shook his head. "We have some news. About Lisa."

The color went out of her face. She sank into the chair. "Lisa?"

"Her remains have been found, Becky."

Becky stared at him. "Lisa?" she asked again.

"Her skull, anyway," Max said.

"Max!" Roger snapped.

"She goes around looking for body parts all the time," Max said. "She a damned ghoul. Won't bother her."

I really wanted to forget my manners and bite him. But I don't think Becky heard him at all. She kept staring at Bob, as if she still wasn't able to take it all in.

"You must have known that if she had been alive all these years, she would have contacted us," Roger said.

She looked sharply at him.

"It's not the same, is it?" Bob said gently. "Imagining what might have happened, and knowing? But we're sure it's her — dental records were still on file with missing persons."

Becky lowered her head in her hands and began to cry. Both Bob and Roger tried to move closer to her, but she batted Roger away. He grew embarrassed at this, and stepped back as she let Bob hold her. I could see from the set of Roger's body, the jutting of his chin, that he was angry, too. His voice was cold when he said, "Don't you want to know what happened to her?"

Becky looked up at Bob, her eyes questioning.

"Fell off a cliff," Max said. "All these years, she's been rotting in some ravine."

"Mr. Court —" Bob began, but Roger interrupted.

"Max," Roger said with exasperation, "you are going to make this detective think you wanted her dead."

"Truth is," Max said, "she was a troublemaker. I didn't miss her then, and I don't miss her now. If I had been up there with them that day, I probably would have pushed her off that cliff."

"That's a horrible thing to say," Becky said.

"Maybe you two should leave," Bob said.

"I begin to think you're right," Roger said. "I'll try to sober Max up before we begin the search. Becky, you know I only want what's best for you. Call me if you need me. Come along, Max."

Grumbling, Max allowed Roger to guide him out.

"Becky," Bob said when they were gone, "we don't know what happened yet, and we may never know. Until we have recovered more of Lisa's remains, we're only guessing. But one thing I can tell you — it doesn't seem likely that she suffered. The forensic anthropologist tells me that from what she can see, there was a blow to the head that would have knocked Lisa unconscious. That fracture didn't heal at all, so most likely, it occurred near the time of death."

Becky was silent for a long time, her face pinched with worry.

"You couldn't have done anything to save her, Becky, even if you had been standing right next to her."

"We argued."

"Don't think about that. She was walking in one of the most beautiful places around here. Don't be so hard on yourself."

Becky didn't answer.

"If you'd rather be alone —"

"No, no, and please, be straightforward with me, Bob. I need to know as much as you can tell me."

"Sure."

"Who found her?"

"The skull was found by a hiker, who unfortunately picked it up and carried it to a ranger station. He had a rough idea of where he had found it, but the rangers weren't able to locate anything more."

"Roger mentioned a search."

"I'm bringing a team up there to-morrow."

"I'm going, too."

"Becky, I'm not sure that's such a great idea. You're upset, and the dogs will pick up on that. You know you can't lie to a dog."

"People lie to dogs all the time."

"You know what I mean. You can't lie to them because they can read the lie. They go along with the program because we've trained them to, or because they're good natured, I don't know. But they pick up on all sorts of cues that we devious humans don't even know we're giving. You can't lie to a dog, and a dog won't lie to you."

She looked over at us, and of course we

wagged our tails. She called to us, and we hurried over to offer what comfort we could, and she held on to us and buried her face in our coats. But then she looked up and said, "I'm coming with you, Bob. Don't you see that I have to? I'll never get closure on this any other way. Besides, you need another dog to confirm any find, and you know there's no better dog over that kind of terrain than Sherlock. You can handle him yourself, if that's what's worrying you."

"Roger has offered to help search."

"You know as well as I do that he is a raw beginner. I've never seen him work, but he's just started training that dog."

"He wasn't going to bring the dog. I'm just asking if you are going to be able to handle being around him if he comes along."

"Of course," she said scornfully. "Just keep him away from my dogs."

In the end, we all crowded into Bob's truck. Becky rode with him in the front, and Sherlock, Happy, and I rode in our crates in the back. Not knowing how long we would be gone, Becky hadn't wanted to leave me behind. I was grateful to her for thinking of me.

Roger met us at the ranger station. So did a forensic anthropologist and some other searchers. From there we drove to the area where the hiker thought he had been when he found the skull. The teams divided up to cover various sections of this area.

As the two-leggers in our team — Becky, Bob, and Roger — studied a topographical map, we were kept in our crates in the shade. I heard Roger say, "This area would have been more than an hour's hike from your campground, right?"

Becky shrugged. "I suppose so."

"Then I wonder if Lisa came here on her own. It doesn't seem likely, does it? I mean, when other people get angry, do they walk that far before they cool off?"

"Some will," Bob said. "But we'll consider every possibility."

"You looked for her that day, didn't you, Becky?" Roger persisted.

"Yes."

"Did you think she might be this far away?"

Sherlock bristled, not liking his tone.

"I wasn't sure what had happened to her. For a time, I even hoped she was getting back at me by making me worry — was hiding, or had found a ride home with someone else," she said. "I didn't want to think of her out here, cold and alone, perhaps hurt." She sounded upset. I wished he would shut up.

"Speaking of which — as I recall, you were hurt, weren't you?"

"It was nothing, really."

"No, I remember. You were quite scraped up — all sorts of cuts and bruises."

"It was just starting to get dark, and I tripped on a tree branch. That was what made me realize I needed to get help while I could still find my way back to the camp."

"You said she might be 'getting back at you' — getting back at you for what?"

Bob sighed. "You want to wait back at the ranger station, Roger? Because you are starting to seriously tick me off."

"It's okay," Becky said, and I heard a kind of strength in her voice then, some new determination. "He knows that Lisa didn't want me to marry him. He knows exactly how determined she was to prevent our marriage. Don't you, Roger?"

There was the slightest hesitation before he answered, "Yes, yes I do."

Becky came over to let us out of our crates. She took Sherlock and Happy closer to where the search would begin. I watched Roger. I didn't trust him. Sure enough, he was lying to Bob.

"I'm sorry," Roger said in a low voice. "I didn't mean to be a pest."

"Oh, I understand," Bob said easily. "I doubt Lisa would have wanted it to be her dying wish, but after all, things turned out her way, didn't they?"

Roger didn't look so pleased about that.

They gave Roger the job of walking with me on a lead. The other dogs were off lead. I tried not to resent it. For my part, I behaved like a perfect blockhead, walking along flawlessly at heel until I felt Roger's attention wander, and then lunging on the leash as if I'd never passed Obedience One. It wore Roger to a frazzle, and more than once he nearly fell. If he shouted at me, I jumped up on him and licked his face. He hated that, and hated Becky and Bob's apparent unwillingness to help him. I worried that they might not see my intent, and would be ashamed of me. But as I said, Becky and Bob are connectors, and they only seemed amused.

Searches always take longer in real life than they do on television. We came back to our base and rested for a while, then started over in the early afternoon. Happy made the first find. A rib.

Bob praised her, and called out to the rest of us. Sherlock found a femur just as Bob was radioing our discoveries to the other teams. Becky looked upset, although she was trying not to. "We're not sure it's Lisa," Bob said. That was true — at least for the humans — but we didn't think Bob believed what he was saying. Sherlock found a pelvis that was undoubtedly female not long after that.

Soon the forensic anthropologist and the ranger joined us, and Sherlock and Happy continued their work. The bones had been moved by scavengers, so it took some time to locate even the biggest ones. The moisture in this area was good for keeping the bones "greasy," though, so we had some luck there.

I say "we" even though I wasn't allowed to search. I was restless, and would have loved to have joined in the activity, but Becky would not allow a dog with so little training to be involved.

After one brief bout of crying, Becky tried to fool us into believing she wasn't bothered, but we knew she was. Bob tried to get her to wait with us on the hiking path at the top of the ravine. She argued, but then he hinted to her that he wanted her to get Roger away from the scene.

Roger kept wanting to pick things up. I barked at him when he tried this the first time, much to his dismay. Bob reminded him that he needed to keep his paws to himself — the professionals were the only ones who could handle evidence, so only Bob or the anthropologist could collect the bones.

Roger was unhappy, but I don't think it was because Bob had given him a correction. He began the climb up the ravine without complaint, although I didn't need to be on the other end of the leash to know he was disappointed.

I was disappointed, too, and began to imagine in my own mind the day when I was a fully trained search dog, a dog who found some vital clue. I thought of the praise I'd receive, of Becky's approval. All the other dogs would look up to me. Sherlock himself would be stunned that so young a dog had made such a find. It would be something important. Something more than an old bit of bone. Something like . . .

Something like blood. I no sooner thought this than I became aware that I *did* smell blood. In my excitement, I lunged forward, and this time I caught Roger so unawares, he fell forward on his face, and let go of the leash. I hardly noticed. I was focused on one thing and one thing only — that familiar scent of blood. It was ahead, lodged beneath a fallen log, not far from the top of the ravine. I dug furiously as Sherlock barked and Becky called out and Roger swore. But I had found a prize: a stick, to which dried blood and a small hank of hair adhered. As much as I wanted it, all my training said I should now give an alert. So I decided to prove that I was not so green after all. I held my head back and gave three sharp barks. I looked back at Becky, expecting her to praise me, to play ball with me as a reward for being such a grand dog.

She stood stock still, horrified.

Sherlock began racing forward, but he was some distance below Roger. Roger reached me first. And delivered a vicious kick to my back end that sent me sprawling, and yelping in pain.

Sherlock leaped on Roger's back, hit him with his full weight, driving him to the ground with a growl so fierce, I stopped yelping and merely whimpered. Sherlock sniffed at the stick, glanced at me, and said, "Keep raising a fuss!" Then, to my shock, he pulled the stick free and ran off with it. I did as he told me.

Becky arrived, and all her concern was for me. She held me and comforted me and called Roger all sorts of names. I put as much drama into it as I could, even as Sherlock disappeared from sight.

Everyone else soon joined us, and crowded around me. Happy took an interest in the place where the stick had lain, so I really went for broke with the pitiful whimpering. It wasn't entirely fake. The jerk had lamed me.

Sherlock came back. Bob looked between him and Becky, but didn't say a word. We got into the truck, leaving Roger to get a ride with the ranger, and the forensic anthropologist and other two-leggers to continue the work of searching and recovering Lisaremains. Bob took us to a vet, who did his best, but said that I might always be lame.

We went home, although it didn't seem much like home after that. Something was wrong between Sherlock and Becky, and he wouldn't tell me what it was. But he stared at her, willing her to do something.

It is in our lineage, you know. Some breeds of herding dogs bark their lambs into obedience. Others simply stare at them, perhaps reminding them that the wolf in us is never far away.

I do not know if Becky saw the wolf in Sherlock, but over the next two days, I saw her growing unhappiness. Sherlock seemed no happier than she.

On the evening of the third day, she looked at Sherlock, and petted him, and said, "You're right, but what will become of you two?"

I could not understand this, but apparently it caused her more worry than anything else that was on her mind. She called Bob, and asked him to come over.

When he arrived, she said, "I want you to take my dogs."

"Are you going somewhere?" he asked.

"I mean, I want you to own them. Will you?"

"Becky, I know you are upset about Lisa —"

"Bob, if you love me, you will agree to take them before I say another word about anything to you."

He stared at her, and I think he read her just as he could read Happy. After a long while, he said, "You promise me that you aren't thinking of killing yourself, and I'll take them."

"No, I won't kill myself. But you have to take ownership of the dogs."

"Okay."

She handed him some papers — ownership papers, I suppose. I was ready to yelp as I never had up in the mountains, but Sherlock hushed me. "It's as it must be, youngster," he told me. He was no more pleased about it than I was, but there was a dignity in him that was beyond any I'll ever be able to manage, even if I live to be twenty.

"What's this all about, Becky?"

She began stroking our fur, saying good-bye with her hands.

"Do you know what my little one found up there in the mountains?"

"No."

"A stick. Sherlock ran off with it before anyone could see it, but it was a good find. I never praised this one for it," she said, ruffling my ears.

"A good find?"

"It was a stick with blood on it."

He went pale, and said, "Lisa's."

She shook her head. "Sherlock wouldn't know Lisa's. It was mine."

"I don't understand."

"I've trained them often enough by pricking my fingers and damping gauze with my blood. Of course they know the smell of it. There might have been some of my hair on the stick, even some scalp tissue. Lisa hit me hard enough to take skin away."

"Are you telling me that Lisa attacked you?"

"I've never told anyone what happened up there — I didn't think anyone would have believed me. I should have trusted you, though. I should have told you a long time ago. Sherlock has been convincing me of that over the last few days."

"Becky, maybe you should have a lawyer."

She shook her head. "Let me say this while I have the guts to do it. I hadn't been on that camping trip for an hour when Lisa started asking me if I really loved Roger. She began to needle me about it. To be honest, I began to wonder if she wasn't right. She kept saying that the only reason Roger want to marry me was because I had money. I hated how likely that sounded to me. But then I began to wonder why Lisa, who had never been especially close to me, was so intent on protecting me.

"We were walking near that ravine. She had picked up a short, thick stick — for firewood, she told me. Then she told me she was having an affair with Roger, and that she'd keep him in her bed even after I married him."

Bob waited, not saying anything, just watching her.

"I was furious, and hurt, and not even certain I believed her. I said, 'Over my dead body,' and I guess she took it as a suggestion."

"She tried to kill you?"

"As I walked away from her, she hit me on the back of the head with a large stick. It wasn't enough to knock me out, but it stunned me. She came at me again, to knock me into the ravine, and I ducked low. I guess I caught her off balance. She went tumbling down that ravine. I climbed down after her, but she was dead when I reached her."

"Why didn't you say something then?"

"I wasn't thinking straight. I was scared, and angry, and I didn't think I could trust anyone. And I couldn't find that damned stick. I figured I couldn't prove it was self-defense, although I suppose the knot she had raised on the back of my head might have helped. Still, I was alive and she was dead, and if the story came out about her affair with Roger — do you see?"

"You know I believe you. And you know it isn't going to be a matter of what I do or don't believe."

"It matters to me."

He looked over at me and said, "I wish to God that dog had never found that damned stick."

So Becky was questioned by other detectives. Roger, however, had not finished his part in all this. He convinced these new investigators that Bob wasn't telling the truth — that Becky had ordered Sherlock to hide the evidence that would have proven Lisa was the one who had been struck by the stick. Others had seen the dog run off and return to her. And that is how Sherlock began to be seen as an accomplice to murder. She was arrested.

I saw how miserable this made everyone in my new household. Bob pretended he didn't hold my part in this against me, but he failed to hide his resentment. I realized that if I hadn't had such daydreams of personal glory, if I had simply been a good dog that day, she wouldn't have suffered. Sherlock tried to comfort me, but it was no good. I had let my pack down. I stopped eating.

One day, when we were out in the yard, a meter reader opened the gate. I made my way out. Sherlock started to follow me, but I bared my teeth at him.

"I could have you begging for mercy in less than a minute," he said.

I stared at him, just as he had once stared at Becky.

"You're making a mistake," he said.

I kept staring.

"Take care, little one," he said, and turned away.

I still had my limp, and so it wasn't hard for the animal control officers to catch me. My tags still said I was Becky's, and so they wrote, "Owner was arrested."

"Bob didn't come to bail you out?" I asked.

"No, and I hadn't expected him to. Strangely, once I was there, I found I wanted to live, even if I didn't go back to Bob. So I put on a show for our two-leggers, and they brought me home to you."

"Well, I, for one, ruffian, am pleased that Bob was so stupid. The day they brought you home, I thought it was Christmas."

He seemed surprised by this. "Truly?"

"Truly. You know I can't lie to you."

I should let you know that I finally had a chance to meet Sherlock in person about a year later. We had gone to the dog beach, and were frolicking on the sand, when a big shepherd approached us. He knew Britches immediately. They greeted one another with a kind of affection that made me just a teensy bit jealous.

"I'm here with Becky and Bob," Sherlock said. "You must come to us. She has worried so much about you."

Britches's ears came up, and for a moment, I thought he would run off with the other dog. But then he hesitated, and said, "She's out of jail?"

"Bob didn't realize you were gone until it was too late to visit the pound. He was busy pressuring Max to confess what he knew about Roger and Lisa's plans."

"Plans?"

"It was no accident that she had taken Becky to a remote spot in the mountains — or that she was carrying that stick. And Bob found evidence in the park ranger's permit records to show that Roger had been up in that area just before Lisa died, undoubtedly scouting out a place where Becky's body might be found. I'll tell you all about it. We have so much catching up to do! Come on, join us, we can be a pack again!"

But Britches only licked Sherlock's lips and said, "Allow me to introduce you to the Captain. I'm in his pack now. I'm happy in it."

Sherlock studied him and said, "I see you are. Bring him back to the sea again someday soon, Captain."

We, for our part, stare our two-leggers into doing just that whenever we want to see The Great Finder.

About the Authors

Ex-journalist **Carole Nelson Douglas** is the award-winning author of forty-some novels and two mystery series. *Good Night, Mr Holmes* introduced the only woman to outwit Sherlock Holmes, American diva Irene Adler, as a detective, and was a *New York Times* Notable Book of the Year. The series recently resumed with *Chapel Noir*. Douglas also created contemporary hard-boiled P.I. Midnight Louie, whose first-furperson feline narrations appear in short fiction and novels. *Cat in an Orange Twist* and *Cat in a Hot Pink Pursuit* are the latest titles. Along with her publisher, Forge Books, she has promoted cat adoptions nationwide through the Midnight Louie Adopt-a-Cat program, which have made homeless cats available for adoption at her book signings since 1996. She collects vintage clothing as well as stray cats (and the occasional dog), and lives in Fort Worth, Texas, with her husband, Sam.

J. A. Jance has written more than thirty mysteries. The first of her J. P. Beaumont novels, *Until Proven Guilty*, was published in 1985. A second series, based in Arizona, centers on Cochise County Sheriff, Joanna Brady. She also has three stand-alone suspense thrillers, *Hour of the Hunter*, *Kiss of the Bees*, and *Day of the Dead*, which also come with a Southwest flavor. J.A. was born in South Dakota, grew up in Arizona, and now divides her time between homes in Tucson and Seattle. Married, she has five children, four grandchildren, and two dogs, Aggie and Daphne — named after her two idols, Agatha Christie and Daphne du Maurier, of course.

Dick Lochte's novels have been nominated for nearly every mystery book award and have been translated into more than a dozen languages. His book *Sleeping Dog* won the Nero Wolfe award. His most recent books include the short story collection *Lucky Dog* and *Lawless*, a legal thriller co-written with attorney Christopher Darden.

Jill M. Morgan is the author of sixteen novels, including *Blood Brothers*, published by HarperTrophy, and the co-editor of eight anthologies, including *Til Death Do Us Part* published by Berkley Prime Crime. She lives in southern California with her husband and children, and is currently at work on a mystery novel.

Marlys Millhiser's newest Charlie Greene mystery is *The Rampant Reaper*. The Hollywood literary agent has learned to put on pantyhose while waiting in gridlock on the 405 but not how to deal with murder at home. *Publishers Weekly* has called it the best in a "winning series." She lives in Boulder, where she has written thirteen published novels and as many short stories. She is currently at work on another series featuring the Lennora Poole of the story published here, her thirteenth published story.

Ed Gorman has been called "One of the most original crime writers around" by *Kirkus* and "A powerful storyteller" by Charles Champlin of the *Los Angeles Times*. He works in horror and westerns as well as crime and writes many excellent short stories. To date there have been six Gorman collections, three of which are straight crime, the most recent of which is *Such a Good Girl and Other Stories.* He is probably best known for his Sam McCain series, set in the small-town Iowa of the 1950s ("good and evil clash with the same heartbreaking results as Lawrence Block or Elmore Leonard" — *Booklist*), which includes *The Day the Music Died,* and *Will You Still Love Me Tomorrow?* He has also written a number of thrillers, including *The Marilyn Tapes, Black River Falls,* and *The Poker Club.*

Jane Haddam is the pseudonym of Orania Papazoglou, who is best known for her series featuring retired FBI agent Gregor Demarkian, who has appeared in more than a dozen novels. She had worked in publishing long before turning to writing fiction, with stints as an editor at *Greek Accent* magazine and writing freelance for *Glamour, Mademoiselle,* and *Working Woman.* She has written books under her own name (*Graven Image* and *Arrowheart*) but it is the Demarkian series that continues to garner the most attention.

Maxine O'Callaghan began her writing career in 1972 after moving to southern California, and sold the first short story she submitted to *Alfred Hitchcock's Mystery Maga-*

zine. She sold others, including one featuring a female private eye who worked in Orange County, California. Her name was Delilah West and she eventually appeared in a novel, *Death Is Forever*, published in 1980. The fifth book, *Trade-Off*, is out in paperback from Worldwide Library; the sixth, *Down for the Count*, is out in hardcover from St. Martin's Press. In between the Delilah West books, she wrote four titles published as horror. The last was *Dark Time*, Berkley/Diamond, in 1992. She has also written two books in a suspense series for Berkley/Jove: *Shadow of the Child* and *Only in the Ashes*. This series is set in Phoenix and features child psychologist Dr. Anne Menlo. Maxine still lives and writes in southern California.

Gary Phillips has published several mystery and crime novels and short stories here and overseas. His most recent works are *Bangers* and *Monkology*, a collection of his Ivan Monk stories. He is past vice president of the Private Eye Writers of America, and sits on the national board of the Mystery Writers of America.

Author of three forensic-based mystery novels, a collection of poetry, and several short stories, **Noreen Ayres** is an editor of technical publications at an environmental engineering company in Washington state. When she's not creating fictional murder and mayhem, Noreen enjoys ballroom dancing, making twig furniture, and watching her cats, Zak and Zeus, explore the many varieties of slugs and bugs in the rich gardens around her home. She threatens to write a story about their antics called, "Terror in the Tulips."

Jan Burke is the bestselling author of ten novels and a collection of short stories. Her novels include *Bloodline*, *Nine Bones* (which won the Mystery Writers of America's Edgar® Award for Best Novel), and *Flight*. She is also an award-winning short story writer — she has twice won the Macavity, and won both the *Ellery Queen Mystery Magazine* Readers Award, and the Agatha Award for Best Short Story. She has also received an Edgar® nomination for Best Short Story. She is the founder of the Crime Lab Project, a group of writers and television producers who work to raise public awareness of the need to better support crime labs. Her books and stories have been published internationally. You can learn more about her and her work at www.janburke.com.

About
the Editor

Jill M. Morgan is the author of numerous novels and co-editor of various anthologies, including *Till Death Do Us Part*. She lives in Southern California with her husband and children.

10-05